FASCINATING
RHYTHM

D1059415

FASCINATING

RHYTHM

BY

ANNE LOUISE BANNON

Healcroft House, Publishers

Fascinating Rhythm is published by Healcroft
House, Publishers, a subsidiary of Robin Goodfellow
Enterprises, Altadena, California, United States of
America.

First printing March 2015

© 2015 by Anne Louise Bannon.

All rights reserved. Please do not reproduce, scan or
distribute in any printed or electronic form without
permission.

ISBN # 978-0-9909923-1-8

Library of Congress Control Number: 2015901675

To Michael and Corrie because you guys are the light of my life

And to my ex-husband Gary Klarner, who not only gave me a wonderful daughter but the space and time to write this book. Thanks.

AMDG

Acknowledgments

Way back when I first started researching and writing Fascinating Rhythm, I did not write down the names of two people who made this book possible. The first was a history professor at California State University, Fullerton, who pointed me toward some excellent books on the 1920s and told me that subway fare at the time was a nickel. The other was a very nice woman whose name I didn't write down simply because I thought I'd still know her when this was published. She kindly answered my call for help when I had broken my elbow and couldn't hold a pencil to write my outline. She took dictation with enormous patience and made it possible for me to at least type one-handed the first draft.

Then there were all the others who helped get this up and printed. There's my beloved spouse Michael Holland, who kept reassuring me and took up extra housekeeping chores, not to mention the countless glasses of wine he poured during the editing process. Oh, and the historical notes, too. My wonderful daughter, Cornelia Ann Klarner, who was my first beta reader, in spite of being embarrassed by the sexy bits. My cousin Cairn Martin Shundo, whose unreserved praise was the shot in the arm I needed. Randee Dawn Cohen and Carol Wuenschell both contributed excellent notes and great corrections. And Petrea Burchard, my copy editor and friend. Any goofs that remain were probably edited back in by me during the final revision. Mea culpa, mea culpa.

Got a little rhythm,

A rhythm,

A rhythm

That pit-a-pats through my brain

So darned persistent,

The day isn't distant

When it'll drive me insane....

Fascinatin' Rhythm

Lyrics, Ira Gershwin

Music, George Gershwin

CHAPTER ONE

Deep into the night of December eighth, nineteen hundred and twenty-four, obsession took the life of Frank Selby. His passing was noted only by his killer, and that with the grim satisfaction of an unpleasant task properly carried out. Leaving Selby on the floor of his Murray Hill apartment, the killer stepped out into the city's bright lights, and hid.

Two days later, Kathy Briscow held her breath as she gazed out the window at Broadway and 23rd below. Flivvers and buses fought with each other on the sleet-filled streets. People on the sidewalks hustled along, bundled tight against the December chill, thousands of them going the same way to different destinations.

"I've got to do it," Kathy murmured, twisting her handkerchief in her hands. She certainly had nothing to lose, no thanks to Frank Selby. The son of a bitch couldn't even die without kicking her in the teeth one last time.

Traces of someone whistling slid in under the door and mingled with the faint rattle of the cars outside and the muted roar of the typewriters and adding machines inside. It was probably Evans. He was always whistling something. Kathy strained to catch the melody, then sighed.

It was that bouncy little number from the new show with the Astaires, *'Fascinating Rhythm'*. That Gershwin fellow had written the music. Kathy had been humming the little ditty ever since she'd seen the show the previous Monday. Once soothing and cheerful, the merry little song now grated on her already raw nerves.

Kathy jumped as the door opened and the clatter of typewriters filled the room, then quieted as the door shut.

The head of Healcroft House, Publishers, entered his office and studied the woman at the window. She had a little healthy padding, and bosoms, a refreshing change from those blasted flappers. Still, like them, her straight brown hair was cut even with her chin. Even more unnerving were the brown eyes that missed little. Her waist-less dark suit was modest, and somewhat predictable. A cut above what the other secretaries were wearing, but more indicative of good taste than overspending.

"Well?" he demanded.

Kathy gazed back, analyzing and evaluating. Mr. Healcroft was of medium build. His gray hair was slicked down. His starched collar was a little wide for the current fashion, and he still wore spats and buttoned shoes. Kathy wondered if he'd looked any different as a young man in the 'nineties. He wasn't very modern-minded, either. On the other hand, everyone said he was open to reason.

"Mr. Healcroft, I realize today was a disaster," Kathy began slowly.

"It most certainly was." He sat down behind the huge dark oak desk. "What did you tell the police?"

Kathy moved around front. "The truth. What did they tell you?"

"All I know is that one of my senior editors was found dead in his apartment this morning, and from the evidence taken at the scene, he died no later than Monday evening. And here it is Wednesday, and you, his secretary, never mentioned that he hadn't shown up for work either yesterday or today." Mr. Healcroft glared at her, one iron-gray eyebrow lifted. "Didn't the police find that a little odd?"

Kathy gulped, then pulled herself together. "At first, yes. But I believe they were satisfied with my explanation."

"And that was?"

Kathy pressed her lips together. She looked past Mr. Healcroft to the windows behind him. The skies were as gray as his hair. There would be snow that night.

"That Mr. Selby was in the habit of not coming into the office if he didn't feel like it, but not in the habit of notifying me or anyone else," she said finally.

"And you didn't question this habit of his, Miss Briscow?"

"Of course I questioned it." Kathy resisted the urge to start pacing the faded Oriental carpet in front of the desk. "But Mr. Selby insisted that all the senior editors did the same, and when I men-

3

tioned confirming it, he strongly hinted that I would find myself out of a job with Healcroft House."

Mr. Healcroft folded his arms. "And you believed him."

"I have no doubt in my mind that if it came down to my word against his, I would be the loser." Her heart in her throat, Kathy caught the publisher's eyes and held them.

Mr. Healcroft looked away. "You're how old, Miss Briscow?"

Kathy swallowed her irritation. "Twenty-seven. I've been with your company since 1919, when I graduated from college. That's five and a half years now, six in June. I've been Mr. Selby's secretary for almost two years."

"Haven't you ever thought about getting married?" Mr. Healcroft put on his most stern glare.

Kathy felt his disgust down to her toes. He'd never believe the truth.

"Of course. I," She thought fast. "I almost have a couple times, but found good reason not to. I'm content to be an old maid."

Mr. Healcroft leaned back in his chair and gazed at Kathy with a perplexed frown on his face. "That's not exactly germane to the issue."

Kathy took a deep breath, secretly pleased. If Mr. Healcroft was going to dismiss her marital status, there was hope he'd hear her out.

She stood tall and took the plunge. "Mr. Healcroft, it was no coincidence that Mr. Selby edited considerably more books after I came to him in spite of his absences."

Both of Mr. Healcroft's eyebrows lifted. "What are you trying to say?"

"I've been doing his work for him."

"That's ridiculous." Mr. Healcroft chortled and shook his head. "You've got some nerve, missy. Here the poor man is dead—"

"It's the truth." Kathy took another breath, then spoke again quickly. "He started having me read his manuscripts almost right away. He," Kathy grasped for a good lie, but chose a small part of the truth. "He said he was having trouble with bad handwriting. Then a few months later, we got a wonderful manuscript. Mr. Selby didn't like it. I told him it would sell with a few changes. He told me to take it over, and when it flopped, he would turn me over to you. Only it didn't. It's already gone into a third printing and made Mr. Lindsey's career."

That made Mr. Healcroft sit up. Kathy noted his consternation with satisfaction.

"Are you saying you accepted and edited *The Young Night*?" he sputtered.

"I did. Only since it's a bestseller, Mr. Selby took the credit for it. I've done most of his books since. I type during the day and edit at night in my room. Mr. Selby keeps, kept, the ones he liked, which were darned few. I did all the rest."

Mr. Healcroft coughed. "This is very disturbing." He looked at her, nervously. "How closely did he work with you?"

Kathy snorted. "Not as closely as he wanted."

"Young lady, must you?" Mr. Healcroft's
response was more perfunctory than appalled. His
eyes darted nervously in the direction of Selby's
office.

Kathy bit her lip. "I'm sorry, Mr. Healcroft.
I wouldn't have wished it on him, but at the same
time I can't honestly say I'm all that grieved by his
passing. I've finally got a chance to get some credit
for everything I've been doing."

Mr. Healcroft shifted in his seat. "I thought
someone else was working for him. But you?"

"I'm a good editor, as good as any man
you've got." Kathy paused, almost losing her nerve.
"That's why I feel I should replace Mr. Selby.
There's no one else that knows his job better, because I'm the one doing it."

Mr. Healcroft went white. "B-b-but, good
gravy, young lady, have you no respect for the dead?
They only found the man this morning."

"I can't afford proper sentiments," snapped
Kathy, twisting her handkerchief into a knot. "And
I've seen darned little of it in the junior editors'
room. The only reason they're not all in here is that
I am, and I want my fair chance at a job I deserve."

"You?" Mr. Healcroft slowly recovered himself. "Why... Eh... It-it's completely impossible. After
all, you... Eh... A lady editor?"

Kathy fought to keep her voice calm.
"There's Mrs. Chase over at Vogue. She runs that
magazine, and there are plenty of others like her."

"That's a ladies' magazine," Mr. Healcroft sputtered. "Books are different. We get all sorts of rough stories in here. They're, they're not for a woman's delicate sensibilities."

"This is the twentieth century, Mr. Healcroft!" Kathy groaned. "I am fully aware of how rough these stories can get. I edited *Pirates on the Main* without blushing, I can promise you that."

Mr. Healcroft gaped. "But, but, Selby let you see that?"

"Mr. Selby had no qualms about giving me objectionable material to read," Kathy blurted out, then immediately regretted it.

"What are you implying, missy?" Mr. Healcroft's eyes narrowed.

Kathy paused, struggling to get a grip on herself. "Nothing. In any case, it doesn't matter how shocking a book is. I've already seen it. You should have seen all the awful things I cut out of *Pirates*. Like that rape scene. You'd have been horrified. I had Carter re-write it three times before it was acceptable."

"You had Carter..." Mr. Healcroft gulped, then paused, his mind working. "You truly did edit those books."

"I did, and I deserve Selby's job. I'm working on Mr. Little's book right now, *The Old Money Story*. It's a good book, and I can make it the wonderful novel it should be."

"I see." Mr. Healcroft fidgeted. "And just how closely did Mr. Selby work with you?"

"If you think he was holding my hand at every page, you'd be seriously mistaken," said Kathy, her pique rising again. "Believe me, Mr. Healcroft, I was just as happy to be left alone. Sloth may have been chief among Mr. Selby's vices, but it was only one among many, and I know the breadth of them."

At that, Mr. Healcroft went white again. Still fuming, Kathy didn't notice. She was too annoyed at herself for saying so much. Mr. Healcroft swallowed, then got control of himself.

"That's very bold, missy. But I can't promote you to senior editor. The junior editors would lynch me if I promoted a secretary, let alone a woman secretary, over them."

"But the *The Old Money Story*?" Kathy leaned on the desk in front of him. "You can't let a total stranger take that over. I've just sent Mr. Little a letter telling him the changes he needs to make. Another editor will only confuse him."

Mr. Healcroft pulled back. "A lady editor?"

"I've signed all my correspondence K. Briscow, when I didn't use Mr. Selby's name. No one needs to know."

Mr. Healcroft sighed. "Poor Frank." He brooded some more, then sat up straight. "Miss Briscow, given this afternoon, to grant you a promotion now would be an untoward example to the other workers in this company. However, I, eh, cannot afford to lose a good editor, even if she is a woman. We'll give the office a few weeks to forget this afternoon. After that, you'll be made a junior editor."

"But what about Mr. Little's book?" Kathy yelped in spite of herself. "I can't give that up."

8

Mr. Healcroft went pale again for a second. "No. No. Of course not." He re-gained control of himself. "I'll expect you to continue your work on Mr. Little's novel, in the name of your new boss. I'll explain to him, as soon as I decide who Mr. Selby's replacement will be. It shall remain between the three of us. As far as anyone else is concerned, you are just a secretary until you are duly promoted. And you have my word on that promotion."

"Thank you, sir. You've been very generous."

"You're welcome. You'd better get back to your desk." Mr. Healcroft paused. "And, missy..." His eyes bore into her. "I am counting on your discretion."

"Of course, Mr. Healcroft."

Kathy hurried out. Though she hadn't gotten all she wanted, she'd gotten more than she'd expected, and possibly more than she had a right to expect. She paused in the hallway to savor her victory. Her brain recounted the interview in exact detail, but her emotions lagged far behind. Reality didn't seem to have sunk in, or perhaps she was still unnerved by Mr. Selby's demise and the visit from the police.

Or perhaps it was Mr. Healcroft. He had seemed more frightened than shocked when she'd told him she'd been doing Mr. Selby's work. But that didn't make sense. Nor did the way he had promised her that promotion.

Kathy looked back at the office. He was probably hiding something, but what could it be that would make him give in to her requests? And how would her doing Mr. Selby's work pose a threat to him? She could understand him being surprised, and given his stuffy attitudes, confused by it. But scared? Shaking her head, she took a deep breath and went on down the hall.

CHAPTER TWO

In the cluttered antechamber outside of Mr. Selby's office, Frederick G. Little, III, sat and waited, smoking in long, relaxed drags. Seated on a battered dark leather sofa across from a series of filing cabinets, he was the picture of patience.

Freddie Little's mind, however, was rapidly flitting from thought to thought to thought. He had intended to take advantage of the unexpected wait for Mr. Briscow to contemplate the installation of the new landing gear on his plane. The landing gear had failed the week before, causing no little damage to the belly of the plane, and Freddie desperately wanted to go out to the airfield to supervise the nice gentlemen from the Curtiss factory who were doing the actual repair. But there was also the problem of how to keep his friend Lowell's ex-wife, Victoria, out of both his and Lowell's hair. One didn't want to be rude, butVictoria was definitely getting more and more pushy. And then there was the odd reaction from the office receptionist when he had asked for Mr. Briscow.

The receptionist, a young blonde with shingled hair, had first looked at him blankly and said that no Mr. Briscow worked there. Freddie had then explained that he was the author of *The Old Money Story*. The receptionist had paused again and explained that Mr. Selby was his editor, but that there had been a terrible accident and Mr. Selby was dead.

"Oh, dear," Freddie had said. "I'm so sorry. But may I still talk to Mr. Briscow?"

"Who? Oh. You must mean..." the receptionist had replied with a puzzled frown on her face. "Uh. Sure. Why not?"

So she'd escorted him to Mr. Selby's office, or rather the small outer office.

"She'll be right with you," the receptionist said, nodding at the secretary's desk. The secretary who should have been seated there was absent.

Freddie seated himself on a sofa facing the desk, glancing idly at the file cabinets on the side wall.

The firm was in quite a tizzy, because it quickly became evident that Mr. Selby's accident had been no accident, which perhaps explained the receptionist's behavior. As he waited and smoked, the rumors cascaded in through the open door, and largely centered on Mr. Selby and "you know who." It seemed that everyone knew that the unnamed young woman certainly did not mind working late, and that she was covering up for him. Of course, everyone knew how Mr. Selby was, so naturally that was why she killed him, although why Mr. Selby would take up with someone so full of herself was anybody's guess.

Freddie had a fair idea of who "you know who" was, or at least of her position at the publishers. He knew exactly when she approached the office. As the voices stilled, he snuffed his cigarette in the ashtray next to the battered leather sofa and put the cigarette holder in his suit coat.

Kathy was surprised to find she had a guest. She wasn't sure if her jangled nerves were ready for dilettante millionaires, assuming the gentleman on the sofa was indeed the named author of *The Old Money Story*.

She'd seen Mr. Little's picture time and again in the Sunday rotogravure of the Times. In the flesh, what little there was of it, he seemed calmer and more dignified than the *roué* one saw, and certainly taller. He had the figure of Abraham Lincoln, with contented gaiety replacing the haunted look of the former president. A crisply tailored dark gray three piece suit covered the long limbs and body that rested on the office couch. The strawberry blond hair, neatly parted down the middle and slicked down, had seemed darker in the rotogravure, too.

According to the society pages he had graduated summa cum laude from Harvard, class of '17. But high honors could be purchased, as could ghost writers, and Mr. Little had enough money to buy as many as he wanted. Then again, Kathy had decided it didn't matter whose name went on the title page as long as the work itself was good.

The moment Mr. Little saw Kathy enter, he rose, curiously graceful for something that was all arms and legs.

"May I help you?" Kathy asked as she came around to her side of the desk.

"I'm Freddie Little. I'm looking for Mr. Briscow," he said, rhyming the last syllable with

13

how.

"Oh." Kathy forced a smile, wondering what she should do.

"I got his letter yesterday. It was wonderful, but I've got a great many questions and I'd like to talk to him at his earliest convenience."

"Oh." Kathy sighed. She did not need this. Authors were supposed to stay away from the office, or at least only talk to the senior editor. Why, of all days, did this fellow not only have to come in, but ask for her and not Mr. Selby?

Freddie looked at her with a worried frown. "Very well. Could you tell Mr. Briscow—"

The phone on Kathy's desk rang and she lunged for it, grabbing the candlestick base and putting the mouthpiece to her face even before getting the separate ear piece to her ear. Rumor had it the office was supposed to be getting new phones with the mouth and ear pieces all on one handset.

"Mr. Selby's office," she said quickly. She smiled briefly at Mr. Little, then turned her back to attend to the call.

"I need to speak to Selby," growled the voice on the other end of the line.

Kathy all but broke into tears. Mr. Trimble ran the printing house most often used by the publisher. He only accepted orders directly from the senior editors and flatly refused to speak to secretaries beyond getting his calls put through. Which for Kathy made him an exceptionally sharp thorn in her side, since not only was Mr. Selby seldom around to take Trimble's calls, Selby rarely knew what Trimble was calling about. Kathy took a deep breath and got her customary sang-froid back.

"I'm afraid he's not here," she said.

"He's never there," Trimble complained.

"And he's never going to be again," Kathy said, wincing as she realized she was slipping again. "I'm afraid he met with an unfortunate accident. We've only just found out. What did you need from Mr. Selby?"

"Who are you?"

"This is Miss Briscow, sir, as always." Behind her, Kathy heard a soft chuckle. She bit back the whole canon of swear words.

"I need someone who knows what's going on."

"I assure you, Mr. Trimble, I know everything that Mr. Selby was working on as well as he did." Propping the earpiece against her shoulder, Kathy turned and began looking through the stacks of paper on her desk. "Is there a problem with the print run on Mr. Dryer's book?"

"Have Mr. Selby's replacement call me back." Mr. Trimble hung up.

Her heart in her throat, Kathy turned around. Mr. Little was still on his feet. His grin was a little smug, but delight danced in his green eyes. Kathy hung up the phone and put it back on her desk, on the corner next to the overflowing desk tray.

"That solves one little mystery," Mr. Little said. "You are K. Briscow."

15

Kathy winced at the mispronunciation. "It's Briscow, with the long o. And obviously, it's not mister. You, however, were not supposed to know that."

"Whyever not?" Freddie paused. "Oh. Is Mr. Healcroft afraid I might object to a woman as an editorial assistant?"

"Something like that."

Freddie nodded. "And you wrote that letter yourself."

"Yes, I did." Annoyed at being doubted, Kathy straightened up and glared at Freddie. "And if you have a great many questions, I am the one to ask."

Freddie stepped back. Miss Briscow was obviously distraught, as well she might be after the day's discovery, but she was no wilting flower, either. Freddie wondered how far he could push her.

"I'll be..." he muttered. It was the best he could do. Swear words came to mind, but one simply did not swear in front of ladies.

He took another good look at her. She would not be easily fooled by his affectations. Slowly, a mischievous grin spread across his face.

"I was going to tell you how intelligent I found your letter," he said. "But I'm afraid now it would only sound patronizing."

Kathy silently sighed in relief.

"It was intelligent," Freddie continued. "I was so glad that at least the editorial assistant had some brains. I knew Mr. Selby, and was not impressed."

"He's bright enough in his own way," Kathy conceded, then swallowed. "Or he was."

"Yes." Freddie's forefinger nervously rapped the desk. "Not exactly a good day for me to drop by, is it? At the risk of sounding disrespectful of the dead, does this mean you're the one who's editing my book?"

Kathy smiled weakly. "I'm not sure how much I should tell you. I was given orders, you understand. But I suppose I can at least reassure you that your book is being handled by the same person who was handling it before the, uh, accident."

Freddie's face fell. "Not you? But you just said you wrote that letter yourself, and if I had questions, you were the one to ask."

Kathy glared at the coat tree on the opposite wall by the door, suddenly wishing she hadn't said so much. Outside her ante-chamber, clocks all over the main office were chiming the end of the work day. Chatter replaced the clatter of office machines.

"Yes I did." Kathy glanced back at the inner office behind her and then her guest. "I suppose there's no point in protecting him now." She took a deep breath. "'Assistant Editor' in this case meant I do all the work, with Mr. Selby getting the glory. And just between the two of us, it's supposed to remain that way for the time being."

"That hardly seems fair." Freddie nodded in sympathy, but inside was feeling relieved.

"Perhaps. But it's the best I've got. Now, Mr. Little, why don't you pull up that chair and we can go over your questions."

Freddie hesitated. "If you're certain this is a good time."

Kathy folded her arms, feeling angry and betrayed. "Mr. Little, if you wish, I can arrange for your book to be handled by another editor."

"No!" Freddie stammered. He turned away, reached inside his suit coat, changed his mind, and pulled his hand out empty. Recovering himself, he turned back to Kathy. "No, Miss Briscow. If you indeed wrote that letter, then I do not want anyone else handling my book."

Kathy looked at him, puzzled by how strongly he had reacted.

"You merely seemed somewhat distraught, as you might be," said Freddie, pulling his watch from his vest. "I didn't wish to intrude. Also, I see it's after your quitting time. Might I take you for a late tea?"

"That's a generous offer, Mr. Little, but I don't mind staying." Kathy sat down, trying not to sound as angry as she felt. On one hand, he seemed to genuinely care about his book and how it was edited. On the other, it was always possible he expected that because she was a woman, he would be able to pull the wool over her eyes. "As it happens, I do most of my editing at night anyway."

"So you are Mr. Selby's secretary, then." Freddie nodded, glad that he hadn't missed his original guess after all. "I'll have to take the matter up with Mr. Healcroft the next time I see him. He's a stuffy old bird, but not immune to reason."

Kathy looked away, biting back her anger, then pulled herself together again.

"The white knight treatment is kind of you, but I would appreciate it if you didn't," she said. "You're not supposed to know what's going on."

"Oh, that's right. I am so sorry." Freddie pulled a chair up to the front of her desk and sat down.

"Apology accepted." She looked him over, calculating. That last thing she needed was for Mr. Little to take up her cause. "Besides, I have taken the matter up with Mr. Healcroft and am satisfied with the outcome. Now, Mr. Little, may we get on with your questions?"

Freddie didn't doubt the outcome was satisfactory. She certainly moved quickly, given how recently Selby's demise had been discovered and the rumors he'd heard. But one couldn't put much stock in rumors, and Freddie had a feeling he knew more about Mr. Selby's death than anyone there would guess.

"Here's your manuscript," said Kathy, pulling the box out from under another stack of papers. She took a deep breath and gathered her thoughts. As she did so, the knots in her stomach began to release. It was the book that was important, nothing else. "I believe I told you in the letter why I think you need some of the stylistic changes."

"And you're right." Freddie leaned forward. "I hadn't realized how often I digressed from my point."

And not just in his writing, it seemed. Kathy sighed. Either Mr. Little's ghost writer had somehow managed to capture his voice in the writing, or there wasn't a ghost.

19

"Why did you write this book?" she asked suddenly.

Freddie squirmed, and reached again for the flask in his suit coat, and again decided not to get it out. Her gaze reminded him of the only person who had ever taken him seriously.

"My friend told me to," he said simply.

Kathy watched his green eyes shift from her and dart everywhere else. The lazy smirk was gone and so was the carefully cultivated detachment.

"Obviously, I don't need the money," he continued, his voice a little bitter. Then he smiled at her, somewhat chagrined. "By all rights, I ought to be starving."

"You'd be surprised how few authors do." Kathy looked at the manuscript and again felt the joy of a good story being made better. "You've got a good piece of work here."

"I'm glad you think so." He paused. A cigarette would be good, but a lady didn't smoke in the office, and it would be rude to smoke when she couldn't.

Kathy took a deep breath, pushed aside her own inner turmoil and put on her most business-like expression.

"It's not perfect yet. That's my job." Her grin was a little wicked. "As far as the digression problem is concerned, it's mostly a matter of cutting out what isn't completely connected to the story. Such as this scene." She flipped through the sheets of typescript until she found the place she wanted. "There are others, but it's particularly obvious this one doesn't belong. The one where Thripps tells Meaberry his secret desire to kill people."

"Not that one," Freddie groaned.

Kathy held firm. "I'm afraid so. It doesn't affect the denouement, or Meaberry's character significantly, or even Thripps, for that matter."

"But that's the whole point of the novel, Miss Briscow." Freddie got up and began pacing. "That these rich kids are so bored by life, they go around doing drastic things."

"That point is illustrated so much better in other places." Kathy sat back with her arms folded. "Thripps never actually does it."

"No. He didn't." Freddie looked away. "He killed himself. They said it was an accident, but I find it a little hard to believe one can accidentally hang oneself."

"You mean this happened?" Kathy's breath caught. If Freddie had intended to shock her he'd succeeded, but she wasn't going to let him see it.

"Damn near everything in that book happened," said Freddie. He noticed Kathy and started. "Forgive me. I didn't mean to use such language." He went back to pacing. "I've changed all the names and other things, so it's not recognizable and so it's decent. But I tell you quite truly, Miss Briscow, the people I know are even more depraved than they are in my book."

"That may be, Mr. Little."

He looked at her thoughtfully. "Are you going to insist that I take the scene out?"

21

"I am."

He gazed out the door toward the elevators. "Even if I ask Mr. Healcroft to keep it in?"

"You can ask Mr. Healcroft to get you another editor," Kathy snapped, her temper finally breaking. At least, she managed to keep the tears from spilling onto her cheek. "I haven't got a thing to lose if you do. And I refuse to be bullied into making a mistake just because you can buy out the publishing house."

Freddie grinned. "Thank God! Now, I know you're on my side. Frank Selby would have let me walk all over him."

"Assuming he decided to take an interest in it." Gathering her composure together, Kathy turned back to the manuscript.

Freddie watched her.

"Did you like Selby?" he asked, sitting down.

"Not really. He was fairly intelligent, but very lazy. I was doing almost all of his work for him." Kathy found her curiosity at last rising and returned his gaze. "You say you knew him. How well?"

"He mostly hung on his cousin's coattails. Percy Selby is as well-positioned as I am. He thought Frank was a lot of fun, and I suspect enjoyed the power he had, being magnanimous to the poor relative. Then again, maybe not." Freddie frowned, pondering something, then dismissed it. "I personally found Selby to be witty, but not especially so, a cad when it came to women, and a fair hooch maker, no small thing these days. I assume he threatened to fire you if you let it get out that you did his work."

"He did," Kathy grumbled. She looked at him again. "But why do you want to know?"

Freddie shrugged delicately. "Curiosity, I suppose."

Kathy stood and glared him down. "Curiosity? Or are you worried that I might have killed him? I do have reason to have wanted Selby dead."

"Pray, forgive me!" Freddie sat back in shock. "I didn't mean to imply that at all, especially since I'm fairly certain you're innocent."

"And what made you decide that?"

"A woman who can get a satisfactory conclusion from Mr. Healcroft on her own doesn't need to resort to murder to achieve her ends." Freddie smiled beseechingly.

Kathy folded her arms. "That gives me more reason to have killed Mr. Selby. You cleared me because you think someone else did it."

"That's true," said Freddie after a rueful sigh.

"You don't have to tell me, just the police." Kathy stared at her desk. With any luck, he wouldn't notice how badly she wanted to know.

"Oh no. I don't have any proof that this person did it." Freddie fixed a speculative gaze on her. "I'm thinking of Cousin Percy. Even if I did tell the police that Percy has threatened his cousin with violence more than once, Percy's connections are such that I'd practically have to have a photograph

23

of him doing the deed before the police would even question him."

"New York's Finest swayed by connections?" Kathy let out a mocking chortle. "You'd better start looking for that photograph."

"Or other evidence. Then again, there's always the possibility that Frank Selby was murdered by someone else." Freddie drifted off into deep thought.

"Don't look at me," said Kathy, who hadn't noticed. She leaned back in her chair, finally feeling as though she were safe. "And I don't think anyone around here did it. The police only searched his office this afternoon for the sake of routine. I have every reason to believe they think Mr. Selby was the victim of a burglar."

"At this moment in time, I'm sure they do." Freddie's finger rapped out a steady beat on the desk. "But someone down at headquarters will certainly begin to wonder what Frank Selby had to steal, and you must admit, Miss Briscow, you appear to have the most obvious motive, especially if they make certain assumptions about Mr. Selby."

"If they're going to make that kind of assumption, there are plenty of other women who have more motive than I do." Kathy swallowed back her fear and let rational thought reign again in her head. "Besides, I have good reason to believe that the police will not be looking at me."

"What good reason?" Freddie smiled, but Kathy noted the alert interest in his eyes and decided that pressing the issue would only distract him further.

"I have an uncle on the force, a sergeant," she replied slowly. She held her breath as he mulled the information over, then relaxed when it appeared he either didn't assume that all coppers were Irish (although her uncle was) or was more democratic in his thinking than his status would suggest. "Shall we get back to *The Old Money Story?*"

"We might as well."

But Freddie continued to digress to speculation about the murder. Kathy found herself caught up in the musings, then with no little irritation would force the conversation back to Freddie's book. Finally, even she had to admit her curiosity was overwhelming, and suggested searching the office.

It was a small room, with a wall filled with bookshelves, a faded rose carpet under the medium-sized desk and two straight-backed chairs in front of the desk.

"Not that we have any right to search," Kathy said, going through the desk drawers. "Nor should we be doing police work."

"Nonsense," said Freddie. "You knew Selby better than most, especially as his secretary. You're far more likely to find something important."

Kathy refrained from asking Freddie why he was involving himself. Some minutes later, Freddie laid out the more obvious findings on Selby's desk.

"Some old love letters, two bottles of homemade whiskey, four stray keys, and a buttonhook," said Kathy. "Why would he have a buttonhook? Shoes with buttons went out of style before I got out of college."

"There are a few old fogies who wear them. And," Freddie paused. "It's not something one talks about."

"I have heard of that." Kathy blushed then turned pale. "Oh, my god. That could have been how he was killed. I mean, if he were... Perhaps the woman didn't want to, or felt he was going to kill her."

"Or maybe his partner got too rough." Freddie suddenly remembered with whom he was speaking. "Perhaps we should find something a little less indelicate to discuss."

"Don't be so Victorian, Mr. Little. Everyone talks about sex these days. And I've had to read some very perverse manuscripts." Kathy turned thoughtful. "It was Mr. Selby who insisted I read them, too. I thought at the time he was trying to shock me. I wonder now if he had some other purpose."

"Alas, we can't ask him. I do think I'll have a little chat with Percy Selby in the near future."

"Then I'll leave it in your hands." Kathy went into the outer office, and gathered her papers together. "Frankly, if all that sort of thing is involved, I'd rather not know."

"Very well. Shall I see you home?"

Kathy shook her head. "It's not necessary. I just take the subway to the Village. I only live a few blocks from the stop."

"It doesn't hurt to have a man around." Freddie held Kathy's coat for her. "Besides, after you insisted so vehemently that I not play white knight for your career, the least you could do is give my fragile male ego a boost by allowing me to see you safely to your front doorstep."

"What rot." Kathy put on her hat.

Still, she had to admit she was pleased when Freddie got his own coat and hat from the front of the office and went with her.

CHAPTER THREE

After leaving Freddie on the sidewalk in front of the tall, brick boarding house, Kathy hurried into the house's front hall only to find that her landlady, Mrs. Lynne, was all a-flutter because Kathy had a late guest: her uncle, the policeman. Nonetheless, without any comment, Mrs. Lynne showed Kathy into the receiving parlor, a room filled to bursting with a couch, easy chairs, a piano, and a breakfront, all covered with lace antimacassars or china figurines.

Sergeant Daniel Callaghan was waiting. He was an average-sized man in a brown wool suit that barely hid the paunch he was growing. Kathy had seen his black bowler hat on the coat tree in the foyer. His face was flushed somewhat pink and the veins on his nose were just starting to stand out. His hair had been black, but was now mostly gray and thinning.

"Good evening, Uncle Dan." Kathy dutifully pecked the older man's cheek. "This is certainly a surprise."

"It's always a pleasure to see you, Kathleen," he replied.

There was an awkward pause while they waited for Mrs. Lynne to withdraw. A heavy-set woman, she nonetheless had a fluffy manner and a reedy, sing-song voice. Her graying blonde hair was pulled back into a severe bun at the back of her neck, and she wore a dark blue wool dress that reached her ankles with a white linen and lace standing collar. Like most of Mrs. Lynne's vast wardrobe, it had been new in the mid-teens. The landlady looked from one to the other.

"Are we all comfortable?" she asked, not leaving.

"This is family business," said Callaghan. "So, if you don't mind, it would be a kindness to take your leave. It shouldn't take too long."

"Certainly, certainly." Mrs. Lynne bustled to the door. "Call me if you need me, Miss Briscow."

"I will."

"My apologies for imposing on you, Mrs. Lynne." Callaghan waited until the door was shut, then turned to his niece. "How did you get this place?"

"Uncle Mike found it for me."

Callaghan rolled his eyes. "I might have known. He still hasn't forgiven himself for letting your mother give him the slip when she ran off to marry your father."

"I know. Please, sit down." Kathy waited for her uncle to settle himself on the overstuffed floral chintz couch before seating herself on the nearby matching chair. She sighed. "Why are you here, Uncle Dan? There's got to be something wrong, or you

29

wouldn't have come this late."

"There is." He frowned and nodded. "It's about your boss, Katie-girl."

"Mr. Selby?"

"That's the one. There's some funny business going on with that one."

Kathy's eyes widened. "But wasn't it just burglars? I mean that's what everyone's saying."

"If it were, it was their first burglary. They left fifty dollars on the bureau in the bedroom where the body was found." He sighed again.

The parlor door opened and Mrs. Lynne bustled in and Dan scrambled to his feet.

"Just looking for my tatting," she announced, going over to the end table next to the couch and pulling the lace and thread from a small workbasket under the table. "Here it is. Kathy, are you sure you and your uncle wouldn't like a nice, hot cup of tea?"

Kathy smiled. "I don't think so, Mrs. Lynne. Thank you for asking."

"Mrs. Lynne, if you would please excuse us," said Callaghan.

"Oh, of course." Mrs. Lynne scurried to the door. "I'll just be in the next room if you need me."

Callaghan waited until the door was shut then lowered his voice.

"The problem with your boss, Katie-girl, is the department's thinking is that Mr. Selby was asking you to do more than hide his absences, if you'll pardon me for being so indelicate." Dan eased himself back onto the couch.

Kathy pulled her handkerchief from her sleeve. "Given what I've had to read for my job, I'm hardened to it, Uncle Dan."

"It gets worse, darling." Callaghan looked up at the ceiling. "We believe Mr. Selby was killed Monday night, since that was the last time anybody saw him. Mr. Krinkly, he's the super, he says he remembers seeing a woman leave the building around eleven o'clock Monday night. She was by herself, and he marked it because what woman would be going out alone at that hour?"

Kathy frowned, thinking. "Was she a tenant?"

"Mr. Krinkly knows his people pretty well. She wasn't a tenant. She was in a hurry. Krinkly didn't get a good look at her. She was wearing a tweed coat with the collar up around her face, and a dark hat. All bundled up like that, there wasn't much he could say about her."

"She could have been anyone." Kathy swallowed, twisting the handkerchief around her fingers. "She could have been visiting a sick aunt, or something. She wasn't necessarily visiting Mr. Selby."

"I know." Dan nodded sympathetically.

"It wasn't me. I'm not even sure where Mr. Selby lived, or even how he died."

"Selby's head was bashed in with the poker from the fireplace." Dan shrugged to hide his interest in Kathy's reaction.

The parlor door opened again.

"Sergeant, are you sure you don't want a nice, hot cup of tea?" asked Mrs. Lynne. "It's snowing and it's awfully cold out there. It'll warm you up for the trip home."

"I'll be quite all right, Ma'am. Now, if you'll excuse us?" Dan bounced up.

"Oh, of course." She bustled out.

"I'm sorry about her," sighed Kathy.

Callaghan waved it off and winced as he sat again. "Let's get back to your boss."

Kathy's curiosity overtook her fear. "You know, it could have been self-defense. If it was the woman Krinkly saw, then maybe Selby attacked her, and she reached for the nearest thing handy."

Callaghan laughed. "Now I know you weren't there. Like I said, Selby was found in his bedroom, and he was hit from behind. Nothing was disturbed as if there'd been a fight. I think it was somebody Selby knew, somebody he wouldn't be afraid to turn his back on. I've got a bad feeling that woman has something to do with it, and until we find her, I'm afraid the boys will be looking very closely at you. Can you tell me where you were Monday last?"

"I went to supper then on to see *Lady Be Good*, you know that new show with the Astaires? I didn't get home until almost midnight." Kathy shook her head, knowing what was coming next.

"Did anyone you know see you?"

"No," Kathy said. "I was alone the whole

night. Maybe one of the ushers will recognize me. I don't see how. I didn't speak to any of them, and I found my seat by myself."

"Do you at least have your ticket stub?"

"Why would I keep that?" Kathy shrugged. "I probably left it in the theater."

"All right." Callaghan hauled himself to his feet. "It doesn't look good. But I'm sure you're telling the truth. The only problem will be convincing Reagan. I wouldn't worry. I'm sure I can."

"Uncle Dan, you don't have to crusade for me." Kathy stood, also.

Callaghan put his hand on Kathy's shoulder. "Kathleen, I promised your mother I'd look out for you, and I'd never be able to live with myself if I let her down."

"All right, Uncle Dan. I appreciate the warning."

"I'd better be getting on, then." He yawned. "For my sins, this job is taking its toll. And there's the family, as always. Every little problem, they come to me. Like your Aunt Mary. She's got her back up about another murdered bum in front of her convent."

"Oh no. What's that?"

Dan shook his head again. "It's nothing for you to worry yourself over. Good night, darling."

"Good night, Uncle Dan."

Kathy kissed her uncle, then showed him out with Mrs. Lynne in the background, watching as

Kathy handed Callaghan his coat, bowler hat and knit scarf. Mrs. Lynne tried pouncing on Kathy as soon as she shut the front door, but Kathy yawned and hurried upstairs to her room as fast as she could.

The next morning, Freddie adjusted his fedora and checked the foyer mirror.

"Much better," he said, nodding at the valet. "You were right, Roberts. The other was just a shade off with this suit."

"Yes, sir," Roberts replied. He was an average-sized man of impassive face, properly slicked down hair and anonymous mien. It was his job to anticipate the needs of his employer, preferably invisibly, and he was good at it.

The phone rang and Roberts picked it up.

"Just one moment," he told the other party, then looked at Freddie, holding his hand over the mouthpiece. "It's Mr. Winters, sir. Are you in?"

"Of course." Freddie took the set and put the receiver to his ear. "Lowell, how are you?"

"I'm not in any mood to converse," growled the voice on the other end. "Nine o'clock tonight? The usual spot?"

"Yes. I'm looking—"

The line was already dead. Chuckling, Freddie replaced the receiver and checked his watch. It was almost eleven. Roberts had his overcoat, scarf and gloves ready.

Freddie noticed Victoria Winters at the apartment building's lobby desk as he got off the elevator, which explained Lowell's mood. Victoria wasn't going to let a silly divorce get in the way of taking care of her man, and had obviously decided yet again that Lowell didn't know what was good for him. She had been nothing but trouble ever since Lowell had gotten mixed up with her. Freddie felt responsible because Victoria was from his set, and if he hadn't dragged Lowell to that blasted ball, the two would never have met. Freddie stepped up his pace towards the door, but that only caught her attention and she stopped him with a wave.

"Oh, Freddie, they said you weren't in," she said with a pleasant smile. Her dark hair was bobbed and slicked down under a cloche hat that perfectly matched the fur-trimmed overcoat covering her slender, fashionable figure.

Freddie smiled back. "I'm not. So, what brings you here, Victoria?"

"I was worried. I heard you had an accident in that plane of yours. They said you weren't hurt. I'm glad to see it." Victoria smiled, but Freddie had the odd feeling that she would have been happier if he had been injured

"I'm glad I wasn't hurt, too," he said pleasantly.

She sniffed dismissively. "I tried to speak to Lowell this morning. He was quite abrupt with me."

"Indeed." Freddie decided not to say more.

"He told me he was seeing you tonight. Perhaps you could just tell him a little something for me." Victoria affected her innocent look, which had never worked.

"I'm afraid not, Victoria."

"Oh, Freddie. Don't be so difficult. I'm merely concerned."

"I know you are, Victoria. Now, if you'll excuse me, I do have an appointment, and I see my taxi is waiting."

"Good day then, Freddie." With head held high, Victoria swept out of the building to her car.

Freddie waited just long enough to put Victoria out of his mind, then went to his waiting taxi and began the trip downtown.

He wasn't at all sure he should be going to Healcroft House that morning, but he couldn't get Frank Selby's death off his mind, or Miss Briscow, either. Although he couldn't say why, he felt certain of her innocence, knowing that most of her co-workers were equally certain of her guilt. Worse yet, if Percy Selby had killed his cousin, the police wouldn't be likely to do anything about it and might arrest Miss Briscow just to have someone to blame it on.

Some minutes later, Freddie wandered into Mr. Healcroft's outer office. The door to the inner office just happened to be open. Freddie grinned. The two secretaries who had been solid blocks of concentration moments before were suddenly very busy, but still very quiet. Freddie peeked inside the office. A rather small, dark-haired man in vest, shirtsleeves and visor fumed in front of the aging publisher.

"This is no promotion!" the young man declared. "Little's book is going to sell like hotcakes whether it's good or not, and how does it look if a woman gets the credit for it?"

"I realize it's a little irregular," said Mr. Healcroft nervously.

"It's not irregular. It's ridiculous! I've heard about that book. It's filled with murder, and blood, and all sorts of disgusting things. How can a woman edit that?"

"Miss Briscow has her degree in world literature from Radcliffe, and she graduated magna cum laude. She also edited *Pirates on the Maine*, and did an excellent job." Mr. Healcroft looked up and started. "Excuse me, Mr. Evans, here is Mr. Little, himself."

"Good morning, Mr. Healcroft." Freddie entered and shook the older man's hand.

"Good morning, Mr. Little," Mr. Healcroft replied. "This is Mr. Miles Evans, who will be taking Mr. Selby's place."

"So I heard. May I be the first to offer you congratulations, Mr. Evans." Freddie extended his hand.

"Thanks." Evans shook the proffered hand quickly.

Something about the man's angst tickled Freddie and he decided to tease him a little.

"In fact, might I extend an invitation to you and Mr. Healcroft, of course, to raise a glass in celebration." Freddie turned to Mr. Healcroft. "You know the place, where we met down in the Village. Nine o'clock?"

"I'm afraid I have other plans," Mr. Healcroft said. "But, Mr. Evans, if you'd care to go, please don't avoid it on my account."

"That's a generous offer, Mr. Little." Evans' eyes lit up as he thought of something. "I may just."

"I'll look for you, then." Freddie paused. Evans seemed to be waiting for something. Freddie guessed and thought he'd lead the man on. "I expect we'll be seeing a fair amount of each other, what with my book and all."

"That." Evans' grin got a touch mean. "Apparently Mr. Selby was in the habit of letting his secretary do his work for him. It seems she's working on your book."

Healcroft shifted and shot a quick glare at Evans. "You'll have to excuse Mr. Evans, Mr. Little. He's been looking to Mr. Selby's job for some time, and it was quite a shock to find that he wasn't going to do your book after all. Miss Briscow has already started work on the project. I have been supervising it quite closely, and she is doing very well, surprisingly enough."

"It doesn't surprise me in the least," said Freddie. "I had the pleasure of meeting her last night."

Mr. Healcroft's eyebrow rose. "You did?"

"While I was waiting for Mr. Selby." Freddie paused, suddenly realizing he could get Miss Briscow into trouble. "She didn't tell me she was working on my book, but I commend your perception."

"Ha," snorted Evans. Freddie caught the fleeting scowl. Obviously, Evans' plan had backfired.

"Mr. Evans, that will be enough," Healcroft said. "If you do not wish to take the position, you needn't."

"I'll take it."

"I'd watch what you say regarding Miss Briscow," said Freddie. "Who knows? She might end up as your boss some day."

Evans laughed angrily. "That'll be the day. A lady editor-in-chief. Thank you, Mr. Healcroft. I'm sorry for the outburst."

He left quickly.

"Interesting," Freddie muttered as he sat down in front of Healcroft's desk. "Was Mr. Evans the only one interested in Mr. Selby's position?"

"All my junior editors wanted that job, even if it came with Miss Briscow. Mr. Evans was the most suited."

"Did he know it?"

"That is hard to say. I generally keep my intentions to myself, but someone might have decided that I was favoring him, and let the rumors fly."

Freddie tipped his chair back on its legs. "I take it Miss Briscow is not popular with the rest of the staff?"

"Some of the typists and other women consider her a little aloof, but she does have friends among them. Some of the men," Mr. Healcroft cleared his throat. "They seem to find her intimidating."

"And I don't doubt Miss Briscow would be utterly shocked if she ever found out."

"No doubt. Might I offer you a cigarette?"

"Thank you. Don't mind if I do." Freddie pulled his holder from his suit coat and leaned forward to the case held out by Healcroft. "I hope you don't mind, but I'm rather curious about this Selby affair. How well did you know Mr. Selby?"

Healcroft thought as he lit Freddie's cigarette, then one for himself.

"As well as any man knows his employees, I would imagine. We didn't socialize. Mr. Selby ran with a fast crowd, as you may know."

"I do indeed. I'd met him a couple times. It seems there were some strange rumors floating around. He didn't strike me as that type, but one never knows, does one?"

"It depends on what type." The barest hint of a flush tinged Healcroft's face. He shifted, then appeared to find some safer ground. "I don't care to speak ill of the dead, but Mr. Selby did tend to be rather lazy. Please don't misunderstand me. He was an excellent editor."

"I'm certain he was. But his relationship with his coworkers, what was that like?"

Healcroft shrugged. "He got on well enough, I suppose. He wasn't the most popular man in the office, but he wasn't feared, either. He did tend to keep his nose in the air, on account of his rich relatives..." He sent a suspicious glance Freddie's way. "But why the interest? Surely you're not giving any weight to those murder rumors, are you?"

"As I understand it, he was murdered."

"Yes. By a burglar breaking into his apartment, or so I read this morning."

Freddie tipped his chair back again. "What would a burglar hope to gain by breaking into Frank Selby's apartment? His recipe for bathtub gin? Selby's hooch was good, but not that good."

Healcroft sat up straight. "Mr. Little, I hope you are not planning on implicating any members of my staff in this."

"Actually, I'd like to clear them." Freddie reclined even further. "Although if someone from this office is involved, there's not much I can do."

"But surely you can let the police handle this."

"Indeed I could, and probably should. But there are some nagging questions about this affair that I don't think the police would know to ask. They're busy and I'm not, so I might as well do the asking."

Healcroft shook his head. "Far be it from me to tell you what to do with your time, but boredom seems to be a rather poor excuse for sticking your neck out where it doesn't belong."

"It'll have to do," sighed Freddie. He got up and held out his hand. "I appreciate your taking the time to chat with me."

"Any time, Mr. Little." Mr. Healcroft returned the grasp with an efficient shake.

Freddie ambled to the door, then turned. "Oh, one more thing, Mr. Healcroft. I wonder if you'd know why Mr. Selby would keep a buttonhook in his desk?"

"I-I have no idea." Mr. Healcroft pressed his lips together, emphasizing the slight loss of color in his face. "I keep mine at home. F-for my shoes, you understand."

"Of course. But Selby wore pumps."

"I never noticed. In any case, Mr. Little, I have work to get done."

"Certainly, Mr. Healcroft. My apologies. I've already intruded abominably."

Freddie swaggered out, ostensibly without a care in the world. But his mind reeled with possibilities. The question was where to start?

Kathy yawned for the fifth time as she stared at the cramped writing she was to turn into a neatly typed report. It was on a manuscript that was a vapid attempt at an F. Scott Fitzgerald look-alike, almost a parody of *The Beautiful and Damned*. Kathy would never have bought it. But that wasn't her job, not yet, at any rate. For all Freddie Little's book may have been inspired by *This Side of Paradise*, at least he had the good sense to develop his own style.

Freddie Little seemed to be occupying her thoughts a great deal since the night before. How

odd that he had guessed Selby's death had been
cold-blooded murder, and that she would be suspected. He seemed sincere enough. But he was certainly
more intelligent than he seemed to like most people
to believe.

She forced her mind back to her typing. Half
a page later, she found herself wondering about
Elsie Quinn, who had been Mr. Selby's secretary
before Kathy. He had fired her, claiming she was a
trouble-maker who spread vicious rumors. Everyone
had known it was ridiculous. If spreading vicious
rumors was cause for dismissal, then two thirds of
the staff at Healcroft House, including Mr. Selby,
had reason to fear for their jobs.

Yet, there was that buttonhook, and those
manuscripts. What if Elsie had complained to Mr.
Healcroft? What would have happened? Exactly
what had. Kathy nibbled thoughtfully on a pencil.
Elsie had needed that job. She was a widow with
four children to support, and as fiercely determined
to make it on her own as Kathy was. Brooding over
the injustice of losing her job could have made her
desperate.

Kathy pondered. She and Elsie hadn't kept
in touch much after Elsie had been fired. Perhaps
it was time for a visit. She reached for the phone.
The call took longer than Kathy had planned. Elsie
didn't have her own phone and Kathy had to wait
several minutes while the man who kept the store
on the ground floor of the building where Elsie lived
hunted Elsie down and brought her to his phone.
Fortunately, it didn't take long to make the arrange-
ments for the visit.

As Kathy hung up, Mr. Evans wandered in,
whistling that catchy little tune from *Lady Be Good*.
He stopped as he saw her.

"Personal calls are not to be made from your desk, Miss Briscow," he snarled.

"I beg your pardon, Mr. Evans?" Kathy was puzzled. Mr. Evans had been almost friendly earlier that morning when she greeted him outside the junior editors' room.

"Personal calls, Miss Briscow." Evans folded his arms and leaned on the door jamb.

He was a small man with a round, boyish face. Under his ill-defined chin, he perpetually wore a burgundy and gold school bow tie apparently from some university out West that no one had ever heard of. Like most of the other junior editors, Evans usually worked in vest and shirtsleeves. Kathy noted with a start that he was wearing his suit jacket and no longer had his visor on.

"Mr. Selby may have let you do as you please, but I'm your boss now, and I frown on little deviations from the rules," Evans continued, smirking. "Those reports Mr. Healcroft gave you this morning. Are you done typing them yet?"

"No, Mr. Evans," Kathy stammered, trying to absorb both the news and the request. "I only got them this morning. Even Jess Perkins can't type that fast."

"They need to be done today, as well as the letters to Mr. Selby's authors and other contacts about my appointment. You'll need to write them up, but make sure they're signed with my name." Evans glared at her. "Stay after if you have to, but I want it all on my desk before tomorrow morning."

"But, Mr. Evans, I can't get all this done by tonight!" Furious, Kathy got up and followed Evans into the inner office. "And I have other jobs to complete, too."

"Another job, you mean. That will just have to wait. You are my secretary, and that means my work comes first. I expect you to stay late until everything is finished, and do whatever else comes up, too." Evans struggled with the drawer to the desk. "Damn it to hell! Briscow, do you know how to get this thing open?"

Kathy pressed her lips together. "Slide out the top center drawer a little."

"Right. What is all this stuff? Briscow, get a box and clear out all of Selby's stuff and give it to his family." Evans turned around and around in the office, apparently making a list of other changes he wanted to make.

"What about your letters?" Kathy asked.

He smirked again. "You're staying late. What are you worried about?"

Kathy held back the angry words and her tears and left the office.

Freddie was again waiting for her.

Kathy silently groaned. "May I help you, Mr. Little?"

"I started some of those changes last night," he replied with puppy-like enthusiasm. "I thought you might like to look at them and see if I've got it right. It feels very uncomfortable."

"Good." She pushed past him and headed into the hall. "Now, if you'll excuse me, Mr. Little, I don't want to see any changes until they're fin-

45

ished."

Freddie caught up and stopped her. "You're overwrought, Miss Briscow. What's wrong? Here. This conference room is empty."

He all but dragged her into the darkened room and shut the door. Kathy sank against the edge of the dark wood table. Gray light filtered in through the windows

"Now, what's the matter?" Freddie asked in his most soothing voice.

"I owe you an apology, Mr. Little." Kathy sniffed, vainly trying not to cry. "I'm just so angry now, and I have no right to take it out on you."

"What happened?"

"I'm not sure." Kathy pulled her handkerchief from her sleeve and dabbed at her eyes. "It's Mr. Evans. He's Mr. Selby's replacement. He's given me an impossible amount of work to do, which won't leave me any time to work on your book, unless I forgo eating and sleeping."

"So talk to Mr. Healcroft."

Kathy shook her head. "And all Mr. Evans has to do is deny it, insinuating at the same time that my female sensibilities aren't up to editing a work of such scope as yours, and who do you think Mr. Healcroft will believe?"

"You." Freddie sighed. "But he will act on Mr. Evans' word."

Kathy sniffed. "I'm damned no matter which way I turn."

Freddie winced at the foul language but ignored it. "I have a typist that could help."

"That's what got Mr. Selby into trouble." Kathy dabbed again at her eyes with her handkerchief. "Thank you for your offer, Mr. Little, but I'll manage. Wait. There is a way you could help. I've got an important meeting this evening. If you could arrive at, say five-thirty, I'm sure Mr. Evans will be in. Kindly demand that you take me to supper to discuss your book. Evans knows you're important, and I don't think he'll argue."

Freddie's right eyebrow lifted. "Does this mean I get to take you to supper?"

"I'm afraid it doesn't. But are you still interested in finding out who killed Mr. Selby?"
"Yes!"
"If you'll do me another favor, I'll offer you another tidbit." Kathy took a deep breath. "You know Mr. Selby's cousin, don't you?"

"Yes, Percy." Freddie's eyebrow lifted.

"Then maybe you know Mr. Selby's family, or can at least find out. Mr. Evans has asked me to clear all of Mr. Selby's personal effects out of his office and give them to his family. I know we searched it last night, but we were a little rushed. Maybe we missed something."

"And if the delivery is a little delayed, I just happen to be an irresponsible lout anyway." Freddie chortled. "That's wonderful, Miss Briscow."

"You will tell me what you find, won't you?" Kathy felt her voice getting plaintive and swallowed.

"On one condition. That you give me all the information you have."

"Well," Kathy balked.

Freddie grinned knowingly. "I am willing to put up some good money that your meeting tonight involves getting more information on the matter."

"I certainly have reason to. Even with an uncle on the force, politics and prejudices being what they are, it doesn't hurt to hedge my bets a little."

"Thus nicely continuing my metaphor." Freddie stood up straight. "I will be here at five thirty sharp, and I will see you to your meeting."

Kathy smiled. "I prefer to go alone, Mr. Little. It would probably be easier for my friend."

"I understand perfectly. I won't attend the interview, but I will pick you up afterward, so we can discuss my changes and compare notes on anything we may have learned about Mr. Selby's death."

"All right." Kathy nodded, wiped her nose one last time, then slid her handkerchief back into her sleeve.

Mr. Evans was clearly peeved when Freddie swooped in at five thirty and carried Kathy off. But there wasn't anything he could do. Downstairs, on Broadway, Freddie hailed a taxi.

"West 43rd?" Freddie gulped as Kathy gave the address to the taxi driver. "Good lord, that's Hell's Kitchen."

"And that's where Elsie lives, I'm afraid,"

said Kathy.

"It's a good thing I decided to come with you." Freddie puffed himself up with chivalrous pride, then slumped. His insides were quaking. Kathy knew it, and he knew damn well she knew it. He sulked. "Did you find anything?"

"It's what I didn't find that's more significant," Kathy replied.

"What was that?"

"I'll leave it to you to figure it out."

Freddie decided against pressing the issue and instead asked who Elsie was. Kathy's explanation didn't take long, but neither did the ride. While Kathy was inside the battered tenement building, Freddie went through the box she had given him. What he didn't find were four stray keys, two bottles of whiskey, and a buttonhook.

CHAPTER FOUR

The four Quinn children were as well-be-
haved as one could expect little ones ten years and
younger to be. Still, dinner was an awkward meal.
Kathy was glad that when they finished eating, the
youngsters kissed their mother goodnight and their
grandmother herded them off to bed in the small
apartment's only other room.

"They're such dears," sighed Elsie as she
stacked dishes and turned to put them in the kitch-
en sink. "They're all that keeps me going sometimes."

"I don't doubt it," Kathy replied, silently thanking the heavens she hadn't been foolish
enough to get married. "You're looking well."

She wasn't. Elsie's face had always been
taut with worry. But now it was even tighter. Dark
circles ringed her eyes. Her light brown hair was
unkempt. Her plain dress was faded and the wool
had several darns in it. The holes had been neatly
repaired, but they still showed.

"It's been rough, but the wolf's not on the
stoop yet. Ma takes in washing, always has. I help
out, so we can take in more. I take in typing from

the agency." Elsie shrugged and looked down at the battered wooden table in the corner of the tiny kitchen that served as a dining room. "It's not much, but I get to be home with the kids, at least. It's real hard raising three boys without their dad."

"I can imagine. Do you think much about what happened?"

Elsie frowned. "What do you mean?"

"I don't know," Kathy said. "I'm sure it's rather personal, but if Mr. Selby had fired me for spreading rumors, especially when he was just as bad, I'd have been fighting mad."

"I was. I was real mad." Elsie sniffled and pulled a handkerchief out of her dress pocket. "I even went to Mr. Healcroft about it. But there was nothing he could do. I even told him what Selby really did. He told me Mr. Selby said he didn't, and that left his hands tied."

"What did Selby do?"

"Oh, it was awful, Kathy." Elsie shook her head. "I couldn't."

Hoping to reassure her friend, Kathy feigned disinterest. "Was it something sexual?"

Elsie went beet red. "Look, Kathy, I know you read all that stuff, but... I don't know."

"When I first started working for Mr. Selby, he had me read a manuscript called *The Pain of Pleasure*." Kathy reached over and touched Elsie's hand.

Elsie's face again reddened. "What did you do?"

51

"I read it, then gave him my opinion." Kathy shrugged. "It was poorly written, full of bad grammar and worse syntax, the plot was ill-conceived and the characters were unconvincing."

"What did Selby do?"

"Looked at me strangely, then gave me another to read. After the first three, he started giving me real manuscripts. The next thing I knew I was editing them, with him getting the credit. I'm guessing that you got to read *The Pain of Pleasure*, too."

"I read it." Elsie sighed again and leaned back in her chair. "I told him what I thought of it, and of him. Forcing a Christian woman to read stuff like that. He said I wouldn't have to read anymore, which I didn't."

"Is that what he fired you over?"

"No." Elsie swallowed and decided to continue talking. "Two weeks later, he starts talking dirty to me. I didn't like it, but there was the kids to remember. For them, I could stand a little bad language. Then he started getting real personal. I asked him to stop. He just laughed, and said I liked it and he knew it. Then a month or so later, he asked me to stay late one night. He took me into his office, and asked me to do the most terrible things."

"Did you?"

"I didn't. I'm not that kind of woman. He said he'd fire me if I didn't. So first thing next morning I went to talk to Mr. Healcroft, as if that would help."

"Oh, Elsie, how terrible." Inwardly, Kathy shuddered, trying to suppress her rage.

"Why didn't he do that to you?" Elsie started to cry.

"I think he realized he could get more from me if I did his work for him," Kathy said, keeping her tone even. She paused. "What do you think you would do if you saw him again?"

"I'm a Christian." Elsie sat up straight. "I'd forgive him. I already have."

"That's a blessing, I guess." Kathy traced a threadbare flower on the tablecloth with her finger, keeping one eye on Elsie. "I don't suppose you've heard."

"What?"

"Mr. Selby's dead. He was killed in his apartment last Monday night."

"Killed?" Elsie made a quick sign of the cross. "Lord have mercy, how?"

"They're saying a burglar did it."

"God rest him. He was a terrible man, but no one deserves that."

With a sigh, Kathy decided Elsie was innocent, and murmured the appropriate sentiments. She left shortly after. A taxi, with Freddie in it, waited at the curb.

"Good heavens!" Kathy exclaimed, getting in. "Have you been waiting here all this time?"

"Actually, no. I did go and fetch myself a bite, and one other trifle." Freddie patted a small bulge under his overcoat pocket. Kathy saw that the bulge was gun-shaped and rolled her eyes. With

53

a shrug, Freddie blew out a mouthful of cigarette smoke and signaled the driver to start. "But our driver here will be getting a good fare. I thought it best to hang onto him. Not too many taxis come out to this end of town. Did you eat?"

"I was quite well fed, I'm afraid. I told Elsie not to have supper. But she still put out a Sunday spread for me." Kathy sighed and shut the window between them and the driver, then told Freddie about what Selby had done. "It's so unfair. If I had known how bad things are for Elsie, I might have killed Mr. Selby."

"And I might have joined you." Freddie sucked in a thoughtful drag. "Oh, excuse me. Would you like a cigarette?"

"I don't smoke. I tried it once in college and decided anything that unpleasant couldn't be worth getting used to."

"One does have to acquire a taste for it. But why didn't Selby force himself on you?"

Kathy grimaced. "I suppose when Mr. Selby realized I wouldn't be bullied, he decided it was just as well since I was more useful in other ways."

"In addition, you wouldn't have been quite as much fun." Freddie kept his tone casual and gazed unseeing at the street, the lights of the cars and buildings reflecting in the wet sleet. "Cads like Frank Selby prefer their women to cower."

Kathy shivered. "I can't imagine how anyone could enjoy such a thing. I suppose it has something to do with that psychology stuff. Have you ever read Freud?"

"Who hasn't? He was delightfully Victorian. It all seems to boil down to sex, doesn't it?" Freddie chuckled, then realized he was looking at Kathy's bosom, and that it was a real bosom in spite of current fashion. Startled, he looked away.

Deep in thought, Kathy didn't notice. "Can you think of anybody who hated Mr. Selby? Besides his cousin, I mean."

Freddie laughed. "Any number of people. But most of them are too lazy to waste their time hiring someone to kill him. Wait. That's an angle I hadn't thought of. Consider, Miss Briscow. Frank Selby was known for his hooch. Now, think. If booze is illegal, where does most of it come from?"

"Home breweries, and stills, and the ever popular bathtub. Some of it's smuggled in."

"Anything with a real label on it is." Freddie settled back into a philosophical pose, gesturing with his cigarette holder. "Some of the larger companies still make it for industrial and medicinal purposes, with some of it filtering through to us poor thirsty ones, when we can get our doctors to prescribe it for us. Or —"

"Is there a point in all of this?" Kathy interrupted.

"Of course. I don't generally start an argument without some theory behind it."

Kathy threw up her hands. "That is exactly what I mean when I say you digress. We don't need the whole argument, just the point."

"That does make sense, I think. But how do you know when it's too much?"

"That's what my job is. Yours is to tell the story."

"And the story I was telling was..." Freddie frowned. "Blast it. I've lost my train of thought."

Kathy sighed. "You were on some long diatribe on where speakeasies get their booze."

"Ah, yes. To get to the heart of the matter. Who supplies most of the speakeasies in this city?"

"There's no one person." Kathy looked at him as if he'd just said the moon shone during the day.

"Not a person." Freddie leaned next to her and whispered. "The mob. Mafia. They own and run all of the major distilleries, and they don't like competition. If Frank Selby crossed their path —"

"His body would never have been found in his apartment." Kathy shook her head. "My uncle the policeman has fished enough of their victims out of the East River to know a mob execution when he sees one. Besides, this isn't Chicago."

"But the mob does manufacture and import most of New York City's liquor."

"From what I've heard and seen, most of the speaks are independently owned, and the booze is distributed in neighborhood territories." Kathy gazed out the window at the passing traffic. "That could be an angle, though. If Mr. Selby disagreed with a saloon owner, maybe passed him a bad batch of liquor."

Freddie mused. "No. I can't see Frank passing bad hooch. He drank too much of it himself. And it seems to me, Percy Selby spent a great deal of time moaning how Frank spent so much time with his still. No. Blast. But that's the worst of this thing with Percy. I know he's perfectly capable of killing Selby, even over something as trivial as a drink. But I don't know exactly what the argument was that Percy threatened Frank over."

"And until you know that, you can't say for certain that Percy had a motive, trivial or otherwise," Kathy said. "Furthermore, it's not unlikely that Percy had nothing to do with it. It could have been something else alcohol-related, some other disagreement, territory or a payment, perhaps."

"That seems possible to me. We've got quite a few speaks to investigate, including the ones that Frank didn't usually patronize."

"You'll have to investigate. I've got to work in the morning. I've got reports to type." Kathy growled. "I'm still angry at him."

"Selby?"

"Evans. Although I wouldn't be surprised if Mr. Selby arranged it from the grave that things would go just as they have. I wonder if Evans likes buttonhooks."

"Aha! A non-sequitur." Freddie chortled. "I told you those frequently occur in real life."

Kathy was not cowed. "But they don't work in books. You're not writing life, Mr. Little, you're writing fiction."

"We were talking about Mr. Evans," Freddie replied with a small, injured huff. "Am I to assume from your remark that you'd like to use a buttonhook on him?"

"It could cause considerable pain." A wicked grin crept across Kathy's face as she mused.

"And considerable embarrassment." Freddie sat up straight. "Good God!"

"You thought of something."

"I spoke to Mr. Healcroft this morning. I came in just as Evans was having his say about not getting my book. You were right that he was throwing all that extra work at you, by the way."

"What did you just think of?" Kathy pressed.

"It was..." Freddie pulled the stub of his cigarette from the holder and opened the window a crack.

"You spoke to Mr. Healcroft." Kathy stayed focused on drawing Freddie out even as she shivered from the frigid air.

"That's right." Freddie quickly tossed the cigarette stub in the street, the closed the window. "After Evans left, I asked Mr. Healcroft if he knew of any reason why Mr. Selby would have a buttonhook in his desk. Mr. Healcroft seemed to be flustered by the question, and quickly sent me packing, making me fairly certain he lied when he said he didn't know."

"Mr. Healcroft?" Kathy gaped, then looked out the window to hide her burning face. "He couldn't be involved in... I could see him rum-running sooner."

Freddie chuckled. "He's a repressed old Victorian. It's entirely possible he isn't doing it. He just knows about it, and was terribly embarrassed by the thought."

"That seems more likely." Kathy bit her lip again. "And yet, when I had that meeting with him yesterday, he gave me almost everything I wanted except a senior editing position. And now that I think about it, I probably could have pushed and gotten that, too."

"So why didn't you?"

"Because I was so on edge I didn't realize why he was making all those promises." Kathy's brow creased in a puzzled frown. "He was afraid of me."

Freddie chuckled. "Afraid of you? You're hardly frightening." Then he paused. "But I can see where, shall we say, a lesser man might find you so."

"Briscow the ball buster," Kathy grumbled under her breath, as she glared out the window.

"Miss Briscow!" Shocked to his core, Freddie didn't know whether to remonstrate or laugh himself silly at such crass frankness.

Kathy shrugged. "It's what the junior editors call me, supposedly behind my back."

"If you'll excuse me for being so indelicate, I seriously doubt they have any cause for concern." Freddie hid his blush by lighting another cigarette.

"Of course not. I'm not..." Kathy paused, then flushed as she laughed. "Thank you, Mr. Little. That certainly puts things into perspective." Nervously, she pulled her handkerchief from her sleeve and dabbed at her nose. "But it doesn't entirely explain Mr. Healcroft's behavior. I'll see what I can nose out at the office. You'll have to do the investigating beyond that."

"We'll see." Freddie shifted around and pulled a pocket watch from his vest. "Hmm. It's not late. I know you have to work tomorrow, but I'm meeting a friend at nine at a little speak not far from your place. I think you'll like him. He's a writer, my mentor in a sense."

"Indeed. I would be interested in that. Thank you."

Freddie rapped on the window between them and the driver.

Some minutes later, Freddie helped Kathy out onto a darkened sidewalk on MacDougal Street, in Greenwich Village, then paid the driver.

"The problem is," Kathy was saying, "is that there are so many possible avenues to explore."

The taxi pulled away. The street was deserted, with all of the storefronts shuttered and dark, except for a small grocery store, which had a small line of light coming from under the front window shade. Freddie stepped gracefully between Kathy and the street.

"That's true," said Freddie, gently taking her elbow and guiding her toward the grocery store. "But there must be some way of narrowing things down a bit."

Kathy laughed. "I'm afraid, Mr. Little, that will have to be your job."

"That's Little!" hissed a raspy voice from a shadowed doorway.

Startled, Kathy turned toward the sound. She collided with a fetid, patched coat. For a brief instant, a face crowned by wisps of greasy, dark hair, and scarred and ragged with a toothless mouth, gaped at Kathy. She screamed.

The man pushed her aside. Kathy scrambled after him, tore at his arm and pummeled his back, screaming as if all the demons of hell were after her.

Freddie turned just in time to dodge two similar characters coming at him from another dark doorway. One, he tripped. The other rushed him. Freddie wriggled around and put two good punches in his belly. The man collapsed just as his comrade sprang. A stray gleam from the man's knife sent Freddie dancing backwards, reaching inside his overcoat for his gun.

More annoyed than angered by Kathy's persistence, the gang leader plucked her off himself and tossed her aside. Kathy hit the building hard, and crumpled to the sidewalk.

Freddie's shot ricocheted harmlessly off some nearby brick-work, but the blast sent the hoods scurrying away.

"Sure 'n what's going on here?" A policeman, who had apparently been on patrol on the next block, ran up from behind Freddie.

"After them, officer!" screamed Kathy. "They tried to kill us!"

The policeman took off after the hoods, his whistle shrieking into the night. Freddie dove to

61

Kathy's side.

"Are you all right?" he asked, breathing heavily.

"Yes!" Kathy hissed. "Get that piece away before you get arrested!"

"Oh." Freddie shoved the gun back into his coat. "Good thing I had it, though I didn't expect to use it down here."

"The crime rate is rising all over." Kathy grunted as she tried to get up.

"Are you hurt?"

"No, I don't think so."

"Here, let me help you."

Gingerly, he got Kathy upright, then stood next to her, ready to catch her should she fall, as she slowly tested her weight on one foot, then the other. She nodded. Freddie stepped aside.

"Just a little bruised," she said with a shaky laugh. "Thank you."

Freddie paused. "Somehow 'you're welcome' doesn't seem appropriate."

Kathy started to laugh, but the frightened giggle slipped quickly into tears.

"There ye are," said an Irish brogue even stronger than the first policeman's. The tall copper sauntered down the block from the street above where Freddie and Kathy were. "Me boys are running the scum down now. I'm Officer Murphy. I'm the beat commander. Ye're the ones were attacked, are ye not?"

"Yes, officer," said Freddie. "We were just walking over to, uh, our friend's place."

"I see." Officer Murphy glanced at the nearby door to the grocery. Freddie decided the officer not only knew about the speak inside, he was probably on their payroll and did a fair amount of drinking there. Murphy, a burly man with freckles across his nose, dug into his pocket and pulled out a crumpled handkerchief. "Here, little lady."

Kathy drew back from the offering.

"No, thank you," she said with a sniff. "I have one."

Officer Murphy shrugged and pocketed the kerchief as Kathy pulled hers from her sleeve.

"I should be hearing from me boys soon," said the officer.

"Officer, you've been very kind," said Kathy. "But I'd like to just go home and clean up."

Murphy looked at the door to the speak. "Seeing as how Dooley saw it happen, I s'pose there's no need to swear out a complaint." He pulled a small notepad from his pants, and licked the point on his pencil. "I'll be needing your names."

"I'm Mary Jane Smith," Kathy said quickly. She stepped backwards, pressing her heel onto Freddie's toes. "And this is my gentleman friend, Jim Reynolds."

"That's R-E-Y-N-O-L-D-S," added Freddie.

Officer Murphy laboriously copied it all

down, then left with a shrug. Freddie looked at Kathy.

"I do want to go home," she said nervously.

"Certainly." Freddie took her arm and turned her toward Washington Square.

"I can go by myself." Kathy tried to pull away.

"I see no good reason not to see you to your doorstep."

"But what about your friend?"

"He's frequently tardy, himself." Freddie shrugged. "It's not yet nine. He's probably not even there yet. You don't live far from here. I'll see you home, then return. It's an excusable delay."

"All right." Kathy stopped, and swallowed, then shivered.

"Good. We should be able to catch a taxi on the Square."

"Thank you."

In the taxi, Freddie watched Kathy as she brooded in silence. The attack had an eerie quality that she couldn't quite explain, but it disturbed her to the core.

At her boarding house Freddie told the driver to wait, and walked Kathy up her stoop. Kathy put her key in the lock. Freddie stopped her.

"Miss Briscow, I do have one question to which I believe I have a right to an answer. Why did you give false names to the police?"

"I guess you do have a right to know that." Kathy studied the clasp to her handbag. "I didn't want my uncle to find out about it. Him being a detective and all. I'm already connected to one crime in this city."

"This was just a coincidence."

Sudden pressure squeezed Kathy's heart still.

"But it wasn't." She looked him in the eye. "They were after you."

CHAPTER FIVE

Kathy's fingers raced across the keys of her typewriter. She kept her eyes glued to the handwritten page next to her. It took Mr. Healcroft's shadow to shake her from her work.

"Excellent concentration, Miss Briscow," he said.

"Oh. Thank you, Mr. Healcroft." She looked around. "Mr. Evans hasn't returned from his luncheon yet."

"Have you even gone to yours?"

"I... had some extra typing I needed to get done." Kathy picked up a pencil. "Is there any message you'd like to leave for Mr. Evans?"

"No. But I have one for you. I'll need to see a progress report on Mr. Little's book on Monday."

"Monday?" Kathy yipped.

"Will that be too difficult?" Mr. Healcroft watched the nervous girl carefully.

"No." Kathy regained her composure and

glanced back at Evans' office. "I was just hoping to catch up on some of the typing this weekend."

Mr. Healcroft caught the glance. "I see." He sighed. "Mr. Evans has given you a bit to do, eh?"

"I can manage."

"Indeed." He frowned. As much as Mr. Healcroft would have liked to have been rid of Miss Briscow, Mr. Little had been most adamant about her working on his book. "Miss Briscow, I regret that Evans is taking the situation so poorly. But understand that Mr. Little is a very important author to this firm, as is his book. It is imperative that we keep him happy. Do what you must. But I do not want you at this desk outside of normal office hours. Is that clear?"

"Yes, Mr. Healcroft. I'll have the report for you on Monday."

"Good."

As Mr. Healcroft left, Kathy made a rude gesture behind his back. A short time later the phone on Kathy's desk jangled.

"Mr. Evans's office," answered Kathy.

"Miss Briscow, is that you? This is Freddie Little calling."

Kathy's lips formed a rude reply, even though no sound escaped.

"Miss Briscow?"

"Yes, Mr. Little. How may I help you?" She kept her voice cool and professional.

"Are you still miffed about last night?"

"I gave you my conclusions, and how you chose to regard them is your business, and none of mine."

Freddie chuckled. "You are miffed. I can't blame you, I guess. I apologize if I was rather abrupt. But please understand, it's not pleasant to consider that someone is out for your skin."

"I suppose not," Kathy said softly. "Nor were circumstances the best."

"No, indeed. If it will make you feel any better, I looked over my shoulder more than once last night. In any case, I seem to be perfectly hale and hearty today."

"Thank you for the reassurance, Mr. Little. Is there anything else?"

"No, uh, yes. Oh, da— I mean blast. Now, what was it? Just a moment, Miss Briscow. Ah. I'm working on my book, and I have a burning question. Might we talk?"

Kathy sighed. "If you insist, Mr. Little."

Freddie hesitated. "It's not just that you're miffed. This is not a good time to be calling."

"Oh, no. I apologize, Mr. Little. Any time you like."

"No. This can wait. I'll catch you later."

Kathy hung up slowly.

"Damn you, Mr. Little," she whispered. "There is no good time."

Freddie, for his part, sat looking at his phone for a long time. Something was up. Acquiescence was not something that Miss Briscow tended towards, at least not the Miss Briscow he knew. Why was she so amenable all of a sudden? She wasn't happy. Did it have anything to do with the previous night's argument? She had seemed genuinely concerned.

"Bah!" snapped Freddie.

Everything had happened so quickly, who knew what that voice had said. They were in New York City, for heaven's sakes. One was bound to run into the criminal element sooner or later. Freddie set the phone down and went back to his notes.

It was nicely close to five o'clock when Freddie stepped onto the elevator in the building at Broadway and 23rd.

"Healcroft House," he told the operator as the iron gate shut.

"Yassir."

Freddie ignored the small rush of people waiting to get on as he stepped off. They ignored him. He spotted Miles Evans hurrying down the corridor and into Mr. Healcroft's office. Freddie nodded as he handed his coat and hat to the receptionist. It was just as well. He suspected that any interference from him on Miss Briscow's behalf would in the long run only work against her. The switchboard's cubicle, on the other side of the elevator bay from the reception desk, gave him an idea. He poked his head into the cubicle.

"Uh, miss?"

"Oh!" The operator, a sweet young thing in a green wool dress, jumped and shrieked a little.

"I'm so sorry," Freddie said quickly as he came into the cubicle. "I didn't mean to startle you. I'm Mr. Little."

"How do you do, sir?" She smiled nervously and removed her headset from her short brown hair.

"Be a dear, and ring up Mr. Evans's office for me, will you?" he asked.

She giggled and put the headset back on. "Certainly, Mr. Little."

Kathy jumped when the phone rang.

"Mr. Evans's office."

"Miss Briscow, Freddie Little again. Don't be downcast. I've got good news for you this time. I've just spotted Mr. Evans in Mr. Healcroft's office. Now's your chance to make your escape."

Kathy had to chuckle. "I'll do that, Mr. Little."

"Excellent. I'll meet you downstairs."

There was a pause. "As you like."

Not sure how she felt, Kathy finished covering her typewriter and gathering her coat, hat and some papers. Ultimately, it didn't matter how she felt. He would be in the lobby. Sure enough, as she got off the elevator she spotted the pale pink hair, neatly parted down the middle and slicked down, standing above the crowd.

"There you are, Miss Briscow," he said cheerfully as she approached. He held a black felt fedora in his curiously long, spidery hands.

"Hello, Mr. Little," she said.

"I thought it might be better if I did this in person. May I take you to dinner tonight?"

Kathy held her breath. She did not want to go. She had work to do, on his book, no less. But if Mr. Healcroft found out she'd refused...

"Yes," she said finally. "Thank you."

Freddie chuckled. "No protest?"

"No."

"Very well. But I assure you I will get to the bottom of this."

"Excuse me?" For a brief moment, Kathy's face revealed that she thought Freddie was talking pure nonsense. Then she composed herself. "Never mind."

"I won't then. I'll pick you up at your place at seven-thirty. That should give you enough time to change."

"Change?"

"For dinner."

Kathy frowned. "Oh, dear."

Freddie shook his head. "It won't be anything formal. A party frock will be fine."

71

"Oh." Kathy smiled weakly. "I think I can manage that."

"I'll see you at seven-thirty, then."

"At seven-thirty." Kathy turned and fled.

At the boarding house, Kathy warned Mrs. Lynne of the impending arrival, and ran upstairs. She dropped her handbag on the bed, then dumped the papers on the table under the window. Still more papers littered the table's surface along with all the books that didn't fit on the small overloaded bookshelf next to it. On the adjoining wall were her bureau and mirror. Cosmetics lay scattered over the lace doily on top of the bureau.

Kathy all but ripped her coat off and, still wearing her hat, flung open the doors to the small wardrobe on the wall opposite of the bureau. She gazed at the contents in disgust. There was only one choice: the brown velvet dress. The only other dress that came even close to a party frock was obviously meant for summer wear.

Kathy groaned. She was noted for her quiet, good taste. It was something that did not come naturally to her. She approached clothing herself with the same scholarly bent she turned toward any unfamiliar territory. Sighing, she pulled out the brown velvet dress and tossed it next to her burgundy wool coat, which had landed on the bed. A bath was in order, and after checking the clock on her bureau, Kathy concluded she had time to take one.

By the time she'd taken the bath and gotten dressed, the clock on her bureau said twenty-six after seven. Kathy growled in exasperation and stared at her reflection in the mirror. The bow on her head sagged like a wilted flower.

"This isn't right," she told herself. "I don't know what's wrong. But this isn't right. Oh, hell!" She ripped the ribbon off. "I'll just do without."

Her heart froze. It couldn't have been the front ringing. She listened. Mrs. Lynne wasn't calling. Furious, Kathy whipped her brush through her hair.

But it was the front ringing that Kathy had heard, and Freddie had indeed rung. As Mrs. Lynne opened the front door, she wondered if the gentleman on the stoop had the right house.

"Yes?" she asked, quickly smoothing out the navy blue wool of her dress.

"I'm Mr. Freddie Little. I'm here for Miss Briscow." Freddie braced himself. The fluffy round little woman was probably the landlady and incurably nosy.

"Oh!" She even beamed, damn her. "You're Mr. Little. Do come in."

"Thank you." He followed, removing his top hat, as she fluttered through the inside door into the foyer.

"It is such a pleasure to meet you, Mr. Little. Won't you please step into the parlor for a bit?" She whisked Freddie's hat out of his hands and set it on the hall table. "Of course, you will. And bless me! Let me take your coat." She took the black woolen top coat with the fur collar almost before Freddie could slip out of it. "Oooh! So heavy. Nice. Isn't fur just lovely?" She patted the collar as she draped the coat over her arm.

"Yes." Freddie slipped off his gloves.

"So toasty, isn't it? And leather gloves. Lined, too." Mrs. Lynne smiled as she tucked the gloves into Freddie's hat.

"Yes." Freddie pulled off his scarf before Mrs. Lynne could.

"You do know how to keep warm." Mrs. Lynne did wait for Freddie to hand her the scarf. "Oh, this scarf is just lovely. Silk?"

"From China."

"How utterly rich." She tucked it into Freddie's coat pocket, then hung the coat on the rack next to the hall table. "And what a beautiful hat. It's a pity the weather's so nasty." She brushed the rim of his hat with a little sigh, then turned, clasped her hands to her chest, and sighed beatifically at the splendor of Freddie in evening wear. "My, aren't we the swell!"

"Thank you."

"Oh. The parlor. This way. Would you care for some tea?"

Freddie winced as he followed her into the room. "Not at this moment, thank you. Would you happen to have any seltzer water?"

"Yes, I would. It'll take me just a moment."

"Thank you."

The landlady disappeared through a swinging door at the other end of the parlor. Before Freddie's sigh of relief escaped, someone pounded down the stairs.

"Mrs. Lynne!" called Kathy's voice. "If Mr.

Li— Oh." Kathy stopped in the doorway, both her hands on one ear. "That was you ringing."

"Yes." Freddie kept his face impassive. But the brown velvet dress with long sleeves and a brown satin ribbon around her hips had not been what he'd meant by a party frock.

Kathy looked at the black dinner jacket and black bow tie, and wished she could sink into the floor. Freddie was looking at her dress. She fastened the earring with a defiant twist, and smoothed the velvet.

"It's my best dress," she said.

Freddie nodded. It probably was, which meant her means were considerably more straitened than he'd thought. He smiled warmly.

"It's quite nice," he said.

"You don't have to be kind to me."

"Perhaps not," he said softly. "But I prefer it."

Mrs. Lynne burst through the swinging door with two glasses on a little silver tray. "Here we are. Oh, hello, Kathy. I was just going to call you."

Kathy held back her derisive snort.

"Ah, here's my seltzer water," said Freddie, genially removing the glasses from the tray. "And how kind of you to think of Miss Briscow."

Freddie handed the second glass to Kathy.

"Mr. Little, this is my landlady, Mrs. Lynne." Kathy made a vague wave.

75

"I've had the pleasure," said Freddie. "Now, Mrs. Lynne, I know you have other tenants to tend to."

"You're no trouble, Mr. Little."

"Thank you. But I wouldn't dream of keeping your tenants from your charming presence one minute longer than I must. Thank you."

Mrs. Lynne was flustered. "You're very welcome, Mr. Little."

She backed out towards the front hall.

"He's got money!" she hissed loudly at Kathy as she passed.

Kathy waited until Mrs. Lynne slid shut the doors.

"I apologize for her," she said.

"No apology needed," said Freddie reaching into his inside coat pocket. He pulled out a silver hip flask. "I just didn't think I'd be needing this so soon." Juggling the glass, he opened the flask and held it out. "Would you like some?"

"I suppose. If you don't mind."

Freddie poured, turning the seltzer amber. "Why should I?"

"It's yours. And I know you only offered it to me to be polite." Kathy shrugged as he added some whiskey to her glass. "It doesn't look as though that flask holds a lot."

Freddie replaced the flask. "Miss Briscow, what is going on?"

"What do you mean?" Kathy felt the panic, and fought to stay where she was.

"You. You're so compliant. You don't want to come out with me tonight, and there you are, dressed in your best, ready for heaven only knows what, and not about to complain either. Was it last night? Did I offend you so deeply?"

"Oh, no! You made an excellent point this afternoon," Kathy said, relaxing a touch. "I suppose I was miffed, but not seriously."

"Then what has changed? Because you today are not the same woman I was out with last night."

Kathy took a sip of her drink. He was not going to like the truth. But what else was there?

"I wouldn't try lying," said Freddie. "There isn't one I haven't heard already."

"Then, Mr. Little, please accept my apologies now, and understand that I'm only saying this because you asked, and it's the truth." Kathy turned away, took a deep breath, then turned back. His soft green eyes were warm, and he knew what was coming, and Kathy knew it was going to hurt, and that she still had to do it, and the pressure in her chest squeezed her heart so badly she almost cried out because she did not want to hurt him. "Mr. Healcroft came to me today, and reiterated how important you and your book are to the firm, and I was told to keep you happy. That it was imperative."

"The old bootlicker," whispered Freddie without flinching. He took a sip of his drink. His gaze returned to Kathy, pondering. "I wonder how far you would have gone."

"I don't know, Mr. Little."

"We'll never know now, I suppose." He took another sip.

Kathy felt the hint of a smile on her lips. He would never have pressed his advantage and they both knew it.

Freddie took a deep breath. "Miss Briscow, what will make me the most happy is if you return to your usual forthright self. Rest assured, that is what I value most about you."

"Value?" Kathy stepped back in shock. He valued her? How? And for heaven's sakes, why was that thought sending her stomach into a churning mass? "Damn you!"

Freddie saw the wave of turmoil, and found himself gratified by it. Nonetheless, he laughed to break the tension.

"Now, that's more like it." He paused. "Will you still come out to dinner with me?"

"I suppose, seeing as you went to the trouble to dress for it." Kathy glared, in spite of her own relief. "And why did you say it wouldn't be formal, then show up in a bleeding tuxedo of all things?"

"It's just a dinner jacket and tie."

"Oh, just."

Freddie shrugged. "It's how I always dress for an informal dinner."

"And do you get out the ermine for formal affairs?" Kathy flashed a wicked grin.

"No," replied Freddie, his own smile genial. "Just white tie and tails. Why don't you fetch your coat? And while you're at it, bottoms up." He raised his glass. "We don't want to disillusion your dear landlady, do we?"

"You have a point." Kathy raised her glass. "Cheers."

In the taxi, Kathy corralled Freddie's wandering thoughts, pinned them down to his burning question, and so thoroughly worked through the issue that by the time they arrived at the restaurant, Freddie felt drained.

Kathy, on the other hand, felt slightly unnerved. Huge crystal chandeliers lit up a room filled with ornate scrollwork and tables covered with starched, white cloths. Silver gleamed from the table tops. Freddie was too much of a gentleman to comment on the plainness of the coat he was helping her out of. But the coat was clearly out of place among all the furs in the coat check. Women in rich satins and silks with bejeweled feathers, expertly tucked around their slicked-down hair, glided past Kathy.

She took a deep breath and straightened her shoulders. She'd held her own around all the rich bitches at Radcliffe, albeit never in such thoroughly elegant surroundings. She could hold her own again. And this evening was about business, anyway.

Freddie was asking her about her day at work.

"I'm managing," she answered. "I've got a report to write over the weekend, and Mr. Evans still has a load of typing for me. I'm to keep him happy, too."

"That is rough," Freddie replied as he signaled the maitre d'.

Kathy swallowed. He seemed to treat her as if she were as well-dressed as the other women in the room, which went a small way toward easing her discomfort. Assuming he had even noticed it.

The maitre d' approached, and Freddie was occupied with getting them seated. As the maitre d' turned to show them to their table, Freddie stepped back so Kathy could go ahead. The maitre d' seated Kathy. Freddie signaled the waiter and ordered for both of them right away, without looking at the menu.

Kathy fought to keep her face passive, in spite of her tremendous awe. Freddie was the quintessential gentleman, and at that moment his innate grace and polish were all the more apparent. Kathy had thought she'd known some cultured men before, and perhaps they were. But here, in front of her, was the genuine article.

Freddie smiled. "What were we discussing as we came in?"

"Just my work troubles," said Kathy. "And I'd rather not."

"Then let me just offer my sympathies, and let's move on."

"Thank you. In fact, there is another project that needs our attention."

"Selby." Freddie was unenthusiastic. "Have you nosed anything up at the office?"

"I'm afraid all I did today was work. Have

you had a chance to talk to Percy yet?"

"No, I'm afraid I haven't. I stopped by the funeral home earlier this evening, but he wasn't there. I'm told he's not at all himself. His family is acting rather oddly, too."

"How do you mean?"

"It was almost as if they were deeply ashamed of him."

"Oh." Kathy mused quickly. "I wonder if Percy did kill Selby, and his family knows about it and wants to hide it."

"That might be. But actually I can't see them being ashamed of Percy for killing his cousin. Angry, perhaps. But not ashamed."

"You mean they would assume Percy had good reason to kill Frank Selby."

"Exactly."

Freddie gazed at Kathy, his own thoughts far from the murder of Frank Selby. He was perplexed by the odd woman who sat across from him. Her mind was so delightfully masculine, Freddie often found himself treating her more like a comrade than a lady. Yet why was he so struck at that moment by her femininity? Perhaps it was the quiet dignity of her best dress. It was no party frock, but well cut, and somehow managed to make the finery of the other ladies in the restaurant look overly bright and gaudy.

The waiter brought the soup. Kathy looked at the preponderance of silverware on the table and hesitated. She looked up. Freddie was waiting for her.

"After you," she said quickly.

Freddie chuckled and picked up his soup spoon. He noted how quickly Kathy took the identical piece from her place setting.

"You work from the outside in," he told her with a warm smile.

"Thank you." Kathy's cheeks flushed pink briefly. "It seems so easy for you."

"I'm afraid it was beat into me from the cradle. I may have been born with a silver spoon in my mouth, but I had to know which one it was."

Kathy laughed softly, then glanced around the restaurant, again overcome with how very out of place she was and how very wide the chasm was between her upbringing and Freddie's. She squared her shoulders almost defiantly.

"I obviously wasn't born with a silver spoon in my mouth."

Freddie looked at her, puzzled.

"You may as well know the truth, Mr. Little." Kathy took a deep breath, then the words tumbled out quickly. "I come from humble roots. I did go to Radcliffe, but I have an uncle who's a don at Harvard. He arranged the scholarship. I suspect you were at Harvard my first two years at Radcliffe, but we wouldn't have met because I avoided Harvard men. I didn't exactly fit in with your peers, because my family doesn't have any money. At least, not what you'd call money. We weren't poor. We just weren't rich." She looked at him a little severely. "If it will make you feel any better, my grandfather was one of the town's founders."

Freddie nodded, suddenly aware of the reason behind Kathy's outburst. "He could have been the town drunk, for all I care. I promise you, Miss Briscow, I have very democratic views regarding people. Pedigrees don't interest me in the least, and the only time I'm interested in a person's financial backing is if he's asking me to invest in him."

Kathy blushed. "Perhaps I was a little harsh."

"Not as such. People of my social standing tend to be dreadfully snobbish. It's not unreasonable of you to assume that I am at least somewhat so. I merely differ from most of my peers in that respect."

"In many ways, I expect." Kathy found herself smiling gently.

Freddie looked at his water glass and nodded slightly. The differences were painful. The waiter came to take their plates, and Freddie hoped it had kept Kathy from noticing. But it hadn't. At least, she wasn't saying anything, perhaps because she was no stranger to his kind of loneliness.

"Anyway, you may as well know the worst now," Kathy continued.

"The worst?" Freddie chuckled in spite of himself. "Is this where you tell me that you have a crazed uncle who's an ax murderer?"

"No ax murderers, but I do have one uncle who's a bum. And another who's a saloon keeper, and yet another who's a priest." Kathy looked up at him. "I guess we're going to find out how truly democratic you are. The truth is, my mother came from a big, Irish family. Appalled?"

"Completely." But Freddie's eyes glinted merrily.

"Anyway, they're all here in New York," Kathy went on quickly. "The Harvard uncle, that's Uncle Jonah, is on my father's side."

"And your father's family is in Boston?"

"No." Kathy took a deep breath. "We're in Hays, Kansas. My paternal grandfather was one of the town's founders."

"My, my. Such terrible connections." Freddie laughed quietly. "I don't know why you're so embarrassed. Granted, I've never heard of Hays, Kansas."

"You and everyone else. It's not exactly the big city. They've got a whole street with electric street lamps, and that's a big deal for them." Kathy looked up at him and smiled with small relief.

The fish arrived. Keeping one eye on Freddie, Kathy picked up a knife and fork. Freddie nodded.

"They say the rich are bored," observed Kathy as she delicately cut her fish. "They must be, to make a simple thing like eating such a complicated mess."

Freddie had to stop eating, he shook so hard from the suppressed laughter.

"I take it laughing out loud in restaurants is not done." Kathy's smile was just a touch wicked.

"No." Freddie took a swallow of water to regain composure. "And if you make me do it, we shall be thrown out of here."

"Would you like to go somewhere where you can laugh out loud?" Kathy blurted out without thinking.

Freddie looked at her, puzzled. "How do you mean?"

"My uncle, the saloon keeper. He owns a couple of speaks and knows everything there is to know about liquor in the city. Given the rum-running motive for Mr. Selby's death, he might be able to tell us something."

"That sounds like it might be profitable. Why don't we go after dinner?"

Kathy looked at him and paused. "I guess we'd better run by your place before we do. What you call dinner wear most of these guys only put on for their weddings or funerals."

"Ah." Freddie looked around. "The hotel here should be able to provide a room. I believe we can remedy the situation without the detour." He signaled the waiter. "I need a pen and paper, and the services of a messenger."

The waiter looked at his hand and smiled. "Certainly, sir."

When the pen and paper appeared, the waiter removed the fish plates. Freddie wrote quickly, blew on the ink to dry it, then folded the sheet over once. A boy about 12 years old and wearing the hotel livery appeared at the table.

"You have a message, sir?"

"Yes." Freddie handed him the note. "This goes to 635 Park Avenue, fifth floor. Ask for Mr. Roberts, and wait for a reply."

"Yessir!" The boy hurried off.

Freddie turned to Kathy. "Is something wrong?"

"No!" Kathy colored up again. "You didn't happen to send that boy to your home, did you?"

"As a matter of fact, I did." Freddie watched her, wondering what she was actually asking.

"You mean that's your address?" Kathy tried not to gape and failed. "Lower Park?"

"Between 66th and 67th."

"Criminy! You are rich!"

Freddie pressed his lips together, and put his hand over them, and shook. A minute later, he looked at Kathy.

"You are going to get us thrown out of here," he said, still laughing.

"I'm sorry," said Kathy, feeling a little foolish. "I didn't think you were that rich."

"Given my social standing, I'd have to be."

"But that's society. This is money."

"In the Upper East Side, they're the same thing."

Further downtown, Dan Callaghan sat puffing a stogie on the stoop outside the building where he lived on West 40th.

"You're a fool, Daniel Callaghan," his wife Beth had told him. But she wasn't going to let him smoke his cigar in the apartment, no matter how cold it was outside.

It didn't matter. A good stout overcoat and a good wool scarf, hand-knit by Beth, kept the cold at bay. The streets were quiet and gave a man some peace in which to think.

What to do about his niece? Daniel was sure the girl was innocent, but his captain wanted a solution to the murder, and Sergeant Reagan over at the other precinct was pushing hard to have her arrested. There was just enough evidence to send Kathy to Auburn Prison or worse.

And Kathy was headed for trouble. Daniel had heard about Elsie Quinn from one of the typists at the publisher's office, and had dragged Sergeant Reagan there only to find that Kathy had been there first. The girl was trying to investigate on her own, sure enough. Daniel shook his head as he flicked some ash onto the sidewalk.

A small, hunched-over form slipped up next to him on the stoop.

"Evening, Sergeant," said the young voice.

"Evening, Shorty. Does your mother know you're out?"

The boy coughed. "Ma's passed out in the kitchen again."

Daniel gritted his teeth. Shorty was a bright kid, the kind who could go far. The kind who shouldn't be mere bones with only a thin wool coat to cover him and a patched cap to cover his ragged dirty blond hair. But there was nothing to be done with Mildred O'Connor.

"I got something for you," Shorty said. "The word's out, there's some big ones to be had, but it's not a pretty job. It's all hush-hush and over the phone. A grocer down in the Village is setting it up."

"Really now. Do you know who?"

"Nope." A dirty finger wiped the equally smudged nose. "And I ain't gonna find out either, cause I'm too small potatoes. Word has it, the buyer is pissed off. Hired a couple guys to hit this bootleg-ger in Murray Hill and they botched it. The buyer had to do it."

"Murray Hill? Frank Selby..."

"Yeah, that's the guy's name."

"Do tell." Daniel sucked in, and the ash glowed bright red. "So, if this buyer did it himself, why does he still need somebody?"

Shorty shrugged. "Don't know. Guess there's someone else to be iced."

"All right, Shorty. You run upstairs now to the missus and tell her I said to give you some soup."

"Aw, Sergeant. She always makes me take a bath and sleep over."

"Do as I tell you."

"Yes, sir." The boy clumped up the stairs and into the building.

Daniel fretted as he puffed. A professional hit in the works, and if Kathy was bent on investigating, she was probably the next target. Perhaps he ought to let Reagan arrest her.

CHAPTER SIX

In another part of town, it was early yet. The music was whispering again through the mind of a tortured soul. He checked his wrist watch. It was too early. But again, that evening, he would go out and indulge the rhythm, the music only he heard.

Dinner over, Freddie changed into yet another three piece suit with four-in-hand tie, leaving Kathy for a remarkably short time.

"You're still overdressed," said Kathy as the hotel doorman sought a taxi.

Freddie shrugged. "I can't help it."

The taxi pulled up and the doorman opened the door. Freddie guided Kathy forward.

"And what address?" Freddie asked as he got in.

"11th and 39th, please," Kathy told the driver.

"Not Hell's Kitchen again," groaned Freddie.

"That's where the Callaghans come from."
Kathy settled back in her seat with a small smirk.
"And if you want to investigate speaks, that's the
place to go. They're everywhere."

"Hm. I should have sent for my gun."

"May I remind you this was not where
we had the trouble last night." Kathy watched as
Freddie tried to look stoical. "All right. It is a rough
neighborhood. But I've never had any trouble. They
know me where we're going, and they'll look out for
me."

"If you say so." Freddie slipped the watch
chain from his vest, and tucked it into the vest pocket.

At the corner of 11th and 39th, the taxi driver held his hand out for the fare.

"Why don't you park it and come on in," said
Kathy. "It's a cold night. Bet you could use a nip."

"Maybe I shouldn't leave the taxi," said the
driver.

"I will make it worth your while," said Freddie firmly.

"You fool," Kathy whispered to Freddie as he
helped her out. "That's going to cost you."

"It will be worth it to be sure of a taxi."

"Not when you could have had it for the
price of a drink."

A second taxi drove slowly by. Kathy

thought there was something odd about it, but brushed it aside and turned to the driver of the taxi she'd arrived in.

"See the candy shop with the green shades?" She pointed discretely. "We'll be in there. Tell them you're with us."

Freddie passed the man some money with an insinuating smile.

The candy shop was empty. Kathy knocked on the door in the back. A peephole appeared.

"Look who's here!" shouted a voice on the other side.

The door opened. A stocky teen boy with brown hair hugged Kathy.

"Jimmy, you got put on door duty!" said Kathy.

"Yeah. I'm moving up in the world," Jimmy said proudly.

"This is Mr. Little. Mr. Little, my cousin Jimmy."

"How do you do?" Freddie started to offer his hand, but Jimmy stepped back.

"Ooo. A swell."

"Jimmy!" Kathy chided. "We've got a taxi driver following us. Let him in. Come along, Mr. Little."

The man behind the bar was around Kathy's age, and obviously Jimmy's older brother, sharing the same hair color and build. His shirt sleeves were

rolled up and he wore a long barkeep's apron over
his dark pants.

"Kathy!" he all but hollered.

"Good to see you, Bob." Kathy leaned over
the bar to let Bob buss her quickly on the cheek. She
turned to Freddie. "This is my friend, Mr. Little."

"How do, sir." Bob refrained from personal
comments, although he looked Freddie over with a
glance that meant totaling up.

"I'm fine, thank you," Freddie replied, offering his hand.

Bob wiped his hand on his apron, then shook
Freddie's. "Good to meetcha." He turned to Kathy
and set two shot glasses on the bar. "Where've you
been?"

"Working," said Kathy. "And Uncle Mike
and Uncle Dan have been checking up on me. You
know how they are."

Bob nodded. "Why they don't stop watching
out for you. But they come down here enough."

"I guess they don't want me caught in a
raid," Kathy said.

"Raids are nothing." Bob grinned as he
uncorked a bottle and filled the glasses almost to
the rims. "They shut down Dad's place on 45th, but
Dad got the booze back. Cops let him have the whole
damn load, 'cept the three bottles they needed for
evidence. Only cost him a couple hundred."

"Is your dad in?" Kathy asked.

"He's upstairs. I'll go get him. Mom, too.
She'll be fit to be tied if you get out of here without

93

talking to her."

"Great. Thanks."

Bob left the whiskey bottle next to the glasses he'd poured. Kathy carefully picked hers up.

"Uncle Thomas only serves the best," she told Freddie. "To me, at any rate. In any case, it's safe to drink."

Freddie took a sip. "It's very good, too."

He looked around the darkened room. Battered tables and chairs were scattered around, largely filled with working men talking quietly. In the far corner, a poker game was going on. Freddie saw mostly coins on the table. Nearby, a man lay curled around a beer mug, sleeping it off, snorting every so often.

"Do me a favor and don't offer to pay for it," said Kathy softly. "I'm family. I don't know what the rules of etiquette say about relatives in business. But these folks would be mortally offended."

"There she is!" hollered a new voice.

"Uncle Thomas!" Kathy swept around the bar for two more noisy hugs, one from the balding, heavy-set man with graying hair scraped over his bald spot, and the second from his equally stout and gray-haired wife. "Aunt Jane. This is Mr. Little. Mr. Little, my aunt and uncle, Thomas and Jane Callaghan."

"How do you do?" said Freddie, offering his hand.

"Damn good," replied Thomas, giving Freddie's hand a vigorous shake. The older man wore a yellowing work shirt and suspenders with dark brown pants that sagged beneath his belly.

"Do I know you?" asked Aunt Jane with a puzzled smile. Her dark woolen dress was long-sleeved and had a slight waist to it.

"I don't believe so," said Freddie.

Thomas pulled Kathy aside. "Is he one of Mike's friends?"

"No," said Kathy. "I know him through my job."

"Whew! One lawyer in the family is too damn many as it is. Bob! Set us up a table." Thomas turned to Freddie as he picked the whiskey bottle up off the bar, then grabbed two empty glasses and Kathy's drink. He nodded at Freddie's glass. "Would you like a beer chaser with that?"

"This will be fine, thank you." Freddie smiled gracefully in spite of his unease.

Thomas plopped down at the nearby table even as Bob was still clearing it. Jane followed. Without thinking, Freddie put his glass down and seated Kathy, who blushed.

"Ooo!" cooed Jane. She patted Kathy's hand. "So, darling, when did you meet your new beau?"

"He's not my beau!" said Kathy anxiously as Freddie slid into a chair next to her. "Uh, Mr. Little is a writer. We're here doing research. He's writing this wonderful adventure story all about rum-runners and the like, and, Uncle Thomas, you know everything about liquor in the city. I thought you could help."

"Well, I don't know everything, darling," Thomas said proudly as he poured himself a drink. He gave Freddie a quick glance as if he wasn't convinced Kathy was telling the truth. "I'll tell you what I can, Mr. Little. But we don't get much adventure here. An arrest or two, but nothing in the line of thrilling."

"That doesn't matter," said Freddie. "I can make that up. What I'm after is background information, so the story sounds good."

"They make it, we buy it."

"But who are they?"

Thomas mused. "It depends on what they're making, and where they're selling it. Around here, it's all done in the neighborhood."

"Not the mob?"

"Mr. Madden brings the beer. You don't say no to his boys. But if you're talking Mafia, well, they're mostly in the Lower East Side, some in the Village. I think they supply some of the clubs in Harlem, but I don't know for sure. A lot of the fancy clubs near Broadway are run by gangsters of one sort or another. A small businessman like me, I try to avoid them."

"I can imagine." Freddie paused. "I have heard one name, Frank Selby. What do you know about him?"

"He's not a gangster." Thomas scratched his chin and looked at the ceiling for inspiration. "Selby, Selby, Selby. Frank, you say. I think there's a Selby fellow passing hooch... Ooo. That's way over in Murray Hill. Not much happening there. Mostly residence, you know. But there is one small speak. Nice place, too. A little rich for my blood. It's near Lex and 40th, behind the bookkeeping office. Ask for Petey and give him my name."

Freddie smiled. "Thank you."

Jane sighed suddenly. "Mr. Little, what did you do during the war?"

"Excuse me?" Freddie was startled by the sudden change of subject. "I was in the Army Air Corps."

"Did you fly?" Jane beamed.

"Yes and no," said Freddie. "I did fly, but I was a training officer. I never made it to Europe."

"They sent Dicky." Jane sniffed. Thomas and Kathy waited with solemn faces. "He didn't come back."

"Her son," whispered Kathy softly.

"I'm so terribly sorry," said Freddie with genuine sympathy.

"Thank you." Jane wiped her eye then tucked her handkerchief back in her sleeve. Then suddenly she smiled, and became as cheerful as before. "Thomas, tell Mr. Little about the time Izzy and Moe came to raid."

Over an hour later, Freddie and Kathy had collected their taxi driver, who had spent the time nursing a couple beers, and were on their way home.

"Aunt Jane did take Dicky's death hard," Kathy explained. "But she only does the grieving business to get sympathy."

"She's quite a character," Freddie agreed with a chuckle.

"And you were a training officer?"

"My great shame." Freddie rolled his eyes. "Everyone assumes I bought my way out of going to Europe. But it was actually the result of logic, an occurrence so phenomenal you had to have been part of the army to appreciate how truly incredible it was."

"What happened?" Kathy suddenly twisted and looked out the back window of the taxi.

"I had learned to fly in college. So when they needed people to train the new pilots, they chose me. I spent the war teaching those great flying aces how to fly."

"How noble of you," Kathy said, laughing.

"I didn't have much choice. I was drafted almost the day after I graduated."

"Did you want to go to Europe?" Kathy twisted again, trying to sound blithe.

Freddie turned thoughtful. "I don't know. I told everyone I was waiting to join up until I finished my education, especially since I was so close. But the only reason I went in so quickly was that the Draft Board caught me." He smiled softly. "All those stories tonight. I'm going to have to write them now."

Kathy caught his wistful gaze. "Why did you write your book?"

Freddie shifted and reached for his cigarette case.

"As I said, my friend told me to."

"But why?"

"I don't know if I can answer that." He looked at her, wondering if he could make her understand. "It would be the same reason I've been writing all my life. I just do. I remember when I was nine, I wrote a story. It was an adventure in a jungle, terribly thrilling. Actually, it was just terrible, but not bad for a nine-year-old. I showed it to my mother, who said it was very nice. I told her I was going to be a writer when I grew up. She just laughed and said I didn't have to be anything." He smiled bitterly. "I will be involved in the family business eventually. But Mother was right."

"I suppose so." Kathy mused, and flopped back into her seat after looking out the back window again. "Then again, just because you don't have to be something doesn't mean you aren't. Write your next story. Although, I'd appreciate it if you would just make notes and write it later. You've got work to do on *The Old Money Story*. Let's get that into galleys, and then you can start your next novel."

Freddie smiled. "What makes you so sure there will be a next novel?"

"Your first." Kathy looked at him with a warm, confident smile. "You are a writer, Mr. Little."

"Yes." Freddie mused. "I suppose I am."

Kathy twisted and looked out the window.

"That's the fourth time you've done that," Freddie said.

"I think we're being followed."

Freddie whirled around and looked. "Who? How?"

"That taxi right behind us. I could swear it's the same one that drove by us outside of Uncle Thomas's when we got there."

Freddie leaned forward and rapped on the glass between them and the driver.

"Yeah?" asked the driver, sliding the glass open.

"Excuse me, I believe we're being followed," Freddie said.

"Yeah, that same guy's been following us since we left that restaurant. You want I should lose him?"

"Yes. Thank you."

The sudden turn threw Freddie on top of Kathy. But before he could apologize, another quick turn threw Kathy on top of Freddie. Their eyes locked. Kathy bounced up and looked out the back window.

"He's still there," she hollered to the driver.

"Ain't no one can follow Jim Pearson," the driver replied calmly as he accelerated. "Watch this."

He suddenly turned down an alley. The taxi behind pulled up, almost close enough to touch. Freddie and Kathy gasped as they saw the oncoming headlights of a truck. Jim Pearson only sped up. There was the sound of tires screeching from the oncoming vehicle. Seconds before the taxi would have hit the truck, it lurched into a right turn and sped down 28th. Behind them, the sound of metal colliding filled the night air.

"What'd I tell you?" Jim Pearson said smugly.

"You've certainly earned your fare tonight," said Freddie, gathering together what little dignity he had left.

Back in the Village, Freddie waited to get out of the taxi until he was sure the street was deserted. Even then, he had Pearson wait while he walked Kathy up the stoop.

"So why do you suppose someone followed us?" Kathy asked as they mounted the steps.

"I haven't the faintest idea," Freddie said. "I suspect it was someone's idea of a sick joke."

"Even after last night?"

Freddie looked away from her gaze. "I suppose it might be that someone wants to kill me. There are probably many people who do. But whoever it was would have had a much clearer shot at me outside your uncle's speak. I think somebody just wanted to put a good scare into me, and as we've eluded whoever that was, I don't intend to worry."

"You've got a point about not hitting us at Uncle Thomas's." Kathy got out her keys. "Unless they didn't want any witnesses, in which case, inviting the taxi driver in probably saved us."

"Then let's be thankful for taxi drivers." Freddie paused. "I would just as soon forget the whole incident. In any case, apart from our little adventure, it was quite a pleasant evening. Thank you."

"I should be thanking you," said Kathy. "That reminds me, how much do I owe you? I was obviously the guest at dinner, but there was the taxi fare after, and last night, too."

"Owe me?" Freddie was flummoxed.

"I didn't mean to offend you. It seemed rude to assume you would pay for everything in a joint venture."

"I'm not offended. Not in the least. I've just never been asked that question before."

Kathy stiffened. "Even by men?"

"Especially not them." Freddie snorted. "They know how much I'm worth."

His eyes fell on her. How odd that she expected to pull her own weight, even when her gender made it acceptable for her to insist that he bear the cost.

He smiled softly. "Miss Briscow, you don't owe me anything. Ever."

"Mr. Little, I don't think I can accept-"

"You had the decency to ask."

Kathy bit her lip. "Oh. Thank you. I won't abuse it."

"Nor will I, I promise."

That made her smile with relief.

"By the way," Freddie continued, taking her keys. "I noticed none of your relatives addressed you by your given name."

"They do prefer nicknames. I'm Uncle Thomas's darling."

"I noticed. But your given name. What is it?"

"That's right. I always sign with my initial. It's Kathleen. But everyone who knows me calls me Kathy, except my mother's relatives."

Freddie nodded. "I prefer it when my friends call me Freddie."

There was a short, almost awkward pause.

"I'd better get in," said Kathy.

"Yes. Of course." Freddie busied himself with unlocking the door. He handed the keys back to Kathy. "With your permission, I will call you tomorrow."

"That would be nice. Oh. Tomorrow's my half-day at work."

"I'll call you there, then. Good evening... Kathy."

Freddie held his breath until she smiled in response.

"Good evening, Freddie."

She slipped inside and was gone.

The next morning, Kathy did violate Mr.

Healcroft's order not to be at her desk outside of business hours. She went into the office early. She was usually one of the first workers to arrive at the office anyway, even ahead of Mr. Healcroft. He would have no way of knowing how much earlier she had arrived.

The quiet in the offices made it easy to concentrate on her typing, and she rattled away happily, taking an almost Puritanical delight in the growing stack of reports and letters. It wasn't until the others began to arrive that she allowed herself a short break.

She only made sure she was back at her typewriter when Evans showed. The last thing she wanted was for him to think she was caught up. Not that she was. Better that the bastard not know that she was getting close.

But even her concentration wasn't enough to make her miss the ripple of rumors that went through the office when the police officers arrived. Kathy listened, then decided she could use another ream of typing paper after all, and wandered past Mr. Healcroft's office on the way to the supply cupboard.

"Hello, Miss Briscow," giggled Miss Watkins, one of Mr. Healcroft's secretaries.

Miss Edwards, the other secretary, giggled nervously with an insinuating glance back at Mr. Healcroft's office. Aside from Miss Watkins being blonde and Miss Edwards a brunette, the two were almost identical, wearing the new shorter hem on their work dresses, red lacquer on their nails and short, bobbed hair.

"What's news?" Kathy asked casually. The

girls were obviously as eager to talk as Kathy was to hear.

Miss Watkins glanced back at the office, then leaned over her desk. "There's a couple coppers in Mr. H.'s office."

"So I heard," Kathy replied.

"They're sergeants," said Miss Edwards, scampering over from her desk. "A Sergeant Reagan and a Sergeant Callaghan. They're questioning Mr. Healcroft."

"Who'd a thought?" said Miss Watkins. "Can you imagine Mr. Healcroft killing someone?"

Kathy paused, because she could imagine just that. "I'll be. How long have they been in there?"

"Just a few minutes," said Miss Watkins.

"But that Sergeant Reagan fellow, he looked awful angry about something," said Miss Edwards. "I say he's here to arrest Mr. Healcroft."

Kathy shook her head. "They'd have brought a couple harness bulls with them if they were going to do that."

Miss Edwards giggled. "Ooh, Susie, remember that cute Officer Lampson that came when they found Mr. Selby?"

"Flossie, you do not want to go on a date with a copper," Miss Watkins answered. "Trust me. They're animals."

Kathy smirked inwardly. Animals had their place, if a good toss in the hay was all a girl wanted,
105

and if she could find one scared enough of her uncle to keep his mouth shut. She smiled briefly at the two secretaries, then went on her way in search of paper.

Uncle Dan and his partner were leaving Mr. Healcroft's office as she returned. Mr. Healcroft was in the door, telling Uncle Dan that he would be working in the office all afternoon and couldn't make Frank Selby's funeral.

Kathy pretended not to see them, but something seemed odd about Mr. Healcroft's announcement. She forgot about it when Uncle Dan called her.

He seemed as if he were on pins and needles. Something was not setting well with him. Kathy sensed that it wasn't her but his partner.

Sergeant Reagan was a large man with a beak nose and hard, crystal blue eyes. He'd kept his bowler hat on, even though Uncle Dan had remembered to remove his.

"We need to have a little chat, Miss Briscow," Reagan said even before Uncle Dan could say hello. "If you'll come with us."

Uncle Dan took her arm and patted it reassuringly, even though his face remained grim.

They seated Kathy in the conference room. Dan sat across from her while Reagan paced.

"Miss Briscow, there's a number of funny things that have come up since you first gave your statement to the police," Reagan announced. "Where were you Monday night last?"

"I went to see *Lady Be Good*."

"By yourself?" Reagan glared with arms folded.

"Yes." Kathy answered slowly.

"And what kind of a lady goes to see a show by herself?"

"Kevin," Dan growled.

Kathy swallowed and sat up straight. "This lady does, Sergeant."

"Kevin, that has nothing to do with why we're here," Dan added forcefully.

"And what do you know of Mr. Selby's personal habits, Miss Briscow?" Reagan returned to pacing.

Kathy eyed him, wondering what he was looking for. "Not much, I suppose. Most of his vices he kept outside of the office."

"Vices such as?" Reagan cocked an insinuating eyebrow.

"Surely you know what vices he had better than I do, Sergeant." Kathy shrugged. "I can only surmise."

"Surmise, heh?" Reagan leaned over her. "So do some surmising."

"I can't be sure. I don't know." Kathy thought fast. "I believe he may have drunk alcohol. There-there were even a couple rumors that he was making it."

107

She felt Dan's eyes on her. He wasn't angry, but he knew something. Reagan, apparently feigning non-challance, gazed out the window.

"Rumors, eh?" he replied, turning to her. "What about the rumors that he had a way of imposing himself on women?"

Kathy looked at him blandly. "I'm afraid I don't understand what you mean, Sergeant Reagan."

That was a bald-faced lie and she knew Dan knew it. But she could see a glint of approval in his eyes.

Reagan again leaned over her. "The rumors say that he had you doing the tango with him, as it were. I'm afraid I can't be more exact, what with you being a lady and all."

"Oh, those rumors." Kathy smiled confidently. "He never tried that with me. He found it more profitable to get me to do his work for him."

"So that's why you did it," said Reagan casually.

"His work?" Kathy saw Reagan's gambit as clearly as a lone train signal on a dark Kansas night. "It was work I enjoyed, to be frank. Certainly more interesting than secretarial work."

Reagan harrumphed and resorted to pacing again. "And his drinking. Did he ever ask you to join him?"

"No."

"Did he ever serve you any?"

"No."

"Did you ever want him to?"
"No."

"Where's his favorite speak?"

"Murray Hill?"

Reagan whirled on her. "So you been there?"

"No." Kathy looked at him, suddenly nervous. "Um. I-I just guessed." But why did she guess Murray Hill? All the other editors went to a place across the street from the office. "After all, eh, as I understand it, his apartment was in Murray Hill. Why shouldn't his favorite speak be near his home?"

"Young lady, you're not telling all you know." Reagan hovered over her like an angry buzzard.

Kathy looked over at Uncle Dan. "Sergeant, I'm doing the best I can. I don't know much about Mr. Selby. I did work for him for a couple of years, so of course, I'm likely to know some things. But one thing I do not know is who killed him or why. I can promise you that."

There was a knock on the door. "Sergeant Reagan, if you're in there, there's a telephone call for you."

Reagan burst out of the room, leaving a trail of fury.

"Uncle Dan..." Kathy reached for him.

"Now, now, Katie-girl."

"Uncle Dan, he wants to arrest me!"

Dan patted her hands. "It won't happen, darling. That's why I'm here dogging him."

Kathy sank into herself. "So what evidence is there? What have you found out?"

"Not much more than I've told you." Dan was evading her.

"What more?" Kathy pressed.

"Katie-girl, that is for me to worry about. I don't want you putting your nose in this mess." He actually shook his finger at her. "This is police business."

Reagan appeared in the doorway. "It's Chelsea again. They found the stiff on the docks."

Dan cursed under his breath as he slowly got up. "Another bum?"

"Yes." Reagan glared at Kathy. "Don't think I'm done with you yet, young lady. You're not getting away with it."

"Come along, Kevin," Dan growled, physically turning the man. "You take Chelsea and I'll take the funeral."

Shaking, Kathy returned to her desk. Just at that moment, the phone rang.

Kathy swallowed her anxiety down, than answered. "Mr. Evans's office."

"It's Freddie Little, Kathy. And how are you this morning?" he asked, cheerfully.

"Well enough," Kathy said calmly, but inside she was churning. She did not want to deal with

Freddie's wandering banter, so why was she feeling so relieved at hearing his voice?

"What's wrong?" Freddie, as usual, had caught her least nuance.

"The police were here. A Sergeant Reagan and Uncle Dan."

"Did they talk to you?" Freddie asked.

"For near twenty minutes," Kathy replied nervously. "Reagan asked all sorts of questions about Mr. Selby's personal habits. Most of them, I couldn't answer. But given all that we know, I've been able to make some guesses, and I think I answered a couple questions a little too well. That didn't sit at all right with Sergeant Reagan. I'm sure he thinks I did it. Uncle Dan knows I didn't, but he's worried."

"Frankly, so am I."

"The only reason I wasn't arrested is that Sergeant Reagan was called to Chelsea to check out some bum that got murdered. That, and I don't think Uncle Dan would have let him." Phone in hand, Kathy wandered around the office as far as the cord would let her.

"Did your uncle let out anything they might have?"

"No." Kathy checked down the hall again. "I did get to talk to him privately afterward. He was fairly close. I'm almost positive he knows I've been asking questions about Frank Selby."

"Did the coppers talk to anyone else?"

"They questioned Mr. Healcroft before they

talked to me." Kathy thought. "It was odd, too. I heard him tell Uncle Dan that he had to excuse himself from the funeral because he needed to spend the afternoon in his office working."

"Working?"

"That's not so unusual. Mr. Healcroft is always the last to leave on Saturdays. He must have paid his respects to the family last night."

"But why would he make sure your uncle knew that he'd be working this afternoon?" Freddie asked.

"I haven't the faintest idea. Have you been able to talk to Percy Selby since last night?"

"Good lord, Kathy, I just got up, and I'm an early riser compared to Percy."

Shocked, Kathy looked out the door at the hallway wall clock. "Freddie, it is nearly eleven thirty!"

"When one does not have to get up to go to work in the mornings, one develops the habit of staying out all hours of the night." Freddie said evenly. "If I'm not at a party or with my friends, I'm still up into the wee hours of the morning. That's when I do most of my writing."

"Hm."

"I'm no sluggard, Kathy. I don't sleep more than eight hours a night. I just do it at a different time than you, as do my friends. They probably sleep more. They are lazy."

"In any case, when are you going to talk to Percy?" Kathy asked. "It had better be soon. Given this morning, I don't think I have much time left."

"I'll try to arrange it for tonight. Would seven be too early for you?"

"Oh, Freddie, I don't think I can go out tonight. I've got to get some sleep, and I do have your book to work on."

"Very well. I'll take care of it myself. Would you like me to telephone you with the results?"

"That would be nice. You can call me at Mrs. Lynne's. Thank you." Kathy gazed out down the hallway once more. "What's...? Freddie, I'll have to call you back."

"Kathy?"

But she had already hung up. She grabbed her coat, hat and handbag, and ran off down the hall. Silently, she slid through the stairwell door and peeked down the stairs.

What was Mr. Healcroft doing, slipping out of the office when he had made it plain he was going to be there, and sneaking down the stairs to do it, at that?

There was only one way to find out. Kathy put on her coat and hat, checked quickly that her uncle and company had gone, and took off after Mr. Healcroft.

Freddie clicked the receiver arm again. "Kathy?"

Still nothing. Freddie replaced the receiver, and put the phone back on the hall table. Bothered, he tightened the knot on his dressing gown.

113

"Roberts?" He turned, looking for the valet.

"Yes, sir?" Roberts appeared from the bedroom hallway.

"What time is Frank Selby's funeral?"

"One o'clock."

"I'll just have time. I believe I shall attend. Is my bath ready?"

"Yes, sir."

As he dressed, and all the way to the funeral, Freddie pondered Kathy's sudden hang-up. The most logical explanation was that someone, probably Evans, had walked into the office, and Kathy had felt she could not continue the conversation. But it seemed as though she had seen something, and Freddie could only hope it would not put her in danger.

The funeral, held in a small church in Midtown, was what he expected: somber, and attended mostly by humbler folk, most of whom he didn't know. He hung about after the service, watching carefully, although he wasn't sure what he was watching for. He noted that he wasn't the only one watching.

The man wore a working man's tweed suit with a bowler hat. The face was lined and the figure somewhat padded, but the skin had the fair cast of the Irish, as did the nose. There was something familiar about the alert eyes, too. The eyes settled briefly on Freddie, then appeared to dismiss him.

A second later, Freddie ran across Miles Evans. Evans was surprised to see Freddie.

"Did you know Frank Selby?" he asked.

"Not well," Freddie conceded. "But we came into contact from time to time. I presume you are here representing the company?"

"Yeah. And Frank was a pal. So. How is work progressing on your book?" Evans flashed him a snide grin.

"Very well. I'm quite pleased." Freddie watched with gratification as Evans' face fell. "If you will excuse me?"

"Of course."

Freddie stepped around Evans, and sorted through the mourners waiting to go to the cemetery. Percy Selby was not among them, but Percy's father was. He was dressed in an all-black morning suit with a fur-trimmed overcoat and top hat. His hair was white and he peered at everyone dolefully through a pince-nez. Freddie walked up.

"Good day, Mr. Selby."

The senior gentleman brightened. "Ah, Freddie, my lad. What brings you here?"

"Paying my respects." Freddie looked around. "I don't see Percy around. I hope he's not ill."

"Percy!" snorted Mr. Selby. "I'm afraid he's not well. Freddie, if you would be so kind as to step around to see him. Maybe you can snap him out of it."

"I'll do my best."

"I don't understand the younger generation.

115

Can't imagine what's gotten into him. He's not the boy I knew."

As if he had ever known his son. But Edward Merritt Selby had paid even less attention to his offspring than Freddie's father had, if such a thing were possible. And yet, if Mr. Selby was upset enough about Percy that he had asked Freddie to intervene, then Percy must be in sorry condition indeed.

His curiosity burning, Freddie quickly made his escape and went straight to the Selby mansion on Fourth. A tall, aging butler admitted him into the cavernous foyer lined by dark wood paneling and lit by two huge crystal chandeliers.

"Is Mr. Percy in?" Freddie asked, removing his gloves.

"He, eh..."

Freddie pressed his lips together. How grave was Percy's condition if even the old retainer seemed discomfited by it?

"Mr. Selby asked me to drop by," Freddie explained.

"Ah." The butler took Freddie's coat and hat.

Freddie took a calling card from his suit coat.

"If you will give him this." Freddie dropped the card onto the silver tray offered by the butler.

"I've no use for calling cards!" bellowed a voice.

Percy Selby emerged from the drawing

room, his face red with rage. Small, with dark coloring, he wore only pants and an open shirt. He slapped the tray from the butler's hands.

"Percy!" Freddie stepped back, shocked.

The tray clattered across the marble floor and spun noisily. Silently, the butler withdrew.

"I've no use for any of it!" Percy ranted. "It's all dung, Freddie. Eating at us like festered sores, stealing away our immortal souls!"

"I'm sorry, Percy." Freddie grasped at the first possible explanation for Percy's incredible behavior. "I didn't know you were that close to your cousin."

"Poor Frank." Percy turned on Freddie. "It's too late for him, Freddie. He's rotting in hell. But it's not too late for us. Freddie, you've got to repent! Forsake your sins, and kneel down before God Almighty!"

Freddie tried not to wince. Percy's problem was all too clear.

"I'll give it some thought. Actually, your father asked me to stop by. He thought you could use some cheering up."

"He's damned," sniffed Percy. "The poor fool is damned."

Freddie put his hand on Percy's shoulder. "Percy, he may yet make it, after all. It's not as though he's dead."

"But Frank is." Percy wrenched himself away.

"Far be it from me to pry, but, Percy, could some of your remorse be based in the fact that you and your cousin were not on the best of terms? At least you didn't appear to be the last time I saw you together."

"When was that?"

"The sixth, I believe. The Saturday before he met with his accident."

"Oh, that night." Percy's gaze swept heavenwards. "The most blessed, happiest night of my life."

"You didn't seem that happy when I pulled you off your cousin."

"That was another time. I was another man, a poor, wretched creature."

Freddie studied his fingernails. "What were you two fighting over, anyway?"

"It doesn't matter, Freddie. That was before. I am a new man, a new creation in the Lord, Jesus Christ."

"I was just wondering. It could be important, you know."

"If it is, it's because it led me to salvation. It made me see what a worm I was, what a worthless, vile excuse for a human being." Percy sighed. "I can't remember what it was, anyway."

"I see." Freddie found himself silently cursing all religionists, and wondering how he was going to summon the butler and get his coat back.

"No, you don't, Freddie. I was like you. Blind." Percy grabbed Freddie's arms. "Blinded by the curse of riches. You can be saved, Freddie! Repent. Renounce this vile way of living, and come to the Lord!"

"Percy, I promise, I will give it my utmost consideration." Freddie delicately disentangled himself. "However, at the moment, I'm afraid I do have another appointment. Might I get my coat back, please?"

As Percy dispiritedly waved Freddie away and retreated into the drawing room, the butler appeared with coat in hand, looking as though Percy had died.

"He may yet snap out of it," Freddie said.

"Thank you, sir. Very kind of you to say so, sir."

The butler didn't seem to hold much hope. Freddie didn't either, and took his leave feeling considerably more unsettled than he would have thought.

The problem was, Freddie did want to renounce his way of living, or at least some parts of it. He looked back at the mansion. Perhaps religion did hold some answers, but not Percy's brand. Almost without thinking, Freddie found himself walking downtown.

But could Percy have killed his cousin? Percy said he had seen the light, as it were, the night Freddie had caught the two fighting. That was the Saturday before Frank Selby had been killed. Or had Percy taken up religion on Monday night after he had killed Frank?

And what about Kathy's strange behavior

earlier? Freddie felt a hard knot in the pit of his stomach. It was hard to say what was more disturbing, the possibility that Kathy had come to some harm or that he was in such a dither over it. On the other hand, there was no reason he shouldn't stop in at the boarding house.

Near 77th, he started to hail a taxi when he paused, disgusted with himself. He had no solid reason to believe that anything was wrong. There was certainly no reason to rush. But walking to the Village was too slow and too cold, and a light snow was falling. There was a subway stop nearby. Shrugging, he fished out a nickel from his pocket and went down the stairs.

CHAPTER SEVEN

Mrs. Lynne was thrilled to see Freddie on the doorstep. Freddie was not pleased with the news she had.

"She's not here," said Mrs. Lynne, showing Freddie into the parlor. "I haven't seen her since breakfast."

Freddie checked his watch. "She should have left work three and a half hours ago."

"I wouldn't worry, Mr. Little. She often steps out in the afternoon."

But not this afternoon, not when she was so worried about getting her work done.

"Has she called at all?"

"No. She almost never does." Mrs. Lynne tittered. "She's quite the free spirit."

Who could be in a great deal of trouble. Or probably not. Freddie couldn't understand why he was so worried. There was no reason Kathy shouldn't go elsewhere before going home. If only she hadn't hung up so quickly.

"Perhaps I'd better leave," he said, and headed for the foyer.

"Oh, please, wait, Mr. Little. She should be home soon. She usually is."

"I think not." Freddie took his coat from the rack.

The outer door slammed shut, and Kathy burst in through the foyer doo.

"Oh, wonderful!" she said, grinning when she saw Freddie. "You're here. Now, I don't have to phone you."

She was out of breath, her cheeks flushed with the cold, holding a brown paper sack with grease stains leaking through.

"Are you all right?" asked Freddie, replacing the coat.

"Perfectly," she replied with a happy smile, then noticed the landlady. "Mrs. Lynne, Mr. Little and I need to talk privately in the parlor, if you don't mind."

"No. I suppose not."

"Thank you." Kathy herded Freddie into the parlor, and quickly shut the doors. "You will not believe the afternoon I've had. Freddie, I have really found out something."

She dropped her sack and handbag on the lamp table and took off her coat and hat, tossing them on the end of the couch.

"Oof! It's cold out there." She shivered a little, then smoothed her dress. "And snowing, too!"

"I was somewhat concerned when you hung up so abruptly this morning."

Kathy plopped onto the couch. "Freddie, I am so sorry about that, but I had to leave at that instant. There wasn't time to explain."

"Obviously." Freddie's sigh was a little sour.

"Do sit down, will you?" Kathy paused as Freddie morosely sank into a wingback chair across from her. "Oh, dear. You didn't think I got arrested, or something, did you?"

"Or something. I don't know what I was thinking, Kathy. I wasn't that concerned until I got here, and found you weren't."

"Poor thing. Oops!" She put her hand to her stomach. "I haven't eaten since breakfast."

Freddie scrambled to his feet. "Don't let me stop you."

"Oh, sit down. You're not. Have you had your lunch?" Her little wicked smile lit up her face. "Or should I say breakfast?"

Freddie had to smile also. "I've eaten. Thank you. But if you're hungry, please go ahead. Don't mind me."

"I won't then, thank you." Kathy all but fell on her bag. "I'm ravenous. You know, you could have checked with the police if you thought I'd been arrested."

She opened the bag and unwrapped a large sandwich cut in halves, and a pickle.

"I thought I'd wait a bit before I did that,"

123

Freddie said, wondering why they were still in the parlor. "I had things to look into, myself."

"Oh, dear." Kathy looked at her food. "I'm not going to be able to eat all this by myself. Are you sure you wouldn't like some?"

"What is it?"

"Pastrami on rye, with extra mustard."

Freddie thought it over. "I suppose I'll give it a try."

Kathy handed him a half. "You've never had pastrami before?"

"Not that I recall." Freddie wound his hand around the awkward sandwich. "Do we need to fetch plates or go to the dining room?"

"Nope," said Kathy, after swallowing a bite. "I can't believe you've never had pastrami before. You've lived in this city all your life, at least that's the impression I got."

"I have, except for college and the army. People from my set don't tend to patronize delicatessens." Freddie took a bite.

"More's the pity." Kathy licked mustard off her fingers. "I got my first pastrami the day I arrived in New York, and I've been eating them ever since."

"They are good." Freddie grimaced over a fallen piece of meat. "Even if they are graceless."

Kathy grinned. "Which is why you don't patronize delis. What things were you looking into this afternoon?"

"Things?" Freddie swallowed a bite of sandwich. "Oh. Well, first off, I went to Frank Selby's funeral this afternoon."

"Damn! I was going to go to that."

Freddie winced at the language. "You have mustard on your chin."

"Thank you." Kathy wiped the mustard off with her finger and then licked it. "Was Percy Selby there? Did you talk to him?"

"He wasn't, but I did talk to him." Freddie sighed. "Poor fool."

"Oh, no. Has he cracked?" Kathy asked around a mouthful of pastrami.

"Worse. He got religion."

Kathy groaned. "The hellfire sort?"

"In blazes." Freddie paused to swallow another bite, then wiped his fingers with his handkerchief. "And according to him, it happened the Saturday before his cousin was killed."

"That doesn't make him innocent. Maybe he thought he was saving Mr. Selby. Or meting out God's justice." Kathy sucked thoughtfully on the pickle.

Embarrassed, Freddie shifted his gaze elsewhere. "I've been considering that possibility. In any case, Percy has definitely consigned the soul of Frank Selby to the eternal flames of perdition, and has given me over to the same fate. Not that I don't go to church."

Kathy laughed. "Do you think I care? I certainly don't go. Sunday's the one day I get to sleep in. Would you like some pickle?"

"No! Thank you." Freddie shifted. "What is your great revelation?"

"That." Excited, Kathy kicked off her shoes and tucked her feet underneath her. "Mr. Healcroft is not the Victorian prude we thought. I happened to glance down the hall and there he was, dressed to go out, and walking so softly. He went to the stairwell, too."

"So that's why you hung up on me."

"Yes. I wanted to follow him. For heaven's sakes, first he makes a big show about being in all afternoon, then he's sneaking out? Why couldn't he have just walked out as always? No one would have thought anything of it."

"Unless he had good reason to want people to think he was in his office all afternoon."

"Exactly."

Freddie leaned forward. "So where did he go?"

"I know where he ended up. I followed him down to East 22nd, when I realized I was being followed."

"Oh, no." Freddie swallowed.

Kathy rolled her eyes. "It wasn't some evil gangster. It was a harness bull. My uncle has assigned one of his beat cops to keep an eye on me. Good heavens, he was even wearing his uniform. I had to let Mr. Healcroft go on down Fifth Avenue. He turned on East 21st, but I didn't see where he went after that. I just kept going down Fifth as if I were doing some shopping. That's what took so long. If Uncle Dan finds out I've been doing any more investigating, he might let Sergeant Reagan arrest me just to keep me out of trouble."

"Oh. So you didn't find anything out about Mr. Healcroft." Freddie frowned.

"That's just it. I did." Kathy grinned. "I eventually wound up at Macy's. Fortunately, the crowds there were so heavy, I was able to ditch the harness bull. I've never run so fast in my life! And wouldn't you know, it had to start snowing. Anyway, I went back to East 21st, in the hope that I just might be able to discover something, and I saw Mr. Healcroft leaving a brownstone there."

"Do you remember which one?"

"I even went there after I hid to be sure Mr. Healcroft didn't see me. I made up a little story about a lost parcel, but I never got to use it. Freddie, it was so embarrassing, even for me. The lady who answered the door was only wearing this little nightgown, and I could see right through it, and she had nothing else on!"

"Do you know what that place was?" Freddie watched her carefully.

"It was a whorehouse. What else could it have been? I suppose it could have been just someone's house, but I heard enough girls, and other stuff to make me fairly sure. Can you believe it? Mr. Healcroft at a whorehouse." Kathy blushed. "I tell you, it's one thing to know about these sorts of things intellectually, but to find them in real life..."

Freddie shrugged. "I'm wondering if they

127

specialize at that house."

"Specialize?"

"In buttonhooks, and other painful things of that nature."

"That's right." Kathy shivered. "But how are we going to find out?"

Freddie wiped the last of the mustard from his hands, and got up.

"We'll ask."

"Oh, no. I'm not doing that. I don't think they'd tell me anything, anyway."

"I'm sure they wouldn't. But they may tell me."

"Freddie, you're not going in there." Kathy bounced to her feet. "I wouldn't dream of letting somebody do something so disgusting."

"My, aren't we the Victorian all of a sudden."

Kathy snorted. "It has nothing to do with that."

"I wouldn't put any money on it." Freddie smirked.

"You actually want to go, don't you?"

Freddie carefully folded up his handker-chief. "Kathy, I'll admit I have darkened the doors of more than one house of ill-repute, but believe me or no, it was not to use the services rendered."

"Then how do you— Never mind." Kathy's

color deepened.

"I generally take a mistress," Freddie said calmly, guessing what the question was, although he was not at all sure why he was answering.

Kathy groaned. "Isn't that the same thing?"

"Perhaps. It is mostly a trade issue, as opposed to a bourgeois cash transaction. There is some exclusivity, and a mistress costs more in the long run. But, most importantly, it is how it is done."

Kathy put on her shoes. "Freddie, I don't have the right to know all this."

"You wanted to know."

"But why are you telling me? It's all too personal." Kathy's heart suddenly did flip flops, and a warmth stirred in her body. "You don't want me..?"

"Good God, no!" Freddie stepped back, in utter shock, then realized his reaction could be equally insulting. "Kathy, forgive me. What I am trying to say is that you are not a candidate simply because I couldn't insult you that way. I assure you, I think very highly of you. The thought of putting you in that position never entered my mind."

"I hope not." Kathy finished with her shoes. "Do you still want me to take you to that brownstone?"

"It would confirm Mr. Healcroft's presence there, which I suspect you were not able to do, and what exactly he was up to in respect to that missing buttonhook."

"I suppose that sort of taste is not common enough to assume that because Mr. Healcroft visits whores, he has it." Kathy glared at her feet. "My shoes are wet. I should get my others."

"By all means and let us be on our way." Freddie's tone was grim.

Kathy ran upstairs.

Freddie stretched and looked idly out the window. A police officer, in blue uniform, stood outside near the stoop. The snow had stopped and the copper lit a cigarette, glancing idly at the boarding house. Kathy's feet pounded back down the stairs. Freddie quickly turned out the parlor lights.

"What are you doing?" she asked, crossing into the room to get her coat.

He parted the lace curtains. "Look."

"Oh," said Kathy. Her eyes grew round as a second man, in plainclothes, approached the officer. He wore the traditional tweeds, overcoat and bowler hat and had a pronounced beaked nose. "That's Sergeant Reagan."

"Would a quick exit be in order?"

"I think so. Would you mind leaving through the back?"

"Not in the least."

Kathy led Freddie to the kitchen just as the front bell rang.

"Now what?" asked Freddie as they entered the alley.

"Let's find that whorehouse. I need all the evidence I can get."

For a distance of a little over ten blocks, Kathy decided hailing a taxi would not be worth it. Freddie's objection that it was nearly four o'clock, and that darkness would be falling soon, went unheeded. Her pace was quick, and even Freddie's long legs had to step lively to keep up. He left her at a bookstore on Fifth Avenue.

"This shouldn't take long," he explained.

"If you're in there longer than, say, thirty minutes, I'm coming after you. I mean, you never know what kinds of thugs are around."

Freddie smiled. He suspected that Kathy didn't entirely believe his distaste for ladies of the evening.

"I'll be back long before then." He turned to go.

"Wait, Freddie." Kathy pulled him back. "You've got mustard on your face."

Quickly, she licked her thumb twice, scrubbed the offending spot just below the corner of Freddie's mouth, then lightly brushed over it.

"All clean," she announced triumphantly.

"Thank you."

Freddie left the store with his mind in turmoil and the rest of him uncomfortably aroused by the lingering sensation of Kathy's thumb on his chin. The unpleasantness of the coming interview was bad enough. But why had Kathy's mundane, sexless, little scrub job stirred him up so strongly? The idea of her as his mistress revolted him. It had to be the circumstances.

Kathy wasn't sure what was more unnerving: Sergeant Reagan's visit or the way her insides felt when Freddie took her arm as they walked together. It was simply a mundane, perfectly polite gesture and yet it stirred her to her very core.

Sighing, she looked around the bookstore and noticed that the owner had a telephone on his counter. She had to give him two bits, but he let Kathy make a call. Kathy held her breath, hoping that her uncle was in the precinct house.

It took a couple of minutes but she was switched through, and Dan picked up the phone.

"Callaghan," said the familiar voice.

"Uncle Dan, it's Kathy. I've a small complaint to lodge."

"You do?"

"I know you're trying to take good care of me for Ma's sake, but did you have to assign a harness bull to keep an eye on me?"

"Katie-girl, what in the name of all the saints are you talking about?"

"When I left the office this afternoon, there was a copper following me. Are you afraid I'm going to be accused of shoplifting?"

"Kathleen, I didn't assign any of my men to follow you."

"You didn't?" Kathy's heart stopped for a second. "Then who did?"

"I think I know."

"So do I. It was Sergeant Reagan, wasn't it?"

"What makes you so sure?"

Kathy swallowed. "He came to the boarding house a little while ago. I was just leaving, so I, uh, I left through the back so I didn't speak with him."

"Much as I don't like seeing anyone evading the law, you were smart to do that, Katie-girl." Callaghan hemmed and hawed for a second. "I'll see what I can do."

"He thinks I killed Frank Selby, doesn't he, Uncle Dan?"

"Katie-girl..."

"On what evidence? I have the right to know that, don't I?"

"It's thin, but it could stick. There was that woman the landlord saw, and the way you were covering for your boss. And Mr. Healcroft said you were quite forceful the day after the body was found."

Kathy yelped.

"Now, I know you had good reason to be," Callaghan continued. "And there's other evidence, which Reagan knows, which clears you."

"Such as?"

"Now, Katie-girl, don't be worrying your—"

"Uncle Dan, I've got a copper hot to arrest me. I have a right to know what's going on and what clears me."

"All right, Katie-girl." Callaghan paused as he formed his words. "Word's out that the Selby murder was supposed to have been done by hired thugs, and there's plenty of money to be had for another hit. I'm telling you this because I don't want you sticking your nose where it doesn't belong. Now, the thugs botched the job. But whoever hired them has enough money to be dangerous. I'm sure he wouldn't think twice about icing you."

"But what about Sergeant Reagan? If he knows this, why is he still coming after me?"

"We're all under a lot of pressure at the moment. Reagan thinks it would make him look good if he got the Selby matter cleared up right away, so he's looking for the easiest answer whether or not it's the right one. I'll talk to the captain and see if I can't keep him off your back. But I want you to promise me you'll watch your step."

"I promise, Uncle Dan." Kathy smiled to herself. "Thank you."

"You're welcome, Katie-girl."

"Give Aunt Beth my love, and 'bye."

Twenty minutes later, Freddie returned to the bookstore to find Kathy humming some little ditty as she browsed through a series of guide books.

"Well?" she asked.

"Let's get out on the street. It's chilly, but not too bad."

"If we keep walking, we should stay warm enough."

Outside the air was crisp, and the street was

lost in the shadows of the fading day.

"Let's walk up to 22nd, and over to Broadway," Freddie suggested.

"All right." Kathy waited a moment. "You seem disturbed."

"It was not pleasant. But I am untouched, somewhat lighter in wallet, and fully informed as to Mr. Healcroft's activities at that place of business."

"What are they?"

"The sort that cause pain and you don't want to know the rest."

"Do they include buttonhooks?"

Freddie shuddered. "Yes."

"Then given that we found the buttonhook in Mr. Selby's office, and that it was gone the next day, and the fact that Mr. Healcroft certainly had access to it, which strongly implies that Mr. Selby was somehow blackmailing Mr. Healcroft, we now have a strong suspect."

"Quod erat demonstrandum."

"But what about the woman the landlord saw?"

"Something regarding Mr. Healcroft's tastes leads me to believe he would not mind dressing as a woman, and he is not a large man."

Kathy giggled. "That's just too ridiculous. The image, I mean. I'm sure it's quite possible. Then again, the woman could be completely unrelated to the crime."

"True. So, now what?"

"I suppose we should try to find out if Mr. Healcroft has an alibi for the night of the murder. But how?"

"Have your uncle ask."

"Oh no." Kathy shook her head. "I managed to phone him from the store. He didn't make me promise not to investigate, but he'll be pretty darned angry if he catches me at it."

"Perhaps I can find a way to find out." Freddie got out his holder and cigarettes. "Did your uncle tell you anything of interest?"

"A lot." Kathy told him about the conversation. "The good part is that I have a reprieve from Sergeant Reagan, but that doesn't mean I'm going to take any chances on that score. But this business of someone hiring thugs to kill Selby, it doesn't make sense. I'm not sure what to do about it, especially with all the information we have on Mr. Healcroft."

"At the moment, I don't care." Freddie finished his cigarette and lit up another. "I have just been engaged in some extremely nasty business, and I would like to find a way to wash the unpleasant taste out of my mouth."

Kathy debated asking why he was smoking then, but remembered there were those who actually enjoyed the activity.

"We could find a speak on Broadway," she offered instead.

They turned up Broadway. Freddie gazed at the glow of lights a few blocks ahead.

"Would you settle for an evening of theater?" he asked.

"Can we get tickets for anything?"

Freddie shrugged. "We can try."

"Anything but *Abie's Irish Rose*. I've seen it, and I agree with Mr. Benchly."

"Benchly? Oh, the critic. We are of one accord on that issue."

But even *Abie's Irish Rose* was sold out, as were the better vaudeville houses. Kathy was going to suggest a movie, when they stumbled onto a man trying to sell his tickets to *Lady Be Good*.

"I have seen it," Kathy admitted. "But I do like Adele Astaire. I wouldn't mind seeing it again."

"Are you sure?" asked Freddie.

"Do you want to?"

"I haven't seen it, and right now even the *Irish Rose* is sounding good."

Kathy laughed. "I'd stay home, sooner."

It was by then too late to change to evening clothes, but it didn't matter. The seats were not the sort that required it. They ate dinner at a small restaurant near Times Square. Later, Kathy again left the theater humming the catchy little ditty, *Fascinating Rhythm*.

"I have heard that song before," remarked Freddie. "Someone was humming it not too long ago. I just can't think who."

137

"I was, in the bookstore."

"Not you. And it was a few days ago. Before Wednesday."

Kathy shrugged. "It's a nice tune."

Freddie hailed a taxi.

At the boarding house, Kathy asked Freddie not to call the next day.

"I've simply got to get that report done, and there were some things I wanted to do on your book before I did," she said.

"I shall probably see you Monday, then," said Freddie. "I'm going to try and gain an interview with Mr. Healcroft."

He opened the door for her and she went inside.

Sunday at the boarding house was the cook's day off. More accurately, it was Mrs. Lynne's day off, since she was the cook and the cleaning staff. But since she liked to keep some pretense of gentility, the tenants pretended not to notice, and usually referred to the servants as if they did exist.

On Sundays, the tenants took turns running out and fetching food for the others. At least those who were there did. That Sunday the three other young working girls, Misses Timms, O'Leary and Felt, were presumably with beaux or their families. The widowed Mrs. Johnson always spent Sunday with her grown son and his family.

That left Kathy and Mr. Robb, a gentleman in his fifties that Kathy suspected liked other men, and Mr. Eggleston, who was a Civil War veteran, and often spent his Sundays in the parlor telling stories about his days fighting for the Union, in a loud voice because his hearing was almost gone.

To Kathy's relief, the cook had left pastries for breakfast, and Mr. Robb volunteered to fetch lunch and dinner. His doctor had recently recommended lots of brisk walks in the fresh air. Kathy didn't care. If Mr. Robb hadn't wanted to go, she would have had to, because Mr. Eggleston could barely make it to the parlor.

She spent the day in her room, working. The setting sun threw orange shadows across the pages. Kathy got out another bottle of ink and kept working. The working girls trickled in. Kathy heard Miss Felt, who had the other fourth floor room, giggling with Miss O'Leary before clumping up the stairs.

The blackness of the night wrapped around us, as deep as the void that was our lives. I felt as if I could reach out and touch it, luxuriate in the rich, velvet folds. But my hands only found the gnarled roughness of tree bark, as if the trees stood as sentinels, guarding us, keeping us from knowing the reason, however insignificant, for our existences.

Thripps retched behind a tree, about two yards behind me. I heard his misery and felt no compassion. How cold I had become. He approached.

"Give me the bottle," he said in a husky voice.

"Why?" I asked. "Do you really want to kill yourself that badly?"

"Not really," he confessed. "I'd like to do someone else in."

"Who?" I asked, horrified.

"It doesn't really matter," he said. He took the bottle from me, and drank in long gulps. "I wouldn't kill you, of course. You're quality. I do have some sense of propriety. But it would be interesting to feel someone go limp in my hands, the lifespark gone. It's very easy to snap someone's neck, you know, once you get the knack of it. It's in the rhythm. Pop. Absolutely fascinating."

"You've done it?"

What I could see of his eyes gleamed with bloodlust, then it flickered out in a sigh so profound it touched the depths of the night itself.

"No, I haven't done it," he said. "I only wish and dream. Pop. There goes one. Pop. There goes another. Pop. I can't get it out of my head. Pop, pop, pop, all day long."

I couldn't bear it any longer. Leaving him with the comfort of his bottle, I crawled into the blackness of the bracken and the wood, a darkness that would yet be broken by day. But the darkness of Thripps' soul would know no sunshine, no light.

"He's used that darkness metaphor three times now," grumbled Kathy.

Not to mention the worthlessness of life theme, which was a part of the whole book, but did not need to be stated again. The scene was redundant.

Still, Freddie had thought it was important. Kathy shuddered when she thought how most of it was true. Even if Meabury was based more on Freddie's friends than himself, there were some deep darknesses in Freddie's soul. It was odd how Freddie, himself, remained the perennial optimist. The cheer and bonhomie were occasionally feigned. Kathy saw that much. But Freddie had found some measure of peace, some way of keeping the darkness at bay.

The scene, on the other hand, never fulfilled its threat. Furthermore, the chapter was about Nanette, and Thripps was yet another digression. It had to come out.

"Where can I start the cut?" Kathy muttered, and flipped to the previous page. A few more scratches, and she laid the page aside.

The boiler rattled again and again as the others bathed and washed up. Beneath Kathy, Miss Timms' gramophone scratched out her favorite jazz songs, and then a couple of ballads. Snatches of a German lullaby drifted in as Miss Felt made her way to the bathroom. The gramophone eventually stopped. The plumbing whooshed, then the lullaby got louder and softer. Silence slowly settled on the house, broken only by the scratching of Kathy's pen, and her soft mutters.

Downstairs, the grandfather clock banged out its chime and struck two. Kathy looked at the clock on her bureau. Its hands agreed, and a sweet, tinkling chime confirmed it. She yawned. Blinking back the heaviness in her eyes, she wrote two more sentences, then surveyed the results.

"Good enough," she grumbled.

Not that it mattered, but she decided to wash up before changing into her nightgown. Out-

141

side the house, a car chugged by. A horn honked, and Kathy made out the sounds of male laughter.

"Damn college kids," she grumbled, turning on the faucet.

She was brushing her teeth when the ringing started. There was a short ring first, then a prolonged one, as if someone were leaning on the front bell. She rinsed quickly and charged downstairs.

The only tenant not gathered around the front door was Mr. Eggleston.

"We want to see the lady editor," someone drawled.

"I told you not to wake them." It was Freddie's voice, but thickened and overly deliberate.

Kathy forced her way to the door. Mrs. Lynne, in wrapper and hairnet, stood staring at a crowd of five men dressed in evening wear and weaving about on the stoop. They were led by Freddie and another man who seemed a little younger. Freddie was holding the younger man up, or maybe leaning on him, it was hard to tell.

"Dah-dee-dah-dee-dah-dah!" the younger man sang tunelessly. "Dah-dee-dah-dee-dah! Dah-dee-dah-dee-dah-dah! Duh-duh-duh-duh-dah!"

Kathy barely recognized the tune from *Lady be Good*.

"I'm sorry," said Freddie. He looked as though he was working as hard to stay straight as he was to speak clearly. "I did tell them not to wake you."

"Mr. Little, you're behaving so peculiar,"

said Mrs. Lynne.

"He's drunk!" snapped Kathy.

"I'm afraid so," said Freddie. "I told them not to wake you, but they wouldn't believe I wrote a book. I told them. I even told them I had an editor. They wouldn't believe me. So, we just drove by to look at your house."

"Is that her?" asked Freddie's friend.

"Yes, Edmund. M-Miss Briscow, Edmund Markham."

Edmund looked at Kathy, then stumbled around the other way.

"I'm sick," he announced, and promptly proved it all over the stoop.

Freddie gazed at the mess philosophically while the others cheered. Edmund fell forward, but was caught by his companions.

"Now what do we do with him?" asked one.

"Take him to his sister. She likes taking care of him."

"She's why he's drinking."

"Good ol' Victoria. Has to take care of baby brother, the old bitch."

"Get them out of here!" Kathy's voice rose with her anger. "Get every last stinking one of them out of here this instant. And if I ever see any of you here again, I swear I'll fill your hides with buck-shot!"

143

She slammed the door shut. With a deep breath, she turned. The eyes of her fellow tenants were glued to her.

"Well, boys will be boys," said Mrs. Lynne.

"If you'll excuse me, I'd like to go to bed now," said Kathy calmly. "I'm sure you all would, too. Good night."

Holding her head as high as she could, she stepped through the crowd.

CHAPTER EIGHT

Kathy woke up late the next morning. It was annoying having to scramble through her morning rituals, but it did save her the trouble of facing her housemates at breakfast. She merely dashed through the dining room pausing just long enough to grab some toast before running outside.

The last thing she expected to see was Freddie Little calmly supervising while a young maid mopped up the stoop.

"What are you doing here?" Kathy demanded coldly.

"Making amends," he replied, just barely wincing. He looked at Kathy. "At least I am to Mrs. Lynne. I did think of bringing you flowers, but something told me that would not do it."

"Not by half." Kathy picked her way around the maid. "If you'll excuse me, I'm late for work."

"I've got my car."

"I'll take the subway, thank you."

Kathy stepped up her pace. Freddie said

something to the maid, then hurried after.

"Kathy, what I did last night was abominable," he said, wheezing a little.

"It was humiliating." Kathy kept her eyes straight ahead. "Heaven only knows what the others are thinking."

"I know." Almost frantic, Freddie ran beside her down the subway steps. "Kathy, if you never want to see me again, just say the word and I will understand. But will you at least allow me to apologize, and then I will leave you alone."

"That's not going to do me any good. I still have to edit your book, and if you take it away, I will never get a chance to edit another."

"Yes, that would be the perfect apology," Freddie said sarcastically.

She glared as he paid her fare.

The train pulled in. In the press, Freddie got separated from her. Kathy fumed all the way to 23rd. She could see Freddie at the other end of the car, and hoped she could lose him again at the station. As if it would do any good. Her fate was tied to him whether she liked it or not. Unless she got arrested for murder.

He caught her halfway up the stairs to the street.

"Wait," he gasped, and steadied himself. "My head is pounding."

"It's not pounding near enough for me!" Kathy pushed past him. "Damn it, I'll be late for work."
146

Freddie turned after her, but she was gone. Fortunately, he knew where she was headed. He stopped long enough to get the heaving in his stomach under control. Workers streamed around him, some of them in the same condition he was. Slowly, he finished the ascent and went to wait in the lobby of the building where Kathy worked until he was certain she was at her desk and couldn't easily avoid him.

Mr. Healcroft had left a note asking Kathy to come to his office right away. Kathy had expected that. What she did not expect was what he said.

"Your report is excellent," he told her after reading through it. "But I'm afraid I do have some rather bad news for you."

"How so?" Kathy's heart pounded. Had Freddie phoned him already?

"As you know, the police were here Saturday morning. Mr. Selby's death has been a scandal for this house. Now it appears that you are one of the main suspects."

"The police do not have any evidence of that, Mr. Healcroft," said Kathy, feeling more angry than afraid.

He leaned back in his chair. "Nonetheless, it is a risk this company cannot afford to take. As of now you are suspended from your duties, Miss Briscow. It is only temporary, until such time as you are cleared. I am advancing sufficient salary to get you through the end of next month." He held out a sealed envelope.

"You can't do that!"

"I most certainly can, and I am." He dropped the envelope on the edge of the desk closest to Kathy.

Kathy got to her feet. "There is no evidence! And I promise you, Mr. Healcroft, I did not kill Frank Selby."

"I am confident you did not, Miss Briscow, which is why I am advancing you your salary."

"Then why are you treating me as a common criminal?"

Mr. Healcroft swallowed. "I have a company to think of. You are not my only employee."

"No, but I get to be the sacrificial lamb. This is completely unjust. It may look like I have a motive, but I'm hardly the only one here who does. Mr. Evans had just as much reason to kill Mr. Selby, perhaps more. I won't stand for this!"

"That is enough, Miss Briscow. You are dismissed." Mr. Healcroft turned to some papers on his desk.

Kathy snatched up the envelope. "You've got a strong motive, too, Mr. Healcroft." She stomped to the door. "I remember seeing a buttonhook in Mr. Selby's desk."

She slammed the door shut behind her without looking for Mr. Healcroft's response. In her office, she collected as many of her things as she could carry. As she pulled her coat on, she noticed the deep white manuscript box on the corner of her desk. It contained the only copy of *The Old Money Story* currently at the publishing house. Kathy had the other copy in her room.

She grabbed it and ran. As the elevator opened in the office lobby, Kathy heard Mr. Evans furiously shouting her name. She got on.

"Please, take me to the ground floor without stopping," she begged the operator.

The little man shrugged. Kathy dug into her purse.

"Please?" She pressed two quarters into his hand.

He smiled. The elevator crawled, but it did not stop. The other elevators were no faster. When the doors opened onto the lobby, Kathy ran.

Freddie, was still waiting in the lobby, caught her. "What's the matter?"

"I'm stealing your book!" she hissed.

She started toward her usual exit, but Freddie pulled her away to the doors that opened on the opposite side of the building from the subway stop. He held her back just outside of the doors where she could not be seen, and looked back into the lobby.

Evans burst out of an elevator and went straight for the subway. Freddie smiled and pushed Kathy down the street a ways while he hailed a taxi.

"Where to?" asked the driver as Freddie helped Kathy inside.

"Just keep driving up Fifth," Freddie told him, and shut the glass partition.

Kathy was shaking. Freddie put his arm around her shoulders. The tears started slowly, but gained force.

149

"This is the worst day of my life!" she sobbed.

"There, there." Freddie gently squeezed her as she cried.

Her sobs finally abated as they neared 57th. Freddie offered her a handkerchief.

"It's clean," he said softly.

Kathy took it and blew her nose. "I can't imagine you offering anything less." She wiped her nose again and glared at him. "You're the last person I wanted to be with."

"I'm sorry. Would you like me to get out? I'll see that your fare home is paid."

"No. Right now, I'm glad. Oh, Freddie, I'm so furious I don't know whether to cry or scream."

"Kathy, I don't blame you. What I did last night was unforgivable. I do apologize. I just hope you can somehow find it in your heart to forgive me."

"We can worry about that some other time. I've got bigger problems now."

"Is it something at work?"

Kathy sniffed and nodded. "I got suspended. That bastard Healcroft is afraid of the scandal because the police suspect me. As if he doesn't have any motive!"

"Did you tell him that?"

"I was so angry. I barely stayed calm enough to take my pay envelope."

"Oh no," sighed Freddie.

"The son of a bitch. So magnanimous because he advanced my salary through January. If you ask me, that's a cheap way to get rid of a possible scandal."

"Does Healcroft know anything about your suspicions?"

"I only told him that I'd seen the buttonhook in Mr. Selby's desk."

Freddie groaned. "Kathy, if Mr. Healcroft did kill Selby, you just told a cold-blooded killer that you think he did it. And even if he didn't, it's not likely he'll give you your job back."

"Do you honestly think I'm going back there?" Kathy screeched. "As soon as I calm down enough to think, I'm getting a copy of the Times and looking for a new job. I wonder how much it costs to advertise for a situation."

"That's assuming Mr. Healcroft is not now looking to kill you." Freddie glanced out the window. "What we need to do first is make sure you're safe."

"I'm safe," Kathy grumbled. "Uncle Dan's got half his men making sure I stay out of trouble, and there's Sergeant Reagan and the other half trying to arrest me. If you're worried, the best thing to do would be to find the evidence to convict Mr. Healcroft, or find the real killer, if he isn't the one. In the meantime, I've got to find a new job."

"You've got 'til the end of January." Freddie paused, then got out his cigarette holder. "And if worse comes to absolute worst, I might be able to arrange something."

"Freddie, if you try to offer me money..." Kathy growled.

"Kathy, where does my family's money come from?"

"You're digressing again."

"No, I'm not." Freddie lit his cigarette. "Do you know?"

"From your forebears. I have no idea. Will you get to the point?"

"The point is if you need a job and can't get one by yourself in time to avoid eviction and starvation, I will get you a job."

Kathy sneered. "What are you going to do? Buy a new company and give it to me to run?"

Freddie blew out an angry mouthful of smoke. "I'm trying to do this so that you are reassured but your blessed pride is not offended. Sarcasm does not help."

Kathy shriveled and sniffed. "Damn it. I'm sorry, Freddie. I'm not being fair, am I? All you're trying to do is help."

"Kathy, my family has been in textiles almost since the industry first came to America a hundred years ago. We own a lot of mills and such, and there is a big corporate headquarters here in New York. They always need good secretaries. If you want to run a company yourself, I'm afraid you'll have to earn the privilege."

Kathy smiled softly. "Do you think I could?"

"I've no doubt of it."

"There's only one problem. I have eight uncles, including husbands of aunts, in this city, who could also get me a job, at a good salary."

Freddie smiled. "Then you shall have your pick."

"I don't want that. I want to do it myself."

"I promise I won't do a thing for you until you are down to your last penny, and your uncles' offerings are not to your satisfaction." Freddie paused. "I guess what I'm trying to say is that I don't want you to worry. I want you to get your own job, too. But I don't want you fretting, or taking something awful because you're afraid you won't get anything better, especially when I can help. Is that all right?"

"It's more than all right." Kathy started to weep. "It's wonderful. Thank you, Freddie." She smiled at him, then got control of herself. "The only problem now is what are we going to do about your book?"

"That." Freddie grimaced. Thinking, he clicked his cigarette holder against his teeth. "You said you have it, right?"

"Both copies."

"Then let us pursue the following. I will write you a letter of recommendation, and perhaps have my writer friend write a letter also, to counteract whatever Mr. Healcroft might say. You get on with another publisher."

"I'll only get hired as a secretary."

"Then tell them you were editing my book

at Healcroft House when you decided to leave, and that I will follow you. I don't know if it will work. But the publishers seem very interested in it."

Kathy laughed. "They'll do handstands to get it." Her face fell. "Damn. That's not the way I'd want to do it. But it seems like the only way the book will get published."

"I don't believe it." Freddie gazed at her, bemused. "You'll barely sacrifice your pride to keep from starving, but don't question sacrificing it for the sake of a book."

"It's a damn good book, Freddie." Suddenly, she sighed. "I'm not that altruistic. Just a secretary's job is not worth the sacrifice. But your book, Freddie, is my one chance to be taken seriously at a job where I'm doing something important, and not just following someone else's orders. I've always wanted a job like that. Probably the best I could hope for would be running an office. I suppose I could have surrendered to the academic life. It would have been all right. But I couldn't see spending my life in an ivory tower."

"Indeed." Freddie looked out the window, then rapped on the driver's partition. "You can let us out here."

They were at the northern end of Central Park. Freddie paid the driver, then took Kathy's elbow.

"I hope you don't mind," he said.

"You're looking a little pale."

Freddie winced. "The taxi was getting stuffy, and my head started pounding again."

"Poor thing."

"It's no less than I deserve." Freddie ambled toward Eighth.

"I'm amazed you got on your feet so early." Kathy sighed. "I don't know, Freddie. Maybe I ought to just let Healcroft House have your book."

Freddie turned on her. "No! Not without you." He turned away. "It's not the white knight this time. It's for purely selfish reasons. Kathy, you don't know what I've been through with this damn thing already."

"I would imagine laying your life bare on the printed page is not an easy thing to do." Unconsciously, Kathy squeezed the box tighter against her chest.

"You might try watching a group of idiots tearing it apart to make something of it." Freddie gazed over the park, where browned patches of grass poked up through the snow and a breeze rippled around the barren trees. "It was at another house last October. I had no illusions that it was a perfect work. My friend, Lowell, was adamant on that point. He said it was on the edge of greatness, but even he couldn't figure out what was wrong. The editors at that other house couldn't either. I sat in on a meeting where they completely rewrote it. It may have been a better story for all I know, but it wasn't the story I was writing. The only reason I took it to Healcroft House was that Percy had heard about it and suggested I do so, which I did in spite of his cousin. I was not impressed by Frank Selby, but at least he knew what I was writing about."

"Only he never read it."

Freddie smiled. "I'm glad he didn't. I'm glad he was the bastard he was. The day your letter arrived, I cringed. I had to force myself to read it. I had no idea the first paragraph was sincere. It was nothing I hadn't heard before. But the rest. It was as if Moses, himself, had come down the mountain and told me 'This is the way thou shalt go.' Kathy, your letter was the first opinion that actually made sense."

Kathy shrugged. "It's not my job to rewrite your book, just smooth out the rough edges. And there are not nearly as many as you might think."

"I don't care. You understood. I showed your letter to Lowell, my writer friend, and he told me I was not imagining it, and that I should stick with this Mr. Briscow at all costs." He mispronounced her name as he had originally, rhyming it with cow. "Which is what I intend to do."

"You seem to have a great deal of respect for this Lowell person."

"Aside from being a true friend, which I assure you is plenty rare, he is making a good living as a writer, something not easily done, even these days."

Kathy gazed at the frozen park musing. "Lowell, Lowell. I can't place the name."

Freddie laughed. "Lowell Winters."

"The big contributing editor over at Life Magazine." Kathy nodded, smiling.

"And everywhere else. He also had a moderate success on Broadway some three years ago. It wasn't a smash, but it was enough to feather his nest nicely, and get him married to the wrong woman." Irritated by the memory, Freddie went for his cigarette case.

Kathy looked at him severely. "Are you sure he wasn't the wrong man?"

"Perfectly sure." Freddie grimaced. "Victoria is an extremely overprotective woman, practically compulsive. She completely smothered Lowell to the point that near the end he could barely write enough to keep his job at Life, and, like you, his job is very important to him."

"This Victoria wouldn't happen to be related to an Edmund Markham, would she?"

"Her brother. But how...? Oh. Last night." Freddie grimaced again, then sighed. "Kathy, I can't apologize enough for that."

She shrugged. "I was angry, and I can't say I'm looking forward to going home and facing the others. But it just doesn't seem that important now. At the absolute worst, I'll have to move. That's nothing to worry about. Mrs. Lynne's isn't the only house in New York."

"But with your job."

"I'll take it as it comes. If you need to salve your conscience that badly, I'll let you buy me a few newspapers."

"You shall have them all." Freddie brightened, relief spreading through his limbs. "Say, I've got a corking idea. It's getting on for noon. Let's find a place where I can use the phone. I'll call up Lowell and we can all have luncheon together."

"I guess that would be all right, as long as we stay uptown." Kathy smiled weakly. It was not as though she had anything else to do.

"Naturally, uptown." Freddie stopped and sighed. "Oh, that's right. The coppers."

Kathy nodded weakly. "I didn't see anybody this morning but I wasn't looking, either. Heaven only knows how long Uncle Dan can keep Sergeant Reagan off my back."

"But there's evidence that says you didn't do it." Freddie gazed down the street, looking for taxis.

"If Reagan is out to get me, I wouldn't put it past him to make some evidence up."

Freddie shuddered as a taxi pulled alongside the curb. They went downtown to the other end of the park. At one of the hotels there, Freddie got permission to use the phone. Kathy watched as Freddie gave the operator the number, feeling strangely nervous. It was as if she were intruding too far into Freddie's life, albeit at his invitation. Then again, he had met her uncle and his family.

"Lowell, Freddie here," he said into the speaker. "I'm so glad you're in. How about lunching together today?" Freddie waited while Lowell answered. "Now, now. I've got a surprise for you, somebody you've been wanting to meet... We're at the Plaza now. Just come on over..." Freddie glanced at Kathy. "No, the club would not be a good idea... Very well, then. I'll have it sent over to your place, and we'll meet you there." Freddie shook his head as he rang off. "Lowell refuses to be seen in a public place today." He smiled at Kathy apologetically. "Perhaps Victoria's been calling him again. Do you mind?"

"I don't see why," said Kathy, even though she did for some reason.

"I'll have to call the Mayfair." Freddie paused, suddenly debating the wisdom of the venture. "Kathy, I'd better warn you to take Lowell with a grain of salt. He's been practicing to be a curmudgeon for a long time now, and he's gotten rather good at it since the divorce."

Kathy quaked. "I'll do my best."

Lowell's apartment was on the East Side just above Murray Hill. As Freddie and Kathy approached the door, they could hear angry voices on the other side.

"She's here," Freddie sighed with disgust.

"Maybe we should come back."

Freddie shook his head. "I can't do that to Lowell. I'm afraid I'll have to rescue him. I'm sorry I'm dragging you into it."

Kathy sighed. "I suppose one does have to respect a sincere friendship. Go ahead."

The voices stopped abruptly at Freddie's knock. Victoria Winters opened the door. Kathy took one look at her slender, flat-chested figure, the round face, and the perfectly bobbed hair, and hated her as only one can of those they envy.

"Freddie!" Victoria glowed. "What a perfectly delightful surprise. What are you doing here?"

"Lunching with Lowell," replied Freddie with a polite but restrained smile. "I regret I didn't know you were here. Unfortunately, I didn't order anything for you."

159

Victoria flashed an uneasy smile. "I was just leaving." She stepped closer to Freddie. Her voice was lowered but still easily heard by Kathy. "Who is that frumpy little thing you've got with you?"

Freddie stepped away, angry but not visibly so. "This is my editor, Miss Briscow. Miss Briscow, Mrs. Victoria Winters."

"Oh." One of Victoria's eyebrows lifted.

Kathy swallowed. The woman's curiosity was almost overpowered by a deep, seething rage in her eyes. It matched Kathy's.

"It's truly a pleasure." Victoria smiled.

"Likewise," said Kathy.

Victoria turned back to Freddie. "I'll get my coat. Do step in."

"Thank you," said Freddie, taking Kathy's arm and leading her into the apartment.

Victoria shut the door behind them and walked down the hall. "Lowell! Freddie's here. I'm leaving."

"And none too soon!" hollered a voice from the bedroom.

"He is so rude," sighed Victoria, putting on a fur trimmed coat. "I never could break him of it."

Freddie waited in silence as she left. When the door had shut, he went to the bedroom door.

"Lowell?" he called in a raised but still gentile voice. "It's Freddie. She's gone."

"The bitch." A door opened and closed. "She came about her alimony. Can you imagine? I'm already paying through the nose for her, and she's got all the fucking money!"

Freddie loudly cleared his throat. They appeared in the entry way together. Lowell Winters was of medium height, but stout. Next to Freddie, he appeared much shorter. His shirt was open and stretched over a large, rounded belly, on each side of which were suspenders. His dark hair was tousled. Under the prodigious nose was a rich beauty of a mustache. Lowell stopped short when he saw Kathy. He turned on Freddie.

"What is the meaning of this?" he snapped. "I thought you said you were bringing over your editor. Where's Mr. Briscow?"

Kathy sighed at the mispronunciation.

Freddie grinned. "Right here. This is Miss Briscow." He pronounced it correctly.

"K. Briscow?" Lowell demanded, incredulous.

"Yes, that's me," said Kathy, her anger growing.

"Impossible!" Lowell fumed. "A woman? It's preposterous!"

"I beg to differ!" Kathy started forward.

Horrified, Freddie stepped between the two and put his hands on each of their shoulders.

"Now, now," he said in his most soothing voice. "I know you've both had very trying mornings. But that's no reason for you to fly at each other's throats like a couple of alley cats. Lowell, Miss Briscow proves quite conclusively that intelligence among the fairer sex is quite possible. Kathy, I did warn you about Lowell."

"You never told me he was a misogynist," she snapped.

"I apologize," said Freddie quickly before Lowell could respond. "Lowell, has lunch arrived?"

"In the kitchen."

"I'd best see to it." Freddie hesitated. "Can I trust you two alone together for a few minutes?"

"You can trust me," said Kathy. "I'm not the one making insulting comments."

"You're just reacting to them." Freddie held her back as Lowell snorted. "And you're the one making them, Lowell. Now, enough."

He let them go and went into the kitchen. Kathy looked after him, wondering just how badly his poor head was pounding by then. Lowell snorted and mumbled to himself.

"The dining room's this way," he said suddenly, his tone surly.

"After you," said Kathy.

Technically he should have deferred to her, but Kathy wasn't going to let him. Freddie wheeled the lunch into the dining room on a cart just as Kathy and Lowell entered. Papers and books covered the entire surface of the mahogany dinner table. A huge, matching, glass-fronted china hutch stood against the wall nearby, but instead of china, it was filled with empty bottles and books. Freddie cleared the table, piling papers and books on a breakfront on the other side of the table. He started to seat Kathy, but she took it herself.

"Uh, Lowell," said Freddie, hesitating. "It is your apartment. Would you prefer to be the host?"

Lowell looked at Kathy. Kathy folded her arms and silently dared Freddie to ask her.

"Never mind. I'll serve." Freddie quickly set out the plates and flatware.

Lowell tucked in gracelessly. Freddie smiled weakly at Kathy.

"So, Freddie," Lowell said around a mouthful of steak. "Since when have you started supporting the Nineteenth Amendment?"

Kathy stiffened. She looked at Freddie hoping, even praying it wasn't what it sounded like. Freddie squirmed.

"It's a moot point, isn't it?" he said finally. "The amendment was passed a good four and a half years ago."

"And we've regretted it ever since," insisted Lowell. "But I'm surprised at you, Freddie. You used to be the most outspoken opponent of women's votes at Harvard."

"Second only to you," said Freddie. He turned to Kathy, who was looking at him as if he'd changed into a maggot. "That was also some time ago, Kathy. Please bear in mind that Lowell and I did support the concept of women's votes. It was just at the time, the only women we knew were the types who were more interested in clothes, and jewelry,

163

and getting rich husbands than anything else. And so based on practical experience, we came to the conclusion that votes for women was not appropriate."

"Based on the fact that an intelligent woman is rarer than hen's teeth," finished Lowell triumphantly.

"I know something still more rare," said Kathy softly. "An intelligent man. And thus, based on your hypothesis, Mr. Winters, no one in this country should be voting."

Lowell's chewing slowed as he thought it over.

"The woman has a point, damn it all," he said at last. "It was the common man who gave us that bastard, Harding, not to mention Coolidge."

Freddie smiled at Kathy, feeling somewhat relieved. Lowell fixed his gaze on her also.

"Did you truly write that letter?" he asked her.

"Every word," she said.

"That Selby fool didn't help any?"

"Mr. Selby never even read the book. He merely handed it over to me, as he did all his work."

Lowell shook his head. "I don't believe it. A woman with a brain. This world is surely about to end."

"Come now, Lowell," said Freddie. "You weren't always so hard on the fairer sex."

"I wasn't," Lowell sighed. "But the cruel lectures of fate have changed me. You see before you a shriveled, embittered old man."

"You can't be that much older than Freddie if you went to college together," said Kathy.

"He's two days older than me," Lowell confessed, then slurped from his water goblet. "Damn it, Freddie, there's no gin in this glass."

"And whose fault is that?" Freddie, nonetheless, got up. "Don't answer. Where is it?"

"Get out the whiskey. Ladies always prefer that."

Kathy bent her head over her plate, a small smile on her lips.

"Lowell, I would caution you against making assumptions about Kathy based on her sex." Freddie lifted another pile of papers to open the breakfront.

"Well, Briscow," demanded Lowell, mispronouncing her name again. "What is it?"

"At the risk of contradicting Freddie, I do prefer whiskey." Kathy smiled. "Thank you."

"Whiskey, it is, then," said Lowell.

Freddie poured Kathy a generous splash, then gave the bottle to Lowell. He raised the bottle towards his lips, but another throat-clearing from Freddie brought the bottle down untouched. Lowell emptied his water glass into the pitcher on the table, then poured.

"Freddie?" He handed the bottle over.

"No thank you. I'm abstaining today."

Kathy tried not to laugh, and managed a silent giggle.

"Hung again, eh?" said Lowell. "Freddie, how many times do I have to tell you? Moderation in all things."

"Even moderation," said Freddie. He watched as Lowell gulped his glass dry and poured again. "But you're a fine one to talk."

"I don't want any lectures," grumbled Lowell. He turned to Kathy. "You have to understand that Freddie is the finest of men and the best of friends. Stays out of the way when you want him to, but when you need him, he's there. I don't know how I would have made it through the summer but for him. He redecorated his apartment as an excuse so he could move in with me and work on his magnum opus here."

"It was nothing I couldn't have worked on anywhere," said Freddie.

"Bullshit," said Lowell. "The only one who didn't figure out that you were here to keep Victoria out of my hair was the bitch herself. I'd kicked her out in March and she was here every damned day, picking out ties and pants, and going through not only my personal belongings, but Freddie's as well."

"It wasn't entirely an act of charity," said Freddie. "You helped me write an awful lot of that book."

"Don't listen to him, Briscow." Lowell leaned over. "I did no more than any good editor would, as I'm sure you would understand."

Kathy refrained from correcting his pronunciation of her name.

Lowell continued, relaxing back in his chair. "But, alas, I am an essayist, a writer of fact, and occasionally a playwright. Fiction is not my strong suit. Digression. It didn't seem inappropriate for a novel. Actually, I don't think I even noticed it."

"If Freddie was living with you at the time, you were probably hearing it so much, you wouldn't have," said Kathy.

"The woman is a positive fiend at keeping me to a point," said Freddie.

"It would take a fiend to do it," said Lowell. "Damn it, Briscow, you hit the nail on the head with that. Smack on. Incredible."

Shortly after, they adjourned to the living room where Kathy and Lowell became immersed in an extended discussion of Freddie's work. They opened the manuscript box and were soon making notes all over the pages. A loud snore interrupted them.

Freddie had fallen asleep on the couch.

"I thought he was up a little early for being hung," remarked Lowell.

"Poor thing. I wonder that he got any sleep at all last night," said Kathy. "He was drunk, all right. Showed up on my doorstep with his dissolute friends at two o'clock in the morning. They woke up the entire boarding house, then one of them was sick on the stoop. So Freddie brought over a maid first thing in the morning to make amends."

Freddie snored again and snorted.

"Roll over, you old fool," Lowell told him.

With another snort, Freddie did so.

"People look so ridiculous when they sleep," said Kathy with a warm smile. Then she got up. "Well, Mr. Winters, I'd like to thank you for the use of your home, and the whiskey."

"It's Lowell, please." He snorted. "I've never been one to stand on formalities."

"I noticed." Kathy tried not to laugh and failed. "In any case, would you convey my thanks to Freddie for lunch? And tell him that I'll be at home this evening if he'd like to telephone. At least as far as I know, I will be. If I end up elsewhere, I will certainly telephone him."

"Be glad to."

Kathy looked at the mess of papers. "I suppose I should get this manuscript back together. Actually, Lowell, why don't you keep it? I think I can remember everything we talked about, and I'd like to go over it again with you."

"You would?" Lowell looked bemused.

Kathy blushed. "I've been editing for almost two years now, but I've never had the chance to talk it over with another editor. As I mentioned, the only reason I was editing was that I was doing my boss's work for him."

Lowell took a long pull on the whiskey bottle. "I don't know why women have to be so blamed stupid. It makes it damned hard on the few that actually have something to offer."

"You might not believe it, Lowell, but I am of the same opinion." Kathy picked up her coat. "I'll have Freddie contact you when the book is ready."

"Don't bother him unless you want him here. You can call me direct at any time."

"I'll remember that."

Kathy collected her things, shook hands with Lowell and left.

Daniel Callaghan prided himself on being an honest cop, which meant that he wasn't above looking the other way now and again when the situation warranted it. The Italian grocer was just making a little wine. What concerned Callaghan was Shorty O'Connor, whom he held firmly by the collar.

"What do you think you're doing in this neighborhood, young man?" he demanded, as he pulled the boy from the grocer's back room.

"I just come to get some groceries for Ma," Shorty complained.

"Groceries. My left foot, you're here for groceries." Callaghan shook the boy until he howled.

"Okay, I was getting some wine. But Ma wants it, and I gotta get it or she's gonna beat me black and blue. But I got some news for you. Will you let me go if I tell you?"

"We'll see. What do you have?"

"That same grocer let out a while ago that there's a second hit in the works. Don't know who, just that the money's good for the right person."

169

"Grocer?" Callaghan stood the boy on his legs and nodded at the Italian wringing his hands behind them.

"Naw, not him. The other one."

"I didn't think so." Callaghan got a firm grip on Shorty's shoulder. "All right. You're coming home with me."

"Aw, Sergeant!"

"Don't 'aw, Sergeant,' me, you young scamp. Come along before I take you to the station house."

The grocer let out a frantic tirade of pleading, apparently still convinced that Callaghan was there to arrest him for the wine, but Callaghan waved him off and started uptown with Shorty in tow.

Callaghan didn't have to drag the boy much. They both knew the only way Shorty would get back home without a beating would be to wait until Mildred O'Connor had forgotten that she'd sent her son on his errand. He gave the boy a quick shake for form's sake, then fretted silently.

Callaghan wasn't fool enough to think Kathy had stopped looking for Selby's killer. Now there was another hit in the works. The skin across the back of his shoulders tightened.

CHAPTER NINE

Freddie looked at the calling card. Roberts waited silently nearby. According to the card, a Michael Callaghan, Attorney at Law, waited in the building's vestibule downstairs. A professional call, although it was possible the gentleman was not well-versed in the niceties of social versus business cards.

"You say this is the third visit?" Freddie asked Roberts.

"Yes, sir. One this morning, and another around noon time."

Freddie tapped the card thoughtfully. He did not like visits from lawyers. It usually meant a great deal of unpleasantness, and only once in a while was it justified, not to mention the expense.

It was the name that was so odd. Surely not all the Callaghans in New York were related to Kathy. But she had mentioned an Uncle Mike, and somebody had said something about a lawyer. If her uncles were truly as overprotective as she said, then it could be. Which meant there was all the more reason to avoid them, especially if one of them was a lawyer.

171

"I'm not in," he said. He handed the card back to Roberts, and went back to lathering up his shaving soap.

He had been disappointed when he finally awoke to find that Kathy had left, but not terribly surprised. Lowell had said they'd gotten on quite nicely without him, which hadn't surprised Freddie either. He'd been sure they would, once they got past Lowell's recently developed suspicion of females.

A telephone call to Kathy had confirmed it and confirmed that for the moment Sergeant Reagan remained at bay. They also agreed it was too late for Freddie to question Mr. Healcroft regarding the buttonhook, and other things. It was past six already. Mr. Healcroft would have long since left the office, and Kathy had no idea where he lived. She wasn't even sure if there was a Mrs. Healcroft, to which Freddie pointed out that if there were, then Mr. Healcroft had access to women's clothing, not that he couldn't have gotten them some other way.

In the meantime, there were the other speaks to investigate. Freddie selected a dinner jacket and black bow tie. He had suggested that dinner wear would be appropriate for Murray Hill, and Kathy had agreed. That probably meant her brown velvet, but there was no help for that. He didn't dare offer to buy anything for her. He'd promised not to abuse the fact that he had assumed the costs for whatever they did together. Even if the clothing was required for the activity, it would still be improper to pay for it.

In the front of the apartment, the front door opened and shut too quickly for any but one person.

"Freddie!" her voice called. "Come on, I know

you're here."

"I'm finishing dressing," Freddie called.

Honoria Little Wentworth bounded into the room, as graceful as her brother. She had his build, although she wasn't overly tall for her sex. Freddie remembered that as a young teen-ager, she had padded her dresses to make bosoms. Now she gloried in the current fashion that made it so smart for beads to hang straight down her chest. Her bobbed hair was brown, and her eyes hazel. Apart from each other, people rarely recognized them as brother and sister. When they were together, there was no doubt.

"Hallo, Mrs. Wentworth," said Freddie, finishing with his tie.

"Hallo, Freddie."

They gave each other an affectionate, but filial peck.

"What brings you down here?" Freddie asked.

Honoria lived in the apartment above Freddie's.

"I'm bored, Freddie. Horribly, desperately bored."

"Am I supposed to be surprised by this announcement?" Freddie eased his feet into his dress pumps.

"You're supposed to do something about it."

"I'm afraid I can't. I'm going out tonight."

"Tonight?" Honoria's eyebrows raised in surprise. "After last night?"

"What do you know about that?" Freddie filled his pockets with all the things he carried, certain Honoria was well apprised of his condition.

"You came home at nearly three o'clock, drunk as a skunk."

"And that surprises you."

Honoria laughed. "Only that it's been so long. It's been at least a month since you last went on a toot. Freddie, this book business has definitely slowed you down. I don't understand. I thought authors were supposed to be sots."

"I don't know. I'm not entirely sure I'm an author."

"Oh, don't be ridiculous."

"You're too kind, dear sister." Freddie bussed her once more. "But I've got to go."

"Freddie, can I come with you? Please?"

"No."

Honoria gaped happily. "Without hesitation. All right. What's her name?"

"And what makes you so certain I'm going out with a woman?" Freddie stopped and looked at her.

"Not just any woman, a girlfriend. You would have at least considered taking me with you had it been anyone else." Honoria grinned. "So what is her name?"

"She's nobody you know."

Honoria groaned. "Oh, Freddie, not another mistress. Couldn't you at least get married first?"

"Honoria, she is not my mistress. She's..." And there Freddie got stuck. "She's a friend, and nothing more. So don't go marrying me off to her. She would be grossly offended."

"That's too bizarre, Freddie." Honoria looked him over carefully.

"Nonetheless, it is the way it is. And it is high time I left, Mrs. Wentworth."

Honoria watched him go, musing. This was a new twist. But would it lead to a sister-in-law for her? Perhaps Edmund Markham would remember something. It had been his car they were driving.

Freddie rode down to the Village, feeling slightly unnerved. That Honoria kept track of his comings and goings gave him no pause. Her spy system was only rivaled by his. She liked to rub it in because she knew damn well he knew just as much about her. Even with six years separating them, they were so close in thinking that it was impossible for either to hide from the other.

Honoria's assessment of the current state of affairs was what bothered him. It was a strange arrangement, and what was to become of it, Freddie hadn't the faintest idea. In the meantime, Freddie would have to keep Honoria from meeting Kathy as long as possible. It wouldn't be easy, given Honoria's persistent nature. But Honoria was dying for a sister-in-law, and rarely subtle in her efforts to get one. It was possible that Kathy might like taking the position, and that worried Freddie more than the possibility of Kathy being offended by Honoria's wedding plans.

He paid the taxi driver and sent him off. Kathy met him on the stoop.

"Saving face?" he asked.

"Just yours," she replied, smiling wickedly. "You would not believe how full the parlor is this evening."

He took her arm. "And I don't doubt they are peering out the windows even now."

"Knowing that, you still took my arm?"

"Of course." Freddie was baffled. "It would be rude not to."

Kathy's grin became even more wicked. "Not to them. Only a beau would take a girl's arm."

"And I suppose only a beau would help a lady into a car." Freddie did the same, leading her around to the left hand side of the brand new Silver Ghost, as the steering wheel was on the right.

"Or seat her." Kathy bounced on the rich leather seat. "This is yours?"

"Yes. I left it here this morning." Freddie shut the door and went around the front of the car to the driver's side.

"Don't tell me, an electric starter, right?" asked Kathy, getting excited.

"Yes." Freddie pushed it, and after a grind or two the engine roared to life.

"Freddie, this is too elegant."

"It's a damned nuisance in the city." Freddie swerved around a wandering flivver, and braked for yet another. "But the Rolls is the most comfortable car I own. All the better when one must sit in traffic." He glanced at Kathy. "Aren't you bothered that your housemates are making assumptions about us?"

"I don't know." Kathy gazed out at the street. "After Aunt Jane made the same, I knew it would happen again."

"But what have I ever done that would lead them to that conclusion?"

Kathy laughed. "It's what I was trying to tell you. All those fancy manners that are second nature to you mean romance to them. It's kind of funny when you think about it."

Freddie suddenly caught his breath. "Are you trying to tell me you might be interested in turning the appearance into reality?"

"No!" Kathy started, then stopped. "Not that it wouldn't be pleasant. I'm sure you would be perfectly charming. But seriously, Freddie, I'm not interested in being courted."

"I am of similar mind, I assure you. But such a relationship wouldn't have to lead to marriage. You could have a boyfriend, I suppose. Someone to share a few kisses with."

"What a colossal waste of time." Kathy almost added that if she had to deal with a man, he could at least be her lover. But she happened to look at Freddie just then, and realized he could be.

177

It wasn't a bad possibility, she mused. But it would have to be negotiated carefully. She had no intention of becoming his mistress or otherwise being kept.

Freddie felt her eyes on him. She smiled, her eyes glowing with a desire that was not entirely innocent. Freddie felt himself stir, and riveted his mind on the traffic.

Kathy chuckled to herself. Always the gentleman, Freddie would not allow himself passionate thoughts about her while in her presence. But he was passionate, from the soft lips that were neither full nor thin, to the long, spidery fingers that held so much promise. He would make a good lover.

Kathy frowned. There was the book. If they were lovers, the work would be unbearable. Once fully reminded of her femininity, Freddie would never be able to see beyond it, no matter how modern he claimed to be. The book held the only key to her career. Lovers, even good ones, weren't that hard to find.

Dinner was a little strained. By the time dessert had arrived, Freddie had had enough.

"I think it's time we cleared the air," he said.

"About what?" asked Kathy.

"About us. About our relationship to one another."

Puzzled, Kathy looked at him. "What are you proposing?"

"Nothing!" Freddie went completely white. "I'm not proposing anything at all."

Kathy burst into loud laughter, then struggled to contain herself.

"I'm sorry. I know it's not done, but I can't help it." She held back her giggles. "You're afraid of getting married."

"I am not," protested Freddie. "I simply don't like the idea. Given the amount of time and effort I've spent avoiding it, I certainly don't want to capitulate all of a sudden."

"You don't have to worry about me." Kathy smiled. "I think that given the way things are and the work we have to do, it would be much better if we just remained friends. In fact, I'd rather."

Relief filled Freddie. "I'd rather, also. But I suppose for the sake of your friends and relatives we shouldn't protest too much if they insist on calling me your beau."

"I'll just tell them you're not and leave it at that."

After dinner, they went to the speakeasy on Lexington and 40th. It was a much tonier place than Kathy's uncle's, but not quite as elegant as Freddie was used to. The band was good, and the drinks drinkable. Cigarette smoke, music and laughter filled the air. Patrons in evening wear mingled with others in daytime dress.

Uncle Thomas's name brought the owner, Petey, in a hurry. He was a somewhat nervous man who had a large bald spot with strands of hair trailed across it. Freddie recognized him from Frank Selby's funeral. He'd been one of the more grieved mourners.

"How do you know Thomas?" he asked suspiciously.

"I'm his niece," said Kathy. "On my mother's side."

Petey looked at her carefully, then sat back in relief.

"Yeah. I can see the resemblance."

"Mr. Little, here, is a writer," said Kathy, her smile almost coy and teasing. "He's doing a book on rum-running and all that. Fictional, of course, but terribly thrilling. Uncle Thomas sent us to you so we could find out about a hooch maker named Frank Selby."

"If you want to talk to him, you're too late," Petey said, disgusted. "He's dead, died almost a week ago, and it's been damned lousy for me that he did."

"How do you mean?" asked Freddie.

"I bought his booze. You're drinking the last of his whiskey right now. I have a certain pride in my place. Standards. I've tried three suppliers since last Wednesday, and not one of them is passing decent stuff. I'd sure like to get my hands on the broad that did him in."

"Are you certain it was a woman?" asked Kathy.

"That's what they're saying. Kind of funny, though. Him getting his head bashed in. That don't sound like a woman did it to me."

"You'd be surprised," said Kathy. "Mr. Little, do you have any more questions?"

"Yes," said Freddie. "Do you know if Mr. Selby was supplying anybody else, and who they might be?"

"Just a bunch of lollygagging rich kids on the Upper East Side. Least that's all I heard him mention."

"Did he frequent this club?" asked Freddie, ignoring the slur.

"He came in. But he liked hanging out with the rich kids more. You could tell from the way he talked, you know?"

Someone hollered over the jazz band. Petey's head shot up.

"Enjoy your drinks. Gotta go." He jumped up and ran back to the bar.

Freddie looked at Kathy. "Well. We've got three options. We could stay here a while, we could go someplace else, or I could take you home."

"Whatever you like." Kathy smiled, then turned sour. "It's not as though I need to get up tomorrow morning."

Freddie reached over and squeezed her hand. "You have my deepest sympathy."

"You sound like somebody died," Kathy snorted.

Freddie nodded at the bar. "What do you think of our new friend?"

"I almost wonder if he's protesting too much."

181

"No, he seems quite genuine to me. And if your uncle's right about neighborhood stills being the primary source for drinks, he has no reason to want Selby dead."

"That makes sense." Kathy thought. "So, what's our next step? Are you going to talk to Mr. Healcroft?"

"First thing tomorrow."

"Will that be before noon?"

Freddie sent her an amiable glare. "Will you please stop making an issue of my sleeping late? You ought to try it first. You might like it."

"I'm sure I'd love it." Kathy sighed. "I just can't imagine doing it all the time. I've had to rise at the crack of dawn all my life, and everyone I've ever known has had to do the same. It's survival. If you don't, you starve."

"I don't have to worry about starving."

Kathy grinned. "Damn lollygagging rich kid."

Freddie laughed. "Speaking of that, maybe we ought to investigate a few of the speaks my kind tend to patronize."

"Would we be able to narrow down the number of them so as to make the job manageable without too much inebriation?"

"Quite easily." Freddie grinned. "I know which speaks Frank Selby liked. And I think I know his liquor when I taste it. If our host hadn't volunteered the source, I would have asked. There's only one problem." He shifted. "I'll probably have to go alone."

"Why?"

Freddie sighed. "I don't want you to take this as a slight against you. But while your best dress is nice, and perfectly appropriate here, I'm afraid where we'd be headed, it would not fit in."

"You're right." Kathy smiled sadly at him. "And you haven't insulted me. There's no shame in the fact that I can't afford all the things you can. But I did go to the bank before I went home. Two months' salary adds up to a pretty amount."

"Kathy, you're going to need that to live."

She shrugged. "I might. I do have some savings. A party frock is grossly impractical. I don't go to places where I need one. And it would cost something. But not so much that it will break me. I think I will get one. It will be just the thing to cheer me up."

"Are you sure?"

"Yes. I'm feeling fairly confident that I will be employed again long before my money runs out. And if worst comes to absolute worst, I know I can count on a position at Little and Sons Manufactures, Incorporated."

Freddie grinned, highly amused. "You've been doing some research."

"Yes. I spent a few minutes at the library, but only a few. I was surprised to find that you don't have any of your family's money."

"Not directly. Nor am I likely to get it any too soon, the way my grandfather keeps hanging on.

But the pile I do have was built with investments made out of allowances that I get from the family funds. Would you like to dance?"

"No thank you. I hate dancing. I'm terrible at it."

"That's too bad." Freddie gazed at the dance floor. "I've been known to trod a few toes myself. But I do like to stumble through a fox trot or two."

"Oh, all right." Kathy got up.

"You're already fired, Kathy." Freddie grinned at her. "You don't have to be nice to me now."

"I was suspended. And..." Her wicked grin flared up full force. "I have my reasons."

Within five minutes, Freddie knew them. He limped off the floor behind Kathy, and promptly swore he would never ask her to dance again.

As Freddie and Kathy left the speak, a figure with a pronounced beak nose left the shadows near the back room and stepped up to the bar.

"Get Petey over here, will 'ya?" he ordered the bartender.

Shortly, the speak's owner slid over and put a glass in front of the man. Petey fervently wished that Sergeant Reagan had chosen some other speak as his preferred watering hole.

"Evening, Sergeant." Nervously, Petey poured two fingers into the tumbler, then trailed a loose strand of hair back into place. "I got your money. It's right here."

He dropped a fat envelope onto the bar. Reagan looked at it with mild disdain before sliding his hand over it and picking it up.

"The woman in the dark dress with the swell you were talking to." He nodded at the table where Freddie and Kathy had been as he tucked the envelope inside his coat pocket. "You know who she is?"

"Niece of a friend of mine. Why?" Petey swallowed nervously.

Reagan shook his head. "That's Kathy Briscow."

"No!" Petey gazed at the door. "Not that broad you got pegged for offing Selby?"

"The same."

Petey swallowed as he reconsidered. As angry as he was at the woman who killed his best supplier, he hated Reagan at least as much. It was her bad luck that Reagan was in the speak when she came in.

Reagan knocked back the whiskey and refilled the glass to three quarters. Petey swallowed again. Good Canadian hooch, damned expensive, and there he was, paying Reagan for the privilege of watching the copper drink it.

Reagan fixed his gaze on Petey. "So what were you three talking about?"

Petey trailed another loose strand into place. "Oh, the usual stuff. How's your family? Things like that."

"You sure?"

Petey gulped. "Aw, come on, Sarge. I'm not gonna lie to you."

Reagan picked up his drink, then looked again at the table. "Who was the swell?"

Petey sighed. "Some writer fella. Um. A Mr. Little."

Reagan's glass hit the bar hard. "Son of a bitch," he growled in amazement. "Son of a bitch." He glared at Petey. "Damn it, Petey, what the hell were they talking about?"

"Family stuff," said Petey.

"Damn it all to hell!" Reagan's hand whipped out and caught the front of Petey's shirt. "Don't be lying to me, Petey. That Mr. Little is just as mixed up in this Selby business as that bitch Briscow. I don't know how, but he is. Now, what the hell were they talking about?"

"Rum-running," said Petey, defeated. "That's all they were asking. She's the niece of a friend of mine. He sent her here."

Reagan loosened his grip slightly. "Rum-running?" Petey swallowed but didn't say anything. "What about rum-running, Petey? Damn it, tell me or I'll close this joint down."

"For his book," Petey whispered.

"Like fucking hell." Reagan let go of Peteys' front, then turned and sagged against the bar. "What's a swell like that writing a book for?"

"Uh, Sergeant, um, why are you so sure this,

uh, Kathy Briscow offed Frank?" Petey asked.

"Because it's the only thing that makes sense." Reagan grabbed the glass, drained the contents, slammed it to the bar, then glared at Petey. "They must be moving in on Selby's business. And I'll be damned before they do."

"Yes, sir."

"And you. Keep your nose clean and your ears open."

Petey swallowed and wiped his hands on his apron as he watched Reagan stalk out. The question now was what to do. Thomas Callaghan's niece did not off Frank Selby, of that much Petey was sure. Why would she be asking so many questions about which place Frank supplied if she had? But Reagan's fury was no small matter, either. If only Frank Selby hadn't died owing Reagan money. Reagan was one vengeful bastard, and he didn't take too kindly to people icing his cash cows. Petey swallowed again. At least his neck was safe. Perhaps the best thing to do would be nothing.

CHAPTER TEN

The morning was like cut crystal in its brilliance. Without a cloud in the sky, the air was so cold it snapped, filling Freddie with exuberance and life even at the early hour of ten o'clock. The whole city was alive and churning with its business and the myriad businesses of its inhabitants.

Still, Freddie knew he had work to do. He took one last, icy breath, then went into the building at Broadway and 23rd, only partly feigning his bonhomie.

Because of his cheerfulness, nobody at Healcroft House had any idea Freddie was less than happy with the company's owner. He decided it was just as well. He would keep Mr. Healcroft thinking the same. He bantered and flirted with the receptionist who took his hat and coat, then teased Misses Watkins and Edwards, then bounded into Mr. Healcroft's office.

Mr. Healcroft was not there. Freddie poked his head back into the outer office.

"Hallo, girls. Where's the boss?"

The secretaries giggled.

"He's in an editor's meeting," said Miss Watkins.

"Will he be long?"

"Less than an hour, I think."

"Very well. I'll wait in here."

It couldn't have been better. Freddie left the door open a small crack, then looked over the office. It would have to be done carefully. He didn't want Mr. Healcroft to know.

He started with the book shelves at the back of the office and under the windows. It seemed if one had secrets to hide, one wouldn't want them out where they could be found. But the books hid nothing. Freddie checked his watch. He'd been there fifteen minutes. Perhaps the desk.

It was in the bottom drawer. Freddie moved aside a pile of files and found a black leather box. The contents, for the most part, were less than discreet, and certainly consistent with what Freddie knew of Mr. Healcroft. And right near the top was a buttonhook, a familiar buttonhook. Freddie removed it, and replaced everything else.

By the time Mr. Healcroft returned, Freddie was seated in front of the desk, and a good way through the Times. He scrambled to his feet as the older man entered the office.

"Corking day, isn't it?" said Freddie after the greetings had been made.

"It's a bit cold for my old bones," said Mr. Healcroft. "Please, sit down. Would you like a cigarette?"

"Yes, thank you." Freddie sat again in the chair in front of the desk, and the two men went through the lighting ritual. Freddie blew out a satisfied mouthful of smoke.

"What can I do for you today, Mr. Little?" asked Mr. Healcroft, settling into his own chair.

Freddie tipped his chair back and gazed at the older man with a sleepy smile. Healcroft seemed a little tense. Given what had happened with Kathy the day before and the way Freddie knew Healcroft felt about his book, the tension was justified. But was there more?

"I just happened to be in the neighborhood, and thought I'd stop in," said Freddie.

"Naturally, you're anxious about the progress being made on your book. I can assure you, it's going very well. I received an excellent report from Miss Briscow yesterday. Of course, these things always take time."

Freddie grinned. "I'm in no rush. You've got quite a pleasant business here."

"I've done nicely by it." Mr. Healcroft watched him, not quite sure what Freddie wanted.

"Provided well for the wife and children, and all that. Any sons to pass the torch on to?"

"One. He's finishing at Yale this year."

"A fine school. You and Mrs. Healcroft must be quite proud."

"My wife, God rest her, is no longer with us." Mr. Healcroft's sigh was profound.

"I'm terribly sorry." Freddie hesitated. "Has she been gone long?"

"Roughly six years."

"Ah. Yes." Freddie got up suddenly. "It's been a pleasant chat, Mr. Healcroft, but I must be on my way. By the by, what were you doing last Monday night, a week ago yesterday?"

"I was at home, I believe." Mr. Healcroft looked puzzled as he got up, then glared at Freddie. "Why do you want to know?"

"Just a silly bet I made. Good day, Mr. Healcroft."

Freddie slipped out quickly. In the lobby of the building he checked his watch. It wasn't quite eleven-thirty. He didn't have to meet Kathy until one. They were meeting at a tea shop at Fifth and 36th, then would go on to the shops. It had been Freddie's suggestion. He didn't know if Messrs Macy and Gimbel were up to meeting Kathy's needs, not that he had said so, and didn't think it would be wise to leave it to chance. Kathy had been reluctant to go with him at first, but then decided that since she'd committed to the purchase, she might as well.

But for the time being, Freddie was at loose ends. He decided to go on home. The morning mail would be there and would occupy a few minutes of his time. The hailing of a taxi was the work of a moment, and shortly after, Freddie handed his coat, hat and gloves to Roberts.

He took the letters into his study. It was a mundane collection of circulars and invitations. The circulars he glanced at and threw away. He wrote "regrets" across the invitations he did not want to

191

accept and set them aside with the others for Honoria, who kept his social calendar.

There was one letter. It was from Michael Callaghan. Freddie almost put it into the wastebasket without opening it, then remembered Callaghan was an attorney. With a sigh, he opened it. It was dated the previous day, and on personal as opposed to business stationary.

"Dear Mr. Little," it said in an expansive script. "Having been unable to make your acquaintance today, I find myself forced to resort to the evening post. I have been given to understand that you have been entertaining my niece, Miss Kathleen Briscow. As her parents do not live here in New York, I find myself acting as their representative. It is in that capacity that I now write. I would like to make your acquaintance at your earliest possible convenience, and discuss your intentions with regard to my niece. Yours sincerely, Michael A. Callaghan, Attorney at Law."

So the old goat was versed in the niceties of social versus business calls. But he was going to make damned sure Freddie knew he was dealing with someone who had some muscle. He certainly worked fast enough, given that it had been barely three days since Freddie had met the other uncle. There were obviously no secrets in the Callaghan family, and given Aunt Jane's conclusions, no doubt that the attorney's inquiry was valid as far as they were concerned.

But Freddie wasn't Kathy's beau, and she had made it plain she was not interested in him becoming such. Sighing, he got out his letter paper and pen. He checked the letter for the address and copied it down.

"Dear Mr. Callaghan," he wrote, then paused. "I regret to say that you have been seriously misled, albeit innocently, as to the nature of my relationship with your niece. We are certainly not on terms in which a discussion of intentions would be appropriate, nor do I have any. Rest assured, if I did, they would be strictly honorable, as I think very highly of her. But she and I are friends, nothing more. Yours sincerely, Frederick G. Little, III."

Freddie blotted the letter, feeling irritated by the chore and wondering if he was being entirely honest. He addressed the envelope, then gave the whole mess to Roberts to post. He looked at his watch. Twelve-ten. The day was fine, if cold. Perhaps a stroll would restore his spirits.

He went straight to Fifth. Central Park was brown and desolate. It was that rotten time of year when everything had died, but there wasn't enough snow to cover it in white finery.

He began to feel livelier when he crossed 58th Street. Here the Avenue was alive with shops and businesses and people. Freddie had traveled extensively, but had never found a place quite so vibrant as his native city.

The display continued with the art galleries near 55th, the Fifth Avenue Presbyterian Church, the Embassy club, and the Hotels St. Regis and Gotham. St. Thomas Episcopal was at 53rd, Cartier at 52nd. Freddie was no stranger to either place. He went past St. Patrick's Cathedral, then smiled at Saks. He peeked at the bronze statuettes in the window at the Gorham Company at 47th.

He barely noted Budd and Finchley. His clothes were made by a personal tailor. He wasn't overly fond of shopping and so rarely did it for

193

himself. H. Jaekel and Sons did catch his eye. He'd made stops at the furrier's before, usually led by some young woman who had a right to expect presents. Somehow, he found it difficult to imagine bringing Kathy there.

He sighed for the passing of Delmonico's as he crossed 44th, and glanced at A. Sulka and Co. More men's wear, but more in line with Freddie's income. He'd been told one could get a Ford car for the price of a shirt in that establishment. Freddie wondered if it was an exaggeration.

The press of the people carried him across 42nd. He nodded at the lions in front of the public library. It was one of his favorite places to hide when he was hungover and didn't want Honoria bothering him. He crossed 40th and went past Knox's, 39th and the Union Club, to which his father belonged, being a devout Republican. He went past Ovington's, Bonwit Teller, Lord and Taylor, the Brick Presbyterian Church, Mark Cross. As he went past Tiffany's, he made yet another mental note to ask Honoria if she'd changed the typeface on her calling cards to something a little more proper and less artistic. He doubted she would, but one had to follow form.

Near 36th, he spotted a nice party frock in the window of Kurzman's. He looked over at the tea shop, then checked his watch. One o'clock, on the nose. He didn't see Kathy. But with a dozen or so women with hats like hers standing on the corner, not to mention all the other people on the street, there was little likelihood he would.

He walked over. Kathy stood next to the curb, a few yards from the corner, watching the taxis coming from uptown. He smiled. A downtown bus approached. A man wearing a dirty brown coat walked up behind he, then suddenly planted his hands firmly on her back and shoved.

Freddie leaped, stretching with every inch his long limbs gave him. He pulled Kathy back as the bus brushed her coat. His heart still pounding, he got a firmer grip and pulled her still further back onto the sidewalk.

"My," said Kathy with a shaky, forced smile. "The Avenue is crowded today."

"You were pushed," said Freddie grimly.

Kathy bit her lip. "No."

"I saw him do it."

Kathy's face turned an odd shade, and she put her hand to her forehead. Freddie's arms went around her shoulders.

"Let's get you sat down." He all but picked her up.

"No!" Kathy waved him off. "I'm fine."

"You look as if you are going to faint."

Kathy curled her lip. "Nonsense. Vapors are for the Victorians. Just give me a second to catch my breath. There. Are you sure I was pushed?"

"Yes."

"Hm. In a sense it's good news. It means we're getting close to someone."

"Mr. Healcroft." Freddie glared at the crowd of people covering the path of the man who had pushed her. "Damn it, Kathy, you shouldn't have said anything about that buttonhook."

"Freddie, we have no way to prove that Mr. Healcroft was behind this." Kathy straightened her coat. "Who knows? It may even have been a coincidence. Whoever did it may just be some poor sick soul who didn't like my coat."

Freddie looked at her and shook his head. "So now it's my turn."

"Let's not get all hysterical. When you think about it, it's rather ridiculous. How would this person have known to find me here? You were the only one who knew we were meeting."

"Weren't you looking for someone following you?"

"But I didn't see any coppers." Kathy's heart stopped beating.

"Someone was following you."

"I'm not sure." Kathy frowned. "I never saw anything. I just had a creepy sort of feeling. If it were a cop, I'm sure I could have spotted him."

"This was obviously no copper."

"No, he wasn't. But why attack me now?"

"A good opportunity, I suppose." Freddie looked at where it had happened. "You were standing right next to the curb, with plenty of people around to cover his escape, and the bus came by. Come on. Let's get something to eat."

"What I'd like is a drink of water."

"You could use a good stiff drink." Freddie

nudged her over next to the building as he reached into his jacket. "Don't make it obvious."

"Thank you." Kathy took the flask gratefully and took a quick gulp. The liquor burned and she shook her head to clear it. "You are corrupting me, Mr. Little. Honestly, drinking on the street in broad daylight."

She smiled weakly as she handed the flask back. Freddie took a quick sip, then screwed the lid on.

"I do have a reputation to maintain," he said with a sly smile. "I still think a bite to eat would be settling, given the recent trauma. Or have you eaten lunch?"

"I got a frankfurter off a cart a while back. I think I can manage another lunch."

Freddie escorted her into the tea shop. They didn't say much until the waiter had taken their order, and then the conversation turned to the weather and the possibility of snow for Christmas.

"Freddie, I do want to thank you," Kathy said slowly after her beef pie had arrived. "You literally saved my life."

Freddie shifted. "You're welcome. I hope you don't take this wrong, but I'd just as soon forget the whole incident. Gratitude can be quite a deadly beast if it's taken too far."

"Freddie, you saved my life."

"I know. But, Kathy, understand that while I might have run a little faster because I know you and consider you my friend, I would have done the same for anyone. Who wouldn't?"

"There were plenty of people there, Freddie."

Freddie fixed his eyes on her. "I believe I told you you don't owe me anything. And I still mean it."

Kathy swallowed. Freddie had turned back to his steak, and his concentration was locked on how to liberate it from the bone. Kathy was confused. It had been the perfect opportunity for him. She would have done anything for him, even become his mistress. Not that Freddie was the type to take advantage. But that he refused to have her beholden to him, that had been unnecessary. And yet, if she had been a man, Freddie's response would have been perfectly reasonable.

Was it possible? Did he regard her with the same respect he gave other men? Kathy broke the crust on her pie absently, her mind whirling with the possibilities. If he genuinely considered her his equal, then maybe, just maybe...

Deep within her the passion stirred and rumbled. Freddie, still working on his steak, looked up. His lips parted a little, and Kathy could see him catching his breath. He looked away.

"Is your pie to your liking?" he asked casually.

"It's quite good, thank you."

"So, how did you fill your morning hours?" He smiled at her, the moment gone.

"Job hunting. I got the newspapers first thing. Thank you."

"It was my pleasure."

"I visited three publishing houses. Two were not hiring anything, editors or secretaries. At the third, there was an editor who used to work for Mr. Healcroft. I was his secretary for a while. He knows I do good work. I mentioned your book and he seemed interested."

"Excellent." Freddie was pleased, but seemed a little distracted.

"And how did you spend your morning?"

"Ah." A genuine grin spread across Freddie's face. "You will be proud of me. I actually spent my morning up and around and engaged in a profitable pursuit of knowledge."

"You mean Mr. Healcroft?"

"The same. He says he spent the fateful Monday night at home."

"Which is very hard to prove."

"And very hard to disprove. Also, he said that Mrs. Healcroft has gone to her reward, some six years ago."

"Hm." Kathy thought. "Fashions have changed quite a bit since then. I suppose even Mr. Krinkly would have noticed that. Did you ask about the buttonhook?"

"I didn't have to." Freddie's hand slipped into his jacket. "Does this look familiar?"

Kathy gaped. "The one from Mr. Selby's desk?"

"I'll stake my life on it."

"You may have," snapped Kathy. "Good lord, Freddie. Have you lost your mind? I just made a chance remark. What were you thinking of when you took that thing?"

"Evidence. It was in his desk, in a box under some files. He was in a meeting, so I went ahead and searched his office."

"I can't blame you for that. But taking that hook. Freddie, that was insane! He'll know you took it."

"How? No one saw me, and I finished searching long before he got there."

"Who else would have been in that office?"

"Anybody. Believe me, it's no great job to distract those secretaries, and there are always those who work after business hours."

Kathy sighed. "I suppose it's possible. He'll have no reason to believe I've got it, especially since he knows I saw it in Mr. Selby's desk, and I left darned quickly yesterday. Why don't you give it to me?"

"Why not?" Freddie took the buttonhook out and handed it over.

Kathy put it in her purse. "Of course, this only proves that Mr. Healcroft stole the buttonhook back. It doesn't prove that Mr. Selby was blackmailing him."

"It's enough to get the police looking at him a lot more closely if Sergeant Reagan starts bothering you again."

"Let's not bring them into it unless I'm going to be arrested. I can just see what Uncle Dan would do if he found out what I'm doing. Do you think we need to continue searching out the speaks?"

Freddie chuckled. "Are you trying to back out of your planned purchase?"

Kathy blushed. "No. Just going out tonight. But I'm also dying to see how you lollygagging rich kids play when you're not waking people up at all hours of the night. On the other hand, if we're fairly sure Mr. Healcroft is the killer, I wonder if it's necessary."

"That's just it." Freddie frowned. "I'm not that sure. There are too many other possible motives. I agree the booze connection seems to be the weakest. But I think we should continue checking on it, if only to eliminate it."

"That is a good point. I guess our shopping trip is on, then." Kathy suddenly sighed nervously.

Freddie cocked a quizzical eyebrow.

She shuddered slightly. "I'm fine. I just keep thinking about that bus."

Freddie nodded. "Then our little trip is well-timed. We'll ban unpleasantries and focus on the banal in order to cheer you up."

They went across the street to Russek's first. Kathy stopped in front of the windows to admire the mannequins.

"Is that what we're looking for?" she asked, pointing to an evening gown.

"That's a little too formal." Freddie followed
201

her to the next window. "The lacy frock there, the pink one. That's more like it."

"I don't think I'd look good in that." Kathy shook her head. "A girl would almost have to have long hair. What about the blue one with the fur on the bottom?"

"That would be nice."

"I wonder how much it is." Kathy peered in closer. There were small cards on the floor next to the mannequins. "That's got to be a mistake."

"What is?" Freddie looked over her shoulder.

"That card. It looks like the price of the dress, but it can't be."

"It looks right."

Kathy swallowed. "That's a hundred and five dollars!"

"Ah." Freddie stopped, then understood. "More than you were planning on spending, eh?" he asked, suddenly finding the diplomatic response.

"Just a bit," Kathy said sarcastically. "Do you have any idea how many weeks' salary that is?"

"More than one, I gather." Freddie smiled blandly, but inside he winced. He'd had no idea how small Kathy's salary was. And yet he found it hard to think of her as poor.

"Do they have any less expensive dresses?"

"I don't know. I don't shop here. My sister might know." Freddie, himself, had never bothered to inquire after such mundane things as the cost of his clothes. The going rate on a Curtiss biplane engine, his favorite stocks, even an acre of land in Florida, those he could quote. But clothes?

"Your sister?" Kathy looked at him. "I didn't know you had any siblings."

"Just the one." Freddie folded his arms and leaned against the building. At least, Kathy seemed considerably calmer. "She's six years younger than me."

Kathy pondered. "Then why didn't I see her name in the Social Register?"

"Because her name is Wentworth, not Little. She got married in nineteen seventeen to a dough-boy shipping out."

"Did your parents actually approve of this?"

Freddie snorted. "Neither our parents nor I knew of it until the deed had been done, including fully consummated. I was already away in the army by then, which is probably how Honoria managed it. She's always been headstrong. According to my mother, Father demanded on an immediate annul-ment, but Honoria refused to cooperate, as I later learned, by graphically proving the marriage was valid. Then Henry saved everyone a lot of trouble by stepping off the boat in France and getting himself killed."

"Ooph!" Kathy found herself laughing in spite of her tension. "They must have kicked her out of the Social Register faster than spitting."

Freddie chuckled. "No. It turned out that Henry was from a very old and respected Virginia family. Somewhere in the three days between the

203

wedding and his departure, he'd gotten his will made and left her comfortably well-off. A satisfactory turn of events all around."

"Except for Henry."

Freddie nodded. "Except for Henry."

Kathy sighed as she looked at the store. "I wish she were here now."

"Trust me, you don't." Freddie straightened. "We'll make do with window shopping until we arrive somewhere you can afford."

"I've a feeling it will be a long walk." Kathy winced as a bus passed by. "Don't you get along with your sister?"

Freddie stepped between Kathy and the street, but refrained from taking her arm.

"We get along famously. Let's just say she has a remarkable capacity for making my lady friends uncomfortable."

Kathy smiled. "Siblings will do that."

"You sound as if you know." Freddie glanced at her as curiosity got the better of him. "And just how many do you have?"

"Six. Five brothers and one sister. I'm the oldest. Joshua grows oranges in California. Abraham is a law student at Harvard Law. Teresa is married with three children and another on the way, poor thing. Gideon will start next year at Harvard, and Isaac and Gamaliel are still at home."

"Interesting names." Freddie wondered what it must have been like to have such a huge family. To not have a social pedigree. To be, it suddenly occurred to him, normal.

"Pa's an Old Testament man," Kathy continued, not noticing his pondering. "He named the boys and Ma named the girls, which is why we have Irish names and the boys don't."

As Kathy had predicted, it was a long walk. The least expensive dress they saw cost seventy-nine dollars and fifty cents. But as Freddie had predicted, the banality of the conversation had relaxed her.

"I'm sorry, Freddie. I had no idea dresses were so expensive," she said outside of Saks. "I'll pay up to twenty dollars for a good dress, and more for a suit. But almost eighty, for something I'll wear once? I can't do it."

Freddie patted her arm. "Don't worry. I can go by myself."

Kathy pressed her lips together. "There is one other alternative, now that I know what I'm looking for. What time is it?"

"Almost four o'clock." Freddie slipped the watch back into his vest.

"I'll need to go home right away. We're at 50th? I'll get the subway at Sixth."

She started off, but Freddie held her back.

"We'll get a taxi."

"That's nonsense."

"Remember the bus? We'll take a taxi." Freddie already had his arm up.

At the boarding house, Kathy insisted on sending Freddie away. He only went after she promised not to leave the boarding house without calling him.

The next day was not a good one for Freddie. By the time his taxi arrived at Kathy's boarding house, he was almost tipsy. Kathy came out to the stoop again.

"Where have you been all day?" he growled the moment they were seated in the taxi. "You promised not to leave without calling me."

"I did call. Around eight. Didn't you get my message?"

"Yes. You didn't have to leave so early. And where have you been all day?"

"Job hunting. I talked to another editor. And I had a little shopping to do."

Freddie looked at the rich green feathe-trimmed evening wrap.

"I noticed." He sighed, then forced a smile. "So when is the grand unveiling?"

"Whenever we get to where we're going. You don't seem very happy."

"I was merely rousted out of bed this morning by a frantic call from Lowell. Spent the day over there keeping him and Victoria from doing violence. Then you weren't home and I confess, after yesterday, I was concerned."

"Unfortunately, Freddie, I need a job, and

I'm not going to get one sitting at home. I took
a quick walk and no one followed me, so I went
ahead." She paused. "Apparently, it's just as well
I was gone. Sergeant Reagan came by twice today
asking after me. Mrs. Lynne was in a complete dither. I had to call Uncle Dan to calm her down. That's
the only reason I was able to meet you on the stoop
tonight."

"Hmm." Freddie grimaced. "If it wouldn't be
so distasteful, I'd probably agree with your uncle,
and let the good sergeant arrest you to keep you
safe."

"I did leave you the message." Kathy glared
at him.

"I know. That's why I didn't take Lowell
with me and go out looking for you. If I could have
trusted Victoria not to go through everything in the
apartment, I might have anyway."

"Poor thing. You don't like her, do you?"

"She's all right to talk to occasionally. But
she won't let anyone close to her move without her
approval."

Kathy smiled. "She seemed like quite the
bitch to me."

"You don't seem to like her much, either,"
Freddie said with a smile.

They went first to a first class restaurant
near Central Park. Freddie's mood improved considerably when he saw Kathy's dress. It was a shiny
silk shift with a bronze-colored background that
highlighted the Oriental peacocks printed on the
fabric, and feathers matching the wrap on the hem.

"Forty dollars for the whole ensemble, including the wrap," she bragged quietly.

"It's very nice. Which shop?"

"Well..."

Freddie laughed softly. "You can't tell me you have an uncle in the clothing business."

Kathy nodded. "Uncle Morris Klein, my Aunt Bridget's husband."

"Didn't that cause an uproar?"

"Some, or so I hear. But the Callaghan women are very headstrong, and Uncle Morris is a perfect sweetheart."

"He does sell good clothes."

For dinner, Freddie insisted on banning any talk related to anything unpleasant for the rest of the evening. The first speak they went to was near Broadway, and only yielded the suspicion that the place was mob run. The second speak was overfull, and Freddie just barely managed to get them out before a young flapper spotted him.

"She thinks she's going to marry me," he explained to Kathy. "And she is annoying as hell."

The floor show was in progress when they arrived at the last place on Freddie's list. It was quite a spectacle, with scores of women and feathered fans and a full orchestra, but Kathy managed to remain cool.

"What did the owner say?"asked Kathy as Freddie brought their second drinks.   "I talked to the bartender. Apparently, Selby only frequented here. The mob seems to be supplying the booze. It's mostly imported. Oh no, not again." He sat quickly, then glanced around.

"What?"

"I thought I saw Victoria Winters." Freddie looked again. "If it was, she's gone, and thank heavens for that."

Kathy gazed in the direction he'd looked. "Freddie, we might want to leave."

"It's early yet. Wouldn't you like to see the second show?"

"There's not going to be one. That gentleman over there just poured his drink into a bottle."

"So he's bringing some home."

"He's a Prohibition agent. We're going to be raided."

CHAPTER ELEVEN

The screaming started just as Freddie and Kathy reached the hat check. Kathy pulled him back into the speak.

"Behind the bar!" she hissed just under the roar. "There should be a back exit. The front will be blocked."

The speak was in the basement of a block of shops, directly under a jewelry store. In the back room, two men frantically tried to get cases of whiskey and the like up a narrow stairway. Another man smashed barrels, while a fourth emptied bottle after bottle. Kathy spotted a door in the side wall and headed for it.

"That don't go out," yelled the barrel smash-er.

"We can at least hide," said Freddie.

"Bullshit," Kathy hissed, but nonetheless opened the door and shut it after Freddie. "They'll be in here looking for a still."

Freddie glanced around. "Like that one?"

Faint light dully reflected off the metal tank. Kathy spotted the light's source.

"Think you can get through there?" She pointed to the street level windows, where an outside lamp shone through.

"More easily than explaining to my mother why I'm in the newspapers again." Freddie went over and looked out. The lower sill was even with his shoulders. "Just thought I'd make sure they aren't back here also."

"If they are, they'll probably be more tied up with that liquor truck." Kathy watched as Freddie quietly opened the window. "As it is, they're probably still fighting the crowd in the front. But you're right. We'd better be careful."

Freddie took her hand. "It's a little high for you. I'll lift you out. I promise I won't look."

Kathy paused. For all the tension and rush of the situation, Freddie was still smiling and peculiarly appealing.

"Pity," she said with a wicked grin, and reached for the window.

After scrambling through, she looked around the alley, then bent back to the window. Freddie had his shoulders through, but was having some trouble finding a foot hold to boost himself the rest of the way out. Kathy grabbed hold of his jacket and pulled.

"Damn, you're heavy!" she grunted. "How much do you weigh?"

"Not enough." Freddie grunted, and got an

211

arm free. "Or so says my doctor."

He got his other arm free, and the rest was relatively easy.

"This way!" Kathy took off running, away from the liquor truck.

Freddie caught up with her at the cross street.

"I don't think we should go back to the street," he gasped, his breath making white clouds.

"You're right. It's probably lousy with coppers, and they'll spot us in a second without coats. I think if we follow the alley for two more blocks, we should be all right."

She dashed across the street. Freddie ran after her. At the next cross street, Kathy paused again.

"We're being followed," she whispered, looking up and down the alley.

A shadow wavered behind a nearby trash bin, then a dark form rushed them.

Freddie turned just in time to dodge a flashing blade. Kathy was knocked aside. Freddie gulped then danced backwards onto the street as the knife bearer pressed. Breathing heavily, Kathy looked around. A discarded piece of pipe lay nearby. Freddie charged at the knife man to distract him from Kathy, then quickly scurried back. Kathy checked again. There were no more assassins lying in wait.

The knife man pressed again, then grinned when he saw Freddie was not going to leave the alley. He feinted. Freddie dodged and tried to get around towards Kathy. The knife man went straight for the spot, and Freddie scrambled back. Kathy snatched up the piece of pipe.

With a loud yell, Kathy swung the pipe with all her strength. It landed in the middle of the man's back. His eyes bulged with the pain. The knife dropped, and he fell forward.

"Is he dead?" asked Kathy.

Freddie checked the pulse. "No, but I think you broke his back. Get rid of that thing, and let's get out of here."

They ran two more blocks, then Kathy waved for a halt. Her teeth were chattering, though whether from the cold or fear, she didn't know. Freddie whipped off his jacket.

"Don't be ridiculous," she snapped. "You'll freeze."

"I've got more on than you do." Freddie draped the jacket around her almost bare shoulders. The feather trim on her hem hung at an awkward angle in a couple of spots and there were several small tears in the front.

Kathy was too tired and too cold to argue.

"Where the hell are we?" She looked around, still trying to catch her breath.

"West 53rd, I think." Freddie took her arm and they stumbled toward Eighth.

Freddie hailed a taxi heading towards the speakeasy.

"Where to?" asked the driver as Freddie

slammed the door shut.

"635 Park," Freddie answered.

"Freddie, that's your place." Kathy looked at him, a little shocked.

"I know." Freddie shivered. "Pray forgive the presumption, but it's closer, and there are extra coats to be had there."

"Given the emergency, I wouldn't call it a presumption." Kathy pulled the jacket tighter, then sighed. "In fact, I think we shouldn't worry about propriety and see if we can't share your jacket for the time being."

"How?"

Kathy took it off. "Just put it around your shoulders and I'll slide under your arm. That way we'll both be covered and combine our body heat, creating more warmth than if we sat decently apart."

"I see nothing indecent in preventing us from freezing to death." Freddie got the jacket situated and Kathy comfortably under his arm.

It was nice having her there. He could feel the cool of her bare arm through his shirt. Her legs pressed against his. Without thinking, he squeezed her a little tighter.

"How are your hands?" she asked.

"Fine." He flexed one. "Maybe a little numb."

"Damn. I hope you're not frostbitten. It's below freezing out there." She picked up the hand that held her and looked at it in the streetlight. "I can't tell. It is awful cold."

She breathed on it, and rubbed. Slowly, Freddie felt the feeling return.

"It feels better," he said after a moment.

"Good." She tucked it under her arm. "Give me the other one."

The other hand was slightly warmer, but not much. As she breathed on the long fingers, Kathy realized she would have much rather been kissing them. They were headed for his apartment. It was the most logical place to go, and Kathy was certain that was all Freddie had been thinking of when he'd told the taxi driver to go there. But she was also certain there would be no one else there, which would leave them with a great deal of freedom.

But would Freddie desire her? He'd had moments when he'd noticed her passion. But they could have been mere masculine instinct, easily set aside.

At the building, Freddie rushed Kathy inside out of necessity. She felt as though she were being swallowed up into a world more opulent and finer than even the best restaurant could emulate. The elevator man stopped at Freddie's floor without asking which one. The outer vestibule was tiny, but richly papered in dark tones.

"How many neighbors do you have on this floor?" Kathy asked, looking for another doorway.

Faint jazz music leaked out of somewhere.

Freddie opened the door. "None. There's

only one apartment to a floor in this building."

He all but pushed her inside.

"One?" Kathy stopped, and her heart fell.

A man, dressed in a black jacket and tie, with white gloves, stood in the entrance to the circular foyer.

Freddie smiled when he saw him. "Roberts, we'll need a fire in the drawing room. Make that the study. It'll heat up faster."

"Yes, sir." Roberts disappeared into a room to his left.

"A butler?" Kathy grinned in awe.

"A valet." Freddie took her elbow and led her into the foyer.

"Criminy." Kathy stepped gingerly across the marble floor tiles. There was a hall table nearby with a telephone and a vase filled with eucalyptus branches. Over that hung a mirror that had no frame, but was beveled in geometric shapes.

The jazz music rose from a murmur to a whisper, and something thumped in the apartment above. Freddie looked up and shook his head.

"Damn her." He looked apologetically at Kathy. "I'm afraid I have to make a telephone call."

"By all means."

Kathy, who again had Freddie's jacket draped around her, pulled it tighter in spite of the warm room. Freddie picked up the phone, rattled the switch and gave the operator a number.

"Do you mind if I snoop?" Kathy asked, not sure if it was polite to ask and not caring either.

"Be my guest," said Freddie. He turned back to the phone. "Mr. Little calling for Mrs. Wentworth."

"That's your sister, isn't it?" Kathy poked her head into the dining room.

"She's lives in the apartment above me."

Kathy turned on the light and gaped. There was a huge black lacquered table with matching chairs to seat at least ten people. Floor length drapes of gold velvet were held back by simple bronze swags, and there was a painting of a group of people on the wall, only they were put together in odd cube-like shapes. Kathy wasn't sure, but thought the artist might be Picasso.

"Hallo, Mrs. Wentworth," said Freddie into the phone. "You know why I'm calling... I'm sure you're all having a corking time. But if I can hear you, you can imagine what the Petersons are hearing... Are they...? Well, try and keep the noise down anyway. I do not want another tiresome scene with the police, not to mention the nuisance of replacing all that liquor... I thought that might make a difference to you... No, I can't... No... My dear Mrs. Wentworth, I am working on my book tonight... You'll just have to think so. Now, good night." He chuckled and hung up.

Kathy had wandered into the drawing room and was playing the Moonlight Sonata on the black grand piano in there. It was a comfortable room, with leather easy chairs and more modern art on the walls. A large, brightly colored Oriental carpet covered the dark parquet flooring.

"That's very nice," Freddie said.

Kathy yipped, and the chords crashed. "You startled me. I hope you don't mind. It's a beautiful instrument. Do you play?"

"It took five years of lessons to prove that I can't." Freddie laughed. "I keep it for parties."

Kathy stumbled through the melody line of her favorite song from *Lady Be Good*.

"I took lessons from Mrs. Skitchem every Tuesday afternoon since I was seven," said Kathy. "Ma always said just because we lived beyond civilization didn't mean we had to be uncivilized ourselves."

"I thought you said your grandfather was one of the town's founders."

"He was. There's just not a whole lot of town." Kathy turned on the bench and grinned. "One block of Hell's Kitchen has more people than all of Hays. Hell, we could feed the whole gang in that dining room of yours."

Freddie laughed. "Just ten of them."

"Just ten." Kathy snorted and came out. "Mrs. Lynne feeds eight in not even a third of that space."

Freddie followed her back through the foyer to the inside vestibule.

"What's through here?"

"The pantry and servants' quarters. They do not wish to be disturbed."

"Ooo." Kathy batted her eyes. "You've got a valet and servants?"

Freddie shrugged. "Just a cook and house-keeper. I don't need a full staff."

"With as much eating out as we've been doing, you don't need the cook." Kathy wandered to the other side of the vestibule.

"Don't let her hear you say that." Freddie smiled indulgently.

"Bedrooms?" Kathy went down the hall.

"Yes." Freddie ambled after.

"How many?"

"Four."

Kathy turned on him. "For just you?"

"I do have guests in sometimes."

Kathy went into the corner room. "Criminy, you could have a party just in here." She peeked into the bathroom. "Forget that. You can have the party in here, and a barn dance in the bedroom. And that bed is huge!"

It was, with an intricately carved black-lacquer head and foot boards. A dark green silk quilt covered it, with matching pillows at the head.

She suddenly noticed the personal items left out on the black-lacquered bureau. She blushed.

"Freddie, this is your bedroom!"

He smiled. "Yes."

"You could have told me before I came in."

"You were interested."

Kathy looked away. "But, honestly, Freddie. I've been terribly rude, busting my way through your apartment like this. And for all you're perfectly polite, you don't let people walk all over you, unless..."

Kathy's eyes fell on the enormous bed, and her heart caught. Blushing, she pushed on the mattress.

"If only," she said softly. She turned to Freddie. "I'm sorry."

She hurried to the door, and went past him, brushing a bit closer to him than was absolutely necessary. She paused.

"Where did you get such a big bed?" she asked.

"I had it specially made. It fits me."

Kathy looked up at him. "It must be nice."

Freddie smiled, but inside he was puzzled. She had flitted off again, back to the foyer. Shaking his head, he followed. She was up to something, but what he couldn't fathom. One minute she was the complete innocent, entranced by things that he considered quite ordinary, which was why he had allowed her the freedom to explore. Then every so often, the blunt insinuations would pop out, as if she were hinting at engaging in other, less innocent activity.

"The study is this way," he said, directing her.

"I don't know why you wanted a fire," she said. "This whole apartment is perfectly toasty. Oh, Freddie!" She stumbled forward, completely captivated by the filled bookshelves that lined all four walls. "So many books!" She turned around and around. "It must be heaven to be rich. To be able to keep so many books, and have the time to read them." She turned on him. "You do, don't you?"

Freddie smiled softly. "Yes. Don't worry. I can't say I've read everything in here. But almost all of it. I do have to save some time to write."

Kathy spotted the antique writing desk littered with paper. "And this is where you do it." She looked over the notes, and her manner changed again to cool and professional. "Freddie, this is good. You've got it. Just enough description to paint the picture."

"Thank you." Freddie went over to the cherry wood sideboard and removed a cut crystal decanter and two snifters.

Kathy set the paper down, and gazed around the room, lost in rapture.

"Oh, Freddie, this is just too beautiful."

"I'm glad you like it. May I take your coat?" He came over to her.

"Oh. Thank you." She let it slip from her shoulders, still gazing at the shelves. "You're so lucky, Freddie. What I wouldn't give to have a room like this."

"Don't you?" Freddie laid the jacket on the back of a burgundy leather reading chair.

"My room's not even half this size. And I don't have the shelves, and Mrs. Lynne won't let me put up any more. I don't have a fireplace. I have an old dressing table as a desk, and that's the only chair I have, too. And I have to sleep there. Although I wouldn't mind sleeping in here." She slid her hand across a series of volumes. "Shakespeare. All the plays, and in calf bindings. May I take one down?"

"Please."

Kathy pulled it off as if it were the Book of Life.

"Gilt edges." Carefully, she opened it. "*Much Ado About Nothing.* I love that play. When I was ten, a traveling troupe came to town. They must have been awful, but then they seemed like the greatest players in the world. They did this play, and *Macbeth. Much Ado* was the first play I ever saw. I wanted so badly to go with them when they left." She put the book back. "It's funny. No matter how beautiful that volume is, the words inside are what make it so wonderful. But how lovely to have such fine bindings."

Freddie handed her a glass. "And how lovely it is to know someone who treasures the words first, and then the bindings."

He paused. The firelight flickered against her face, softening it, reflecting in the depths of her brown eyes.

Kathy gazed up at him, hungry. It was all she could to keep herself from pressing her lips against his, reaching for him, searching him out.

"Cheers," he said lightly, breaking the moment.

"Cheers." Kathy tapped her glass against his and looked at it. "Brandy."

"For medicinal purposes."

Kathy laughed. "That's what my Grandma Briscow used to say. She and Ma organized the temperance movement for the entire town."

"How amusing." Freddie chuckled.

"Did your mother have a cause?" Kathy asked.

"As far as I know, she did. Mother went in big for charity work. At any rate, she does now. I assume that's what she was doing while I was growing up."

"So you had a nurse, just like in the book. Didn't you see your mother at all?"

"One hour a day in the evenings, and that's quite a bit more than I saw of my father. But I believe earlier tonight I recommended a ban on unpleasant subjects."

"That's right." Kathy sipped. "Oh. Then I guess we shouldn't talk about the other adventure we had."

"Ah. The alley." Freddie shrugged. "I would think it was a coincidence."

"He followed us from the speak, and he mostly ignored me."

"To his undoing." Freddie sipped from his glass.

"But he was after you, Freddie, and it wasn't just for your money. He would have held both of us up."

"So he wasn't sane."

"Like the man who pushed me in front of the bus." Kathy folded her arms.

"It would appear we're even, then. Similar conclusions." Freddie fixed his eyes on her. "And you did save my life tonight."

"You could have gotten away."

"Not easily. Thank you, Kathy."

"You're welcome." Kathy squirmed, then batted her eyes to break the tension. "Perhaps I should take advantage of you now."

"Perhaps not." Freddie watched her, wondering.

The worst of it was, she was so attractive when she wasn't acting so strangely. He found himself thinking of sweeping her back into the bedroom, and was appalled but also very tempted.

"Or we could try to figure out who sent that man to kill us," she said quickly, completely shattering the mood.

"It would almost have to be Mr. Healcroft, wouldn't it?" asked Freddie. "He's the only one who has a reason to fear us, as far as we know."

"But would he have the money to hire a thug or two?" Kathy bit her lip. "Uncle Dan said that Selby was supposed to have been killed by hired thugs who botched the job. And the men we've been attacked by were all different, right?"

"That would make it likely they were hired by somebody. But Healcroft. He's not poor, but unfortunately, I don't know what the going rate is for thugs."

"It wouldn't matter as long as it was less money than paying off Mr. Selby, assuming that he was blackmailing Mr. Healcroft. And why else would Mr. Selby have had the buttonhook in his desk?"

Freddie thought. "Why would Mr. Healcroft keep the damned thing if he knew you were aware of it? It connects him rather closely to the murder."

"I gave him no reason to believe I knew it was gone."

"Still, someone else besides Frank Selby knew about that buttonhook. If I were Healcroft, I'd be anxious to get rid of it."

"Unless he didn't kill Mr. Selby, in which case, the buttonhook is embarrassing, and while it might throw suspicion on him, it won't convict him because there won't be any other evidence. The problem is, Freddie, that man was waiting outside that speak for you, and another tried to kill me yesterday."

"Wait." Freddie tapped his glass thoughtfully. "Why didn't he try to kill you tonight?"

"That's right." Kathy thought. "Maybe we are getting too worked up over a coincidence." Her heart stopped as she set her glass down next to the desk. "No, Freddie. There's a perfectly logical reason. What would I be doing in a speak like that? If somebody called the assassin from the speak, it's entirely possible he never saw me. Freddie, you're so tall and your hair is so unusual, you'd never be missed, and you could be expected to be at that place. Everyone there knew you."

"One of the few things Frank Selby and I had in common." Freddie started to drink, and noticed his glass was empty. Tense, he set it down.

"Freddie," Kathy asked, nervously pacing. "If it's not Mr. Healcroft, then who are we getting close enough to that he wants to kill us?"

"I haven't the faintest."

As she passed him, Freddie saw her hands trembling.

"Kathy," he whispered.

He touched her hands to quiet them, and she slid into his arms. He held her as she shook. His head bent just as she lifted hers. Their lips met.

Relief flooded Kathy as the other, more delicious tension took hold. Freddie's kiss was every bit as exciting and passionate as she'd imagined. Thus fueled, she let her own passion flow at its fullest. She pressed tighter and harder, enjoying the feel of his stiffness against her belly.

Deaf to all that was rational, Freddie let the glorious sensations fill him. Kathy's soft sighs mingled with his, and she writhed, sending him into ecstasy. They parted slightly, just long enough for Freddie to see how beautiful she was, and how badly she wanted him. He kissed her again, wanting her even more. He would have to do it gently. However well-read she was, she was an innocent. It was hard to know how explicit her reading had been.

And there was another part of such activity, the waking up afterwards. How well prepared was she to deal with that? How well prepared was he? Freddie kissed her eyes, then returned to her lips. Her ardor grew, and with it, his excitement.

Yet, there was doubt. Could he do as he so desperately wanted to this girl, this innocent woman? Did she even know what her kisses were doing to him? He pulled away.

"Kathy," he whispered. "I must tell you. I'm not the sort of man whose kisses are to be taken lightly."

Her smile was an off attempt at coy. "I thought that was exactly how they were to be taken."

"In some ways, maybe. But I'm talking more about where they lead."

"So am I." Her smile was so open, so wanting.

Stunned, Freddie stepped back. "I can't take you that way, not lightly."

"Then do it heavily," Kathy groaned. "I don't care. Just take me."

"Kathy, you don't understand. This can be no simple exchange of pleasure."

"Why not?"

Freddie searched for the words, and failed. "I don't know. But something inside me... With every fiber of my being I know that if we did, we would deeply regret it. If you were anyone else, I might. But you... I can't do that to you."

Kathy turned away. "I'm sorry."

"Kathy, it's not your fault. I should have seen it happening. I'll get the coats."

They were both morose in the taxi back to the Village. Freddie had given Kathy a woman's overcoat. She had looked at him bitterly until he explained that it was his sister's, and that Honoria had a habit of leaving overcoats at his apartment, but not the habit of retrieving them.

Somewhere near 37th, Kathy broke the silence.

"Freddie, I do owe you an apology," she said softly. "You'll probably think of me as a tramp."

"No, Kathy, I don't."

"Let me finish." She took a deep breath. "It was no accident that I landed in your arms, Freddie. It's this stupid little game I play. I don't know why I tried it tonight. It must have been all the liquor, and the trauma, I don't know. But you didn't kiss me. I kissed you. I kissed you knowing darned well what it could lead to, and I was hoping like hell it would."

Freddie held his breath. So that had been her game, a clumsy attempt at getting him to think he'd seduced her. It had almost worked. The dear thing had no idea, and probably no practical experience of the activity she had tried to induce.

She was weeping. He got out a handkerchief.

"Here. It's clean."

She smiled a little. "Of course."

"Kathy, I know what you were trying to do. But I can't help feeling you don't want to end up as my mistress."

"I don't." She wiped her nose. "Freddie, I have a dream of a world in which a man and a woman can come together as equals, and know each other as equals, and be lovers, without all the little traps and slaveries of marriage. And tonight, I thought somehow it might come true."

Freddie sighed. "It's a lovely dream, Kathy, but I'm afraid it's quite impossible."

"Oh, I know that. If I ever get another job, I'd get fired for moral turpitude, and you'd have to keep me, and I'd hate you for it. The fact is, Freddie, I don't want to be kept, legitimately or otherwise."

Freddie had to chuckle. "There isn't a man alive who could keep you, Kathy. I pray God, I'll never be foolish enough to try."

"I'd still like to. Oh, Freddie, can't we try?"

His face contorted in an anguished frown. "Kathy, please, don't. You don't know how badly I want to. But it would end up just as you say. We both know it. I won't do that to you, Kathy."

"Damn. You would have to be a gentleman. So, this is it, then. I guess we have enough suspects that if the police want to arrest me, I can prove there are others with better motives. Why don't you take your book back to Healcroft House, and I'll manage on my own?"

Freddie felt his stomach tie into knots. "Is that what you truly want, Kathy?"

She looked away. "I want to make this as easy as possible for you, Freddie."

"But do you want it? I want the truth, and I can tell when you're lying."

Kathy shook her head.

"That's some relief." Freddie's stomach slowly untied itself. "I do need you in terms of my book. And even in the short time we've known each other, I have grown to like you quite a bit. Do you think it would be possible for us to remain just friends?"

Kathy managed a smile. "Yes. It probably would be better. It has been fun, Freddie, most of it anyway. You know, you're the first man I've met who respected me like one. Maybe it's time you started treating me like one."

"It's too late for that." Freddie's laugh was rueful. "It looks like we're here."

He walked her up the stoop and opened the door.

"Kathy," he said before she entered. "Please understand. It's not that I don't desire you. Because I do, very much. It's just that it would not be right for me to leave it at that."

Kathy nodded. "Let's hear it for little traps and slaveries."

"It makes it damned awkward, doesn't it? There may yet be a way around it. Shall I call on you tomorrow?"

"I'll be out job hunting. Maybe sometime around five?"

"Until then."

Kathy reached to put her hand on his shoulder. But he turned to the street, and was gone.

CHAPTER TWELVE

"Freddie!" Honoria slammed the front door to Freddie's apartment, and hurried into the back. "Are you dressing?"

"No," came the sullen reply.

Freddie was in bed with his breakfast tray, morosely dropping jam onto a piece of toast as he sulked over the New York Times.

"Oh," said Honoria upon seeing him. "Last night must have been grim."

"Honoria, I will not be divulging any information."

"Then I'll just confirm what I know." She sat down carefully on the bed next to him.

Freddie glared at her. "You're up awfully early for the ruckus you made last night."

"It wasn't much." Honoria took a piece of bacon off of Freddie's plate. "Elizabeth Dunn and some of her friends. Children, really, but fun. You left rather quickly with your lady friend."

"We were just here to warm up a little and get coats."

Honoria giggled. "Let's see. You got a little too warm, and she was not receptive?"

"You are presuming a great deal. And keep your hands off my breakfast!" Freddie pushed her hand away from his plate. "Will you ever grow up and start using some manners?"

"I use them all the time, darling. You're just so much fun to tease." Honoria sat back and sighed. "Poor lamb. You are bothered about her, aren't you?"

Freddie sighed. "Honoria, the best thing that either of us can do is forget the whole mess until the situation resolves itself."

"You do need cheering up." Honoria picked up the paper and winced. "Another strangled bum in Chelsea. That monster is picking them off almost every night now. That is certainly not going to help you feel better. Ah. There was that raid last night." She flipped through the pages. "I presume you were in one. After all, why else would you come here to get coats, unless you'd had to leave somewhere else in a hurry and couldn't get yours."

"I won't be mentioned." A small smile formed on Freddie's lips.

"You weren't arrested? How terribly boring."

"How terribly *outré*, dear sister. We escaped out the back."

Honoria grinned. "How thrilling!"

"It was mostly a tight squeeze, and damn

233

cold."

"That could have been interesting." Honoria smirked, then realized she was intruding into dangerous territory. "Do you have plans for today?"

"Just a call to make later this afternoon." Freddie folded his arms across his chest.

"And dinner with Mummy and Daddy."

Freddie groaned. "Oh, no. It's not the eighteenth already?"

"I'm afraid it is, dear brother. Now, now. It's just a few hours. Then we'll slip out at the first opportunity and go kick up our heels a little. Maybe we'll drag Lowell along. He's not bad company once he's drunk."

Freddie smiled. But a loud speakeasy with drunken companions did not appeal to him in the least. A quiet saloon with Kathy to talk to sounded much better.

"We shall have to see," he said finally. Given the night before, he had no idea whether Kathy would be speaking to him or not.

"So what are you going to do today?" Honoria pressed.

"I haven't the faintest." There had to be someone else who had a motive for killing Frank Selby that he could check.

"Then you haven't any excuse. You promised you'd take me Christmas shopping, and you shall today."

Freddie sighed. He had promised, and had

been putting her off since Thanksgiving. Shopping was the last thing he wanted to do, but he could see no good reason why he shouldn't.

"If you insist," he conceded.

"Oh, wonderful!" Honoria bounced up and took the tray. "Hurry, hurry and get dressed, darling. We've a hideous list to fill. Oh, this shall be too much fun."

Freddie waited until she'd left, then rolled out of bed. It was a ridiculous chore, buying pointless presents for people who had no use for them, but it had to be done. At least Honoria's occasionally outrageous antics might liven the afternoon up some, and she was remarkably efficient at keeping people and addresses straight, not to mention who'd been sent what, and what year they'd been sent it.

But even Honoria hated buying presents for their parents, the distant, stiff couple who inhabited the drafty mansion near 59th and Madison. It had been a long morning of fruitless searching and the pair had finally found themselves in a bookstore off of Riverside Drive.

"I don't know, Freddie," Honoria sighed over the set of novels.

The bookstore smelled of rich leather, and was filled with the hush of those who liked to read.

"Won't he think Dickens is terribly socialist?" Honoria continued. "Isn't there anything new in the shooting business?"

"Not that Father doesn't already have," sighed Freddie. "As for the Dickens, a good case of apoplexy might just cheer him up."

"Doesn't he already have a set of these?"

"Have you ever seen any?"

"I don't think I've ever seen him read. Oh, hell. I can't think of anything better." Honoria went off to signal the salesclerk.

A large volume struck Freddie's eye. Its fine calf binding was embossed with gold leaf. He opened it. A Complete Works of Shakespeare. The pages were as fine as the gossamer wings of a fairy, and edged in shining gold. Freddie's ears filled with the sound of Kathy's voice bubbling over in joy at his study. How sad, actually, that having so many books and the time to read them was as out of reach as heavenly bliss. How odd that the only thing she envied was his library. Thank heavens he did read. He couldn't imagine anything galling her more than the thought of all those books going unread.

Honoria's giggle crashed through his thoughts.

"Freddie, I don't have your girlfriend's name on my list," she teased.

"That's because she is not my girlfriend." Freddie signaled the clerk. "I'll take the Complete Works. Have it wrapped and sent to my apartment."

"Yes, Mr. Little."

Honoria grimaced. "That's not fair."

"Such gifts are to be presented in person," said Freddie. "Nor am I entirely sure we are on terms where such a present would be appropriate. Furthermore, you are going to have to work a great deal harder than that to get her name out of me."

"Of all the big brothers that ever pained a sister, you are the worst." Honoria sulked.

Freddie chuckled. But Honoria was, if anything, persistent, and like her brother, not likely to give up at the first few failures. She badgered, hinted, cajoled and teased. Freddie remained firm, which told her a great deal more than he would have liked.

Finally, around three-thirty, she convinced him that the shops in Greenwich Village had all sorts of unique gifts that would please various younger, more avant-garde, cousins and friends. As it got closer to five o'clock, Freddie grew tense, and wanted to go home. Honoria guessed why.

"Didn't you say you had a call to make this afternoon?" she asked innocently.

"Yes, which is why I would like to part company, if you don't mind."

"I do mind, Freddie. If my guess is right, your call isn't too far from here. You can't go out tonight, anyway. So why don't we swing by there, you can make your call, and then we'll toddle along home and dress for dinner."

Freddie nodded. Honoria had manipulated him right into it.

"I've a feeling if I sent you home, you'd come back after me," he said.

"Of course, Freddie." Honoria smiled. "I am determined this time."

"Then I will do as you propose, on the following conditions. That you will promise not to call on

237

her, telephone, or write in any way."

"Freddie, that's not fair!" She huffed, but he remained firm. "Oh, all right. I promise. I won't call on her, telephone, or write in any way."

"And that you stay in the taxi the whole time."

"Oh, Freddie! You can't! All right. You can. I'll stay in the taxi."

"Promise?"

"I promise. You're dreadful, you know that?"

Freddie smiled. "Only as dreadful as I need to be. It is after all, Honoria, a delicate situation."

It was, as far as Kathy was concerned, a most awkward and frustrating situation. The worst of it was, Freddie was completely right. As disappointed as she had been the night before, in the light of the morning rationality returned, and she realized how foolish she'd been.

That made things only a little easier. As much as she wanted to hear from him, she began to dread the call she knew would be coming at five o'clock. Freddie, ever the proper gentleman, could decide the whole thing was too hard on her, or on both of them, and call it off. Worse yet, he'd suffer agonies before calling it off just because he was upset.

The only thing to do was to concentrate on other things. Job hunting was dismal, but at least it kept her out of Sergeant Reagan's way. All the more reason to find out who killed Mr. Selby. She wasn't ready to dismiss Mr. Healcroft as a suspect yet. But the buttonhook only proved the motive, and not the crime.

She couldn't believe Mr. Selby had tangled with the mob. They weren't usually that subtle, blatant killings being an excellent lesson to others. Furthermore, she and Freddie would most certainly have tasted a bit of lead long before then.

But who else had a reason to want Mr. Selby dead, and wanted it enough to kill him? Kathy thought over all the possibilities. She was fairly certain Elsie Quinn hadn't. That wasn't like Elsie, and she said she hadn't known Selby was dead. It didn't mean she hadn't, but Kathy thought it unlikely.

Perhaps it was some other woman Mr. Selby had done wrong. There was that woman at the apartment building. But how to find out? Kathy doubted questioning Mr. Selby's mother would do any good. Mothers were notorious for thinking their sons were saints. Perhaps his siblings, if he had any. Maybe even Mr. Evans would know. He and Mr. Selby had not been unfriendly.

But Mr. Evans was, in a way, another suspect. Getting Mr. Selby's job had meant a lot to him, and not getting Freddie's book had infuriated him. Then why was Freddie getting attacked, unless Evans was taking it out on him also?

And lastly, there was also Percy Selby to consider. Freddie seemed to have dismissed Percy. Kathy wasn't so sure. Religion was just too easy to hide behind. But as far as Kathy knew, Percy had no idea she even existed. So either the attack on her had been coincidence, or Percy knew more than she or Freddie suspected. Perhaps she could interview Percy. He might also know other women that Frank

Selby had hurt.

Of course none of her musings mattered until she talked to Freddie. And what was she to do about him? There was no denying she was as fond of him as he seemed to be of her, even apart from the more intimate feelings. Ultimately, that was just lust, which was why she was glad she was not his lover. But the tension remained; would it be intolerable, or could they remain friends in spite of it? The one thing Kathy was certain of was that she wanted Freddie as a friend even more than she wanted him as a lover. His kind of friendship was just too rare to let go of that easily.

Five o'clock drew near faster than she wanted. At four o'clock, she went to one last interview. The man talked on and on about all his different projects, and all the intricacies of the carpet business, and what he expected of her, to tell her at the end that he wasn't interested in hiring anybody just yet, but that he would remember her and call sometime in the future.

Disgusted, Kathy left the office, and checked the clock in the building lobby. It was quarter of five. Fortunately, the subway stop was right there, and she didn't have to change trains. As it was, she all but ran from the station to her block. At the corner, she stopped and looked for lurking coppers while trying to catch her breath.

Freddie's taxi turned onto the street just after she did. He kept his face straight as he saw her, but inside he was smiling. She was obviously anxious not to miss his call. Then he froze.

As she reached her stoop, a man dressed in a dark overcoat sprang out from a basement stairwell behind her.

"Stop the car!" Freddie yelled.

The taxi slammed on its brakes. Freddie was on the pavement before the vehicle had completely stopped.

"Freddie!" gasped Honoria, as shocked by the fact that Freddie had raised his voice as by the sudden stop.

Kathy saw the movement out of the corner of her eye. She turned. A scarf, stretched taut in the man's hand, whipped over her head. Her hand flew up, but it couldn't stop the tightening on her throat. Someone yelled. But the world went spinning, and her throat hurt. She couldn't breathe, then it all stopped.

The next thing she knew, she was on the icy sidewalk. Familiar green eyes looked into hers.

"Are you all right?" asked a voice. It didn't quite sound right.

"You're one up on me," Kathy croaked out, her voice hoarse.

"I don't see how," said the voice, and she laughed.

Kathy tried to swallow, but it hurt.

"Looks like you'll be just fine, though," the woman's voice continued. "Freddie took off running after the bastard. We'll see if he comes back with him. I haven't seen old Freddie this angry in my life."

Kathy's vision slowly cleared. "But you're not..."

"Easy. Don't try to talk, darling,"

The woman was thin, and her face had the same shape as Freddie's. But her hair was brown and bobbed, and her eyes, once Kathy looked again, were actually hazel.

"Do you hurt anywhere?" she asked.

"My throat," Kathy croaked. She tried to sit up.

"Now, now. Let me help. Here we go. Is that all right?"

Kathy nodded.

"Oh, good. I'm Honoria Wentworth. My brother is the one who saved you. His name's Freddie." She grinned. "Although, I think you know that already."

Kathy blushed and nodded.

Breathing heavily, Freddie hurried up and knelt beside her.

"Are you all right?" he asked tenderly.

Kathy nodded. "Throat's sore. But I'm fine."

"Her voice has been obliterated," said Honoria. "Did you catch the bastard?"

"Watch your language," Freddie snapped. "And what are you doing out of the taxi?"

"The poor girl was left lying on the sidewalk!" returned Honoria with equal force. "Did you think I would leave her? I sent the driver after the cops, and came to help."

"Oh, no!" croaked Kathy.

"That's just what we needed." Freddie put his arms around Kathy. "Do you think you can stand?" She nodded. Freddie lifted her. "We'll get you inside right away."

"And the police?" demanded Honoria.

"Let's hope we can get her inside before they come," growled Freddie. Steadying Kathy, he walked her up the steps.

"Damn it, for the amount of money I pay in taxes, we should put them to work!"

"Then you do it," said Freddie. He turned to Kathy. "Where are your keys?"

"It's open," she croaked.

"Oh no, you don't!" Honoria scrambled up the stoop, and beat them to the door. "I don't know what you're up to, Freddie, but I'll be damned if you're going to keep me out of it."

"Watch your language, Honoria."

"Here." Honoria slid under Freddie and picked up Kathy. "It'll look better if I do it. This is a rooming house, isn't it?"

"How...?" Kathy tried to ask.

"People in the window," Honoria replied. "Come along, darling."

Freddie opened the door, and followed the two women in.

"Mein Gott!" screeched Miss Felt, as she saw

them.

Mrs. Lynne scuttled in from the back. "What's going on? Kathy! You look perfectly awful."

"It's all right. It's all right," announced Honoria. "Kathy just had a little accident, that's all. She'll be fine. Can we get her set down somewhere?"

"In the parlor," said Mrs. Lynne, leading the way. "Oh! Hello, Mr. Little. Please come in. I'm afraid we're all at sixes and sevens."

"I understand, Mrs. Lynne," said Freddie.

Mr. Eggleston was in the parlor, a medium-sized man, somewhat stooped, with wild white hair and gnarled hands.

"What's going on?" he demanded loudly. "Kathy, you've been trampled!"

"She had an accident," Honoria yelled at him.

"Accident? Damn fools in their flivvers. They'll kill us all."

"Mrs. Lynne," said Honoria as she made Kathy comfortable on the couch. "Do you have any brandy? For Kathy. It's good for shock."

"Why I..." Mrs. Lynne dithered. "Spirits, no."

"Somebody must have," grumbled Honoria. She was going to ask Freddie, then saw Mr. Eggleston. She yelled, "Sir? Do you have any brandy? For Kathy."

"Brandy?" hollered the old man. "Ah. Good idea. I'll be right back." He tottered forward, then stopped when he saw Freddie. "Nice girl. Doesn't mutter."

"Now see here, young lady," said Mrs. Lynne, peeved at being usurped. "I know you're trying to be kind, but you can't just come in here and take over."

Honoria smiled winningly. "Oh, I'm so sorry, Mrs. Lynne. I was just so worried. Kathy and I are the oldest of friends. I'm Mrs. Honoria Wentworth. We went to school together. Before I got married, of course. That's how she knows Freddie. He's my brother, you see."

"But I thought she was editing Mr. Little's book."

"Of course." Honoria didn't even blink. "That's why he took it to her company. I told him to."

Freddie held his tongue, not sure whether he wanted to laugh at his sister's presumption or strangle her. Kathy couldn't say anything, and was still too dazed to protest even if she could.

"Mrs. Lynne," Freddie said. "If we could clear the room of company, I'm sure Miss Briscow would be much more comfortable."

"Certainly, Mr. Little." Mrs. Lynne paused. "I'll go see what's keeping Mr. Eggleston."

"Isn't he a dear?" said Honoria as she left. "Poor, old thing. It's no fun being deaf as a doornail."

"Honoria, what are you up to?" demanded Freddie.

"Making damned sure you're stuck with me." She turned to Kathy. "I hope you don't mind the little lie, Kathy, darling. But this is just too much fun. Well, not the strangling bit. I'm sure that was terribly nasty for you."

Kathy nodded. "Thank you."

"You're very welcome," said Honoria. "But you shouldn't be talking, and it's Freddie who deserves the thanks. Good God. I didn't think my proper old brother could be so heroic. You should have seen him. It was terribly dramatic. He plucked that fiend off of you, and you fell. They struggled together. The man slipped away. And Freddie went tearing after him."

Kathy looked over at Freddie, her eyebrows lifted.

"It's a surprisingly accurate account," he said, a little chagrined.

"I don't always fib," said Honoria, with a coy smile.

Mrs. Lynne came in from the front hall carrying a tumbler of amber liquid.

"Here it is," she said nervously. "I don't hold with spirits. Never have."

"Oh, posh," said Honoria. "Brandy's good for shock. Doctors give it out all the time. It's no trouble at all to get a prescription. We just saved ourselves the trouble." She helped Kathy drink. "Sip it slowly, dear. There you go."

Kathy winced, trying to get the brandy down.

"Hurts to swallow, doesn't it?" Honoria stroked her hair. "There, there. It won't for long. Look. Your color's coming back already."

Even Mrs. Lynne had to admit Kathy looked better. Honoria fed Kathy another sip.

"You know, Freddie, I think the best thing to do would be to get Kathy upstairs and into bed," said Honoria.

"It probably would be wise," Freddie agreed with a sigh. He stopped Kathy's protest. "You can't tell us anything anyway."

"Here, I'll help you up." Honoria helped Kathy get up from the sofa and led her out of the parlor, with a firm grip on the tumbler. "Thank you for fetching the brandy, Mrs. Lynne."

Feeling all at loose ends, Freddie laid his overcoat across the back of the sofa. Outside, he could see a policeman talking with the taxi driver. They argued for some minutes, then the copper stalked off. If only Freddie hadn't lost that thug.

"Freddie!" screamed Honoria from upstairs.

His heart in his throat, Freddie raced up the stairs.

"Where are you?" he called from the second floor.

"Fourth floor!"

He took the rest of the way three steps at a time. Honoria still stood in the doorway to Kathy's room. Freddie looked at her, and went in.

The room was a shambles. Clothing was

everywhere. Drawers hung open. The wardrobe had been emptied. The little bookshelf had been up-turned, and Kathy's books were scattered all over. The traveling trunk at the end of Kathy's bed had been turned over on top of its contents. A bottle of perfume lay on its side in a puddle on the bureau, filling the room with overpowering sweetness. Kathy's few other cosmetics were scattered. A tube of lipstick lay squashed on the floor.

Kathy stood in the middle of the room, gazing at it all as if she were hoping that by taking it all in, it would somehow disappear. She bent and picked up the lipstick.

"I paid a whole dollar for this," she whispered, the tears slowly dropping down her cheeks.

"We'll get you a new one," said Freddie, softly. "Don't try to talk. Here, sit down on the bed."

The dressing table chair had been smashed. Freddie sat down next to her on the bed and pulled out a handkerchief.

"Here," he said. "It's clean."

"What else would it be?" snapped Honoria. "Good God. Who could have done this? Damn it, Freddie. We're calling the police this time."

"No!" choked out Kathy. "Please don't."

"We'll have to, Kathy," said Freddie. "As soon as Mrs. Lynne sees this, she'll insist."

"I insist," said Honoria. "Kathy, you've just been strangled, and now robbed!"

"Honoria," Freddie cut in. "We think we know who is doing this and why. But we don't have any proof. Kathy's current position with the police is such that involving them now would only hurt her in the long run."

"But why?"

"You'll just have to trust me."

"Hmph!" Honoria folded her arms and leaned against the door jamb. "It looks to me like someone wants to kill Kathy, and knows how to get in here to do it. She can't stay here, Freddie."

"For once I agree with you."

"But where..." Kathy started to protest.

"I've got it," said Honoria quickly. "We've got to eat dinner with Mummy and Daddy anyway. We'll bring Kathy and stay the night. It won't be hard to get the invitation. And it'll certainly be the last place anyone would think to look, even to find us. I'll take care of it."

She disappeared down the stairs.

"Freddie," croaked Kathy.

"Sh. Don't talk."

"Your book, the manuscript..."

"It's all right."

"Freddie, it's gone." She started to cry again.

"It's not the only copy, Kathy."

"But why take that?"

Freddie frowned, thinking. "And why take it

249

in the middle of the day?"

"I'm not home. Front's open. People in and out, mostly out, no one to hear."

"Sh. Is there anything else missing?"

Kathy looked around. At first, she shook her head. Then she stopped. Moving slowly, she got up and bent to the floor. Out from underneath a pair of step-ins, she pulled a burgundy printed bow tie.

"A school tie," said Freddie, taking it.

"Evans."

"Are you sure it's not Healcroft?"

"He's Yale."

"That's right, and this isn't. But why?"

"The manuscript. He's the only one... who would want it." Kathy swallowed. "He probably un-tied the tie... to loosen his collar... and lost the tie."

"Kathy, you're talking far too much for that throat of yours. Why don't you sit down, and I'll get you packed."

"I'll do it myself."

Her eyes held his. Weak, injured, and fright-ened, she still dared him to back her down. Perhaps there was something to be said for letting her take care of it.

"Will you talk to Mrs. Lynne?" she asked.

Freddie paused. He was a little nervous about leaving her alone. But he nodded, and picked up the valise that had been upended next to the bed.

"Here." He opened it and laid it out.

As he left, he checked the window, then the bathroom and the other girl's room on the floor. Kathy waited just long enough to be sure he was gone. Evans, or whoever the burglar had been, had missed one hiding place. She lifted the corner of the mattress and pulled out the twenty-two gauge double barrel shotgun and the box of ammo.

Cocking it open, she wiggled the gun around in the suitcase until it fit, then dumped her clothes in on top. The ammo box she wrapped in clean step-ins. Searching through papers and blouses for a camisole, she found a sheet of typescript with a big ink X drawn across it.

"*The blackness of the night wrapped around us, as deep as the void that was our lives*," it read near the top. "*I felt as if I could reach out and touch it, luxuriate in the rich, velvet folds.*"

The page with the rest of the scene was next to it. Kathy grabbed it, and tossed the two pages in the valise. She shut the bag just as Freddie returned.

"Well, Honoria has managed to convince Mother that taking us in tonight would be a delight and a joy for all of us."

"You're not happy," Kathy whispered.

Freddie shrugged. "What it will be is terribly dull. But then, you go to bed early, you might not notice."

Kathy didn't say anything. Freddie didn't

say much about his parents, and from what he did say, she got the feeling he didn't like them much.

The front rang just as Freddie helped Kathy to the door of her room. As they made their way down the staircase, they could hear Mrs. Lynne twittering like a worried sparrow, with Honoria interjecting a calming word or two.

Just as they started down the last flight of stairs, Mrs. Lynne came into the hallway.

"There you are, Kathy," she announced. "I was just coming to see if you were able to come down. Can you imagine? The police are already here! Now you can report that awful burglary in your room, dear."

"I thought that flatfoot had gone," Freddie whispered to Kathy. "And Honoria must have told Mrs. Lynne about your room."

"I didn't even have to call them," Mrs. Lynne bubbled on.

"Oh no," Kathy sighed.

Sure enough, in the parlor waited Sergeant Reagan and the policeman Freddie had seen earlier.

"Hello, Miss Briscow. I think it's time we had a little chat," Reagan said, as soon as Kathy opened the parlor door.

But before Kathy could answer, Freddie stepped into the room.

"Good afternoon, Sergeant," he said. "I'm afraid Miss Briscow will not be able to speak with you. As you may have heard, she's just had a little accident that has seriously hurt her throat and her voice."

"Maybe if I took her down to the station house it might help," Reagan replied, all but sneering.

"I wouldn't recommend that," Freddie answered calmly.

He was gratified by the ever so slight tremor of hesitancy.

"Miss Briscow is a suspect in a murder case," said Reagan finally. "I need to question her."

"Murder?" squawked Mrs. Lynne. Honoria quickly shushed her.

"That is your right and obligation," said Freddie. "I just hope you have a perfectly watertight case."

Reagan walked over and put his face in Freddie's. The two men were almost the same height, with Freddie having the advantage by a mere couple of inches.

"Are you threatening me?" Reagan snarled.

"I don't make threats, Sergeant." Freddie folded his arms in front of him, forcing Reagan to step back. "I'm merely suggesting that you make sure all your ducks are in a perfect row before attempting to arrest Miss Briscow, because I do have the means to ensure your dismissal from the force if you subject her to a false arrest. Now, I would suggest that you take Mrs. Lynne's report regarding the burglary. We believe that one of Miss Briscow's co-workers is the likely suspect. He left this tie in her room. Nothing of note is missing, but the room is seriously damaged. If you will excuse us, my sister and I will remove Miss Briscow to a safe place. Good evening, Sergeant."

Freddie then picked up Kathy's valise and escorted her outside, with Honoria following.

"He hates you, Kathy," Freddie said softly. "Heaven only knows why, but that copper hates you."

"Freddie, what is going on?" Honoria demanded.

He sighed. "Will you kindly hail us a taxi? I'll explain on the way to Mother's."

Grumbling, Honoria did as she was asked.

CHAPTER THIRTEEN

There was a stillness to the magnificent entry way, a hush, as if the winter twilight had settled in and dared those who entered to disturb it. Marble tiles paved the way, and a grand sweeping staircase rose to the upper floor. Suits of armor stood in silent watch, scattered randomly. The paintings, darkened images of forgotten ancestors, were lost in the shadows. Above, the dim light sparkled in the crystal chandelier.

Kathy shivered. If this was home, it was no wonder Freddie and Honoria didn't like returning to it. Briggeman, the butler, took Kathy's case and disappeared with it. Honoria had taken over, as Kathy was technically her guest. Honoria had made quite a point of emphasizing that.

"We'll dress for dinner in my room," Honoria announced. "In fact, you'll have time for a bath, Kathy, darling. Freddie, I'm afraid you'll have to find some way to amuse yourself."

Freddie smiled indulgently. "Very well, Honoria."

Kathy still didn't have much of a voice, so she couldn't protest.

Honoria shivered. "Oh, this old hall still gives me the creeps. Come along, Kathy."

Honoria's bedroom was even bigger than the rooms in Freddie's apartment. She'd had her things sent, as well as Freddie's, from their apartments, and everything was already laid out. The room looked as though it hadn't changed since Honoria was a little girl, with white French furniture, pink walls and a white cover on the bed that featured small, pink flowers.

Honoria shut the door and looked at Kathy.

"Kathy, you are a dear thing," she said slowly. "And I wouldn't for the world embarrass you. But I did get a look at your wardrobe. It was a little hard to miss. And if that brown velvet thing, and the torn bronze silk and the flowered lawn are the best dresses you have left, then I think we may have a problem for tonight."

Kathy nodded sadly. She hadn't even packed the dresses.

"I can eat up here," she whispered.

"No!" Honoria looked horrified. "I won't have you left alone as if we were ashamed to have you. No. I just took the liberty of having a couple of my dresses sent over. Thank heavens fashions are so baggy these days. No one will know they weren't made for you."

Kathy compared her own shorter, rounder figure with Honoria's slim height and held back her reservations. Honoria insisted she try on the dresses before bathing so the dressing maid would have time to make alterations if needed.

"Myrtle's an absolute wonder with needle and thread," Honoria explained.

Kathy decided the woman would have to be a miracle worker, if Honoria's tale were true. But the frocks, a blue silk shift and a straight dark green lace with short sleeves, fit suspiciously well. Kathy looked at Honoria.

"All right, they're my friend's," Honoria confessed, anxiously. "She's from England. She was visiting last month and went on a shopping spree, then decided she didn't like those dresses and left them behind."

Kathy shook her head. The dresses were too new, and something didn't ring true in Honoria's voice. Honoria bit her lip and sank sadly onto the bed.

"Please don't be mad at me," she said, her voice small, like a little girl's. "It's what I would have done for any of my friends, wealthy or no. I don't care how much money you have, bags do get lost and accidents happen. I just didn't realize it would be awkward for you."

"How did you get them so fast?"

"I peeked at the labels on your clothes to get the size, and called the shop from your place when I was calling Mummy and the others. It wasn't that late, and they didn't mind sending them over. Freddie said you'd be furious."

Kathy shrugged. If he had done it, she might have been. But he'd promised he wouldn't, and she couldn't see him breaking his word.

"Kathy, I didn't want to embarrass you. I don't care if you have a pedigree or not, or money, or

257

anything. To be honest, I hadn't even noticed. I assumed your dinner dresses had been stolen. It never occurred to me that you didn't have any. But my mother does notice things like that. Not that she'd ever say anything to your face. But she can get catty in a very polite way, and it's even worse than if she were out and out nasty. After all the awful things you've had happen to you today, it'd be too terrible to put you in that position."

Kathy nodded. "I don't mind borrowing."

"Oh." Honoria brightened. "Of course. That's the perfect solution. I'll be glad to keep them for you, for any time you need them."

"Thank you."

The steamy bathroom did wonders for Kathy's voice. She chose the blue silk to wear and Honoria wound a blue silk scarf around Kathy's throat to hid the marks that were just starting to come in. Kathy was still hoarse at dinnertime, but could speak above a whisper though she never needed to. Before going down, Honoria reminded Kathy once more to be wary of her mother's snobbism.

To call Mrs. Gloria Derby Little imposing was something of an understatement. She was not overly large. Her children got their height from their father. But she had the presence of a true society matron, with a long face, and dark gray hair piled on top of her head. Whereas Freddie was the true gentleman, his mother was the true aristocrat. She greeted Kathy with what could only be called noblesse oblige.

"Now, don't say anything," she commanded kindly when Honoria had introduced her in the salon. "My daughter told me all about your laryngitis. I wouldn't for the world have you hurt your poor throat."

Kathy smiled and nodded her thanks.

Freddie's father, on the other hand, was so completely self-absorbed Kathy wondered if he even knew with whom he was having dinner. Tall and fair-haired, he carried himself with the confidence of someone supremely convinced of his own rightness. He ranted on the evils of Tammany Hall until it was time to go in for dinner.

There were footmen to seat the ladies. As the guest of honor, Kathy was seated next to Mrs. Little, with Freddie on her other side, and Honoria across the table. Kathy felt a small rush of panic when she saw all the silver on the table, and realized that all the courses to be eaten were represented. This was a simple family dinner?

Conversation was superficial, and centered on people Kathy didn't know, although she'd heard a few of the names. Interspersed throughout were a variety of monologues from the elder Mr. Little, mostly on the joys of having the Republicans back in power, and the inherent evils of Democrats. Kathy could see Freddie wishing he could answer back, but it just wasn't done. Given Mr. Little's talent for bombast, Kathy wasn't sure it was even possible. No one even hinted at the existence of Freddie's book.

During the middle of the meat course, Mrs. Little fixed her eyes on Kathy.

"I must apologize, my dear," she said. "But I don't believe I know any Briscows in New York."

"Honoria, didn't you tell me Miss Briscow's grandfather was the founder of Hays, Kansas?" said

Freddie, leaping in gracefully.

"That's right," said Honoria with a smile. "It's oil money, isn't it?"

Kathy nodded, feeling strangely guilty. She knew Freddie and Honoria were stretching and fibbing to protect her, but it bothered her.

"Kathy, you don't mind if I tell Mummy about your family, do you?" Honoria asked.

Kathy shook her head. Her stomach churned as she wondered what wild tale Honoria would spin.

"Actually, they were in cattle first," said Honoria. "So there's been money for some time. Then the oil fields came in, and you know how it goes."

"Indeed." Mrs. Little's gaze was not directly accusatory of her daughter. But Kathy could tell the matron had her doubts. "Freddie, have you spoken with Edmund Markham recently?"

"Yes," Freddie replied, then caught Kathy's eye, and squirmed. "I spoke with him Sunday."

Kathy kept her eyes on her plate.

"His mother seems somewhat concerned," continued Mrs. Little. "He seems to be avoiding his friends."

"Not that I've noticed," said Freddie.

"Strangely preoccupied," said Mrs. Little. "It's regrettable, and not the sort of thing one mentions, but the cousins in that family married rather closely. There's always been an odd streak in that family."

Honoria and Freddie glanced at each other. As if there wasn't in their family. Mr. Little decided to break in with a monologue on the scandals in Washington, and how they'd been engineered by the Democrats.

At the end of dinner, Mrs. Little stood. "I think it's time we ladies withdrew."

The men stood as Kathy, Honoria and Mrs. Little excused themselves. For another half hour of insipid discussion, the ladies sat in the drawing room with coffee. At last, Mrs. Little begged to be excused to retire for the evening.

"Please, Kathy, feel free to stay up and chat with Honoria if you like."

"Thank you," Kathy croaked.

"Oh, dear, that is nasty," Mrs. Little said kindly. "You're very welcome, darling."

She retired gracefully, then went to listen at the gentlemen's pantry door. There was a loud snore. Mrs. Little cracked the door. Freddie glared at a magazine while his father slept.

"Freddie," Mrs. Little hissed and beckoned.

Freddie put the magazine aside and came out.

"Yes, Mother?"

"If you'd like to join your sister and her friend, I believe they are still in the drawing room." Mrs. Little shut the door. "But first I'd like to have a word with you."

Freddie sighed. "Yes, Mother."

261

He followed her down the hall to her stair-case.

"It's this Miss Briscow," said Mrs. Little. "Do you know how your sister met her?"

"Not off hand."

"Your sister knows nothing about her back-ground. After all, Freddie, there isn't that much oil in Kansas. Do you know anything about her?"

Freddie stopped. He didn't. "Just the one remark. She seems well brought up."

"Perfectly correct, and nice manners. Tried to thank me in spite of her voice. It is in a state, poor thing. At least that speaks well of her. But Freddie, I'm afraid you're going to have to find out more about her. Honoria absolutely refuses to. She's such a trial, that one."

"I understand."

"Very well. Good night, dear." She held out her cheek to him, and he gave it a perfunctory kiss.

"Good night, Mother."

Freddie decided to try the drawing room first. Honoria and Kathy were still there, with Honoria laughing heartily and Kathy silently chuckling.

"It sounds like the evening hasn't been a complete disaster," Freddie said, coming in.

"Just be thankful Daddy didn't start fighting the Great War all over again," said Honoria, giggling. She turned to Kathy. "You don't even whisper the words 'League of Nations' around him. He becomes positively apoplectic."

Freddie sank into the nearest couch. "So what are you two doing?"

Honoria laughed. "I got out the family albums."

"Honoria!" Freddie groaned. "Aren't you presuming a bit?"

"Since when are your baby pictures that revealing? There is that one." Honoria collapsed into giggles.

Kathy caught herself yawning. Freddie caught it before she could stifle it.

"Honoria, you are presuming that Kathy likes to stay up late, and I happen to know she doesn't."

"Oh!" Honoria turned to her. "Did you want to go to bed?"

"If it's all right," said Kathy softly.

"You're the guest, darling." Honoria rang a little bell. The butler appeared immediately. "Briggeman, will you please show Miss Briscow to her room?"

"Yes, Miss Honoria."

Kathy followed the butler out. Her room was almost as big as Honoria's, with a door leading to a bathroom. It was furnished with fine antiques and fabrics that were rich enough, but perhaps more suitable for a younger person. Kathy took her time undressing and putting on her nightgown. She was a little embarrassed to find that her valise had been unpacked for her. But the gun was still in the valise, which had been tucked under the bed.

263

Yawning, she went into the bathroom to wash up. Freddie was sitting on the toilet reading a newspaper. She squawked and scrambled out, banging the door shut behind her. A minute later, she heard the toilet flush.

There was a knock on the bathroom door.

"May I come in?" Freddie called softly.

"If you can face it, I can," Kathy replied, still rather hoarse.

Freddie slid into the room. He'd removed his tie, vest and jacket, but still wore his pants, shirt and suspenders.

"I didn't know they'd put you in here," he said.

"I had no idea you'd be there." Kathy's face was burning.

"Honoria must have set this up."

"I take it she has before."

"No. I've never given her the opportunity. But she has visited other pranks upon my mistresses."

"Oh. I suppose if I were your mistress, that would explain how you know me so well."

Freddie grimaced. "Actually, no. And that's not the assumption she made. It's... Honoria has made the same assumption about you that your family has made about me, which is why you're here."

"My." Kathy digested the thought. "This is

certainly a different way to approach courting." She laughed nervously. "What will the servants think?"

"They have probably assumed you're my latest mistress and are having a fine gossip at our brazenness in bringing you here."

Kathy thought of the shotgun under the bed. "Do they honestly think I'm your mistress?"

"I don't care if they do or not. My father probably does, for which you should be thankful, because if he didn't, he'd be in here trying to make you his."

Kathy rolled her eyes. "How delightful."

"I'm sorry to drag you into this."

"Oh, don't be." She looked at him, then sat on the bed. "Go ahead, take your shoes off. Make yourself at home."

Freddie found a chair and relaxed. He watched her, pleased that she had managed to fit in so well, and yet confused. There were not many respectable women, if any, who could stir his passions like she did.

"It's funny," said Kathy. "I can't think of this place as a home, and yet you grew up here. Did you eat dinner like that every night?"

"No. I ate in the nursery until I went to school. After I was ten I was expected to eat with my parents, unless there were guests in, or they were going elsewhere, which was most of the time."

"It seems so lonely." Kathy thought of the crowd at home in Kansas, and the loud, happy dinners.

"It was."

Kathy smiled. "There was this one photograph of you, let's see, it had to be nineteen-two, in a little suit of blue velvet. I mean, I guessed it was blue. From the book."

Freddie's eyes were elsewhere. "I hated that suit. I'd go out in it to take my daily constitutional, and I ran across some poor boys in the park. They threw rocks at me. Until I tackled their leader and stole his sling-shot. Of course, I was promptly reminded that young men of good breeding did not do such things." He suddenly smiled. "But I kept the sling-shot." He looked at her. "You come from a completely different world than I do, Kathy. A world I shunned right along with my peers, because it threw rocks at me. It wasn't until college that I began to understand why."

"Oh no," said Kathy with her wicked grin, determined to cheer him up. "Have you gone, dare I say it? Socialist?"

Freddie laughed. "I haven't gone that far. But I do not share my father's political views. I used to be terrified he'd find out and cut me off. Which, by the way, was one of the reasons I was so vocally opposed to women's votes."

"You and Honoria both spend an awful lot of time lying to your parents."

"They prefer it," said Freddie with a sigh. "Each of us tried telling them the truth. They were so upset by it, they pretended it didn't exist. They never heard us. So the best we can do is resort to harmless fibs to keep the peace."

"It is another world," sighed Kathy.

"Your voice sounds a lot better."

"My throat still hurts. Am I terribly bruised?"

Freddie looked, trying not to wince. "You've got a few. Do you think it was Evans who attacked you?"

"I never saw him, Freddie. Didn't you?"

"A little. I might recognize him again. I'm pretty sure Evans wasn't the one who tried to strangle you, though."

Kathy thought. "This is so frightening, Freddie. I was thinking just today that Evans might be a suspect. And now the manuscript is gone. It must be important somehow."

"I suppose there are people who might be offended if they knew they were the models for the characters in the book." Freddie mused. "But I did a lot of bending to change things enough so no one would recognize himself. And I can't recall putting anything in so dangerous to someone that he'd start killing people over it."

"Since Evans probably took the manuscript, that's hardly an issue." Kathy fidgeted with a pillow on the bed. "It just doesn't make sense. How could Evans have known you would be at that speak last night? That's not the sort of place he'd go."

Freddie sat up. "But he would have known I was going to be at that speak that first night we were attacked. Remember that group of thugs? I was going to meet Lowell there, and I invited Evans to join me."

"Yes, but where would Evans get the money to pay for the thugs, unless they don't cost as much as we think?"

"Perhaps he is also engaged in the manufacture of spirits. That can make a fair amount of money, if you don't drink up the profits, as Selby did."

Kathy shook her head. "The problem is, there's so little proof of anything."

"Then I shall endeavor to get it." Freddie got up. "Kathy, there have been two almost successful attempts on your life. I know this will not be easy for you, but will you please stay here until I can find someplace else to hide you?"

"Freddie, I desperately hate the thought of having to rely on your protection. I can't say I'm not grateful for the way you stood up to Sergeant Reagan this afternoon. But I felt completely humiliated." Kathy touched her throat. "On the other hand, you do have the argument of safety on your side. I'll try."

"I'll find a better spot for you first thing tomorrow, and try to get Honoria out of your hair."

"She's perfectly fine. We do get on well."

"I'm glad." He smiled.

She was so beautiful in her own quiet way. Not the sort that the screen favored, or the magazines. If Freddie had to be brutally honest, her features did not match the current standards for beauty, standards he'd always accepted. But they didn't apply to Kathy. It was as if the rules for beauty were completely rewritten just for her. There was something so uncommon about her, innocent, yet with a sense of the world that made Freddie's heart race as never before. Freddie sighed.

"There are times when I wonder if honor is worth it," he whispered.

Kathy nodded. "The problem is, Freddie, you were right last night. A friend like you doesn't come along often enough to squander it all on mere animal lust. I don't know if we'll ever find a way we can become lovers. But the friendship is worth a lot more right now."

Freddie smiled. "And there are times when I hate it when I'm right. I was so afraid this morning you wouldn't understand. And now that you do, it's all to the better, I suppose. Sleep well, Miss Briscow. For tonight, you are safe."

"Good night, Freddie. Oh, by the way, my family is in land."

"Land?" Freddie frowned. "I thought you said they didn't have money."

Kathy shrugged. "They're farmers. But Pa does own his spread."

"Good lord, you were dirt poor."

"No. We just weren't rich."

The dart hit the board and embedded itself with a loud thud. Another dart followed it. Honoria, tired of reading, followed the sounds to the game room and entered. Freddie sat in the leather over-stuffed chair, his face grim, a cigar burning in the ash tray next to him and half a glass of whiskey next to the ash tray. He sent another dart angrily hissing into the board.

"Why aren't you in your lady's chamber?" asked Honoria slyly.

Freddie glared. "I believe I told you she is not my mistress, nor do I have any intention of making her such."

"Of course not. You want to marry her."

The next dart slapped sideways against the board and tumbled to the floor. Freddie remained silent.

"Oh, dear. This is more serious than I thought."

"Honoria, will you cease trying to get me married?"

"I have to do something with my life."

"Boredom seems a poor excuse for interfering with how I wish to live."

She came around the chair and hugged her brother.

"It is, but it's the only one I've got. Besides, Freddie, darling, it does upset you so, and it's so much fun to see you with your feathers all ruffled up."

He looked at her. "Do you truly want to see me married?"

She sat down on the floor next to him. "I don't know that I do. Once you walk down the aisle I shall have to find a new project for myself. I suppose

I could do charity work, but those old biddies are so dreadfully dull, and I can't believe they're raising that much money for the causes. I haven't said a thing to Kathy about marrying you. In fact, when I brought her here, I was hoping to scare her off."

"You needn't worry. She does not want to be married."

"So be her lover."

"She wants to be kept even less." Irritated, Freddie got up.

"That's not what I was suggesting."

"With no promises or no contracts?" Freddie stuck the cigar in his mouth and puffed away. "That's a dangerous way to proceed, especially for her."

Honoria smiled. "She doesn't want your protection, Freddie."

"That doesn't change the fact that she still needs it. Too many things can go wrong."

"She won't be any worse off than before."

"If she's fired for moral turpitude, she will be, or worse yet, if she conceives."

"There are doctors to take care of that."

"That is presuming a great deal." Freddie flicked ash in the direction of the ash tray and picked up his drink. "She may not want that alternative. Or I may not."

"You?" Honoria giggled.

"Just because I do not want to get married does not mean I like the idea of leaving no progeny behind me. And there are other consequences. As my lover, she has no recourse to the courts. I could die, and the will be contested."

"You're making excuses, Freddie. The simple fact is, you do not want to take her as a lover." Honoria got up. "Your whole problem is that you're stuck on the idea that there are good girls and bad girls, and you marry the good girls, and take the bad girls as mistresses. Now, I can't blame you for not wanting to marry the bubbleheads. But for the first time in your life, Freddie, you're faced with a real woman, who is neither a good girl, nor a bad girl. She might make you feel like a bad girl does, and that's probably why you're so damned confused. But that's because she's a woman, living, breathing and passionate, and still very much your match for brains. Freddie, deep down in that old fashioned heart of yours, you know she's your soul mate, and you want to marry her."

Freddie refilled his glass. "Alas, Honoria, what I want remains a moot point. She does not wish to marry."

"Why should she? She has everything to lose."

"What?" Startled, Freddie looked at her. "There's nothing I can't give her. Houses, clothes, jewelry, even, not that it matters to her, a pedigreed name."

"And what about her own?"

"What about it?"

"She loses it when she marries you, Freddie.

272

Once you kiss the bride, she becomes Mrs. Freddie G. Little for the rest of her life. And that's only the beginning. What about the pride she gets from supporting herself? That's gone. If she isn't let go because she's a married woman, her job is pointless anyway. You'll be supporting her. And her freedom in managing her affairs the way she likes? Forget that. As her husband, you'll have the right to expect that she puts your wishes first. Good lord, Freddie, even the pittance she owns becomes yours when she marries you. Her only hope for getting back some control is for you to die."

"There's always the divorce court."

"I'll admit a good settlement is worth something. But you're still dependent. Widowhood is still a woman's best chance."

Freddie looked at her. "Like you?"

Honoria sniffed. "Yes. Why do you think I grabbed the first doughboy that seemed bearable? I can't believe I was so heartless, but you don't know how many times I prayed that he wouldn't come back. And yet, everything I have is because of him. All my money, everything, even my name. Mrs. Henry Wentworth. I don't even have my own name anymore."

"I had no idea."

"Of course, you didn't." Honoria took a deep breath. "Freddie, there is hope for you and Kathy. You could start by leaving the word 'obey' out of the ceremony. Beyond that, there's a reason they call it the 'privacy of the nuptial chamber.'"

"It might be worth considering." Freddie sighed. "Right now, I don't think I'm up for redefining marriage for the twentieth century, and I doubt Kathy is either."

"I didn't say do it now. Honestly, Freddie. It's like I said, you walk down the aisle, I have to find another project."

"Do me a favor, Honoria. Find another project now. Your current one not only annoys me, but it could embarrass Kathy."

"It might be worth considering." Honoria paused, then giggled. "Good night, Freddie. I think I've gotten you bothered enough for one night."

"Good night."

They bussed one another and Honoria left. Freddie picked up his cigar and puffed thoughtfully.

CHAPTER FOURTEEN

Kathy took her time bathing the next morning. She knew Freddie was sound asleep in the next room, although she'd locked the door on his side just to be certain. The steam in the closed bathroom brought her voice back to almost normal.

In her room, she considered the alternatives as she dressed and ate the breakfast that had been brought in. She didn't want to stay. Both Freddie and Honoria wanted their mother's good opinion of her, and she was afraid of making a fatal mistake. So she packed her valise.

She had just finished a note to Mrs. Little when there was a knock on the door. She opened it.

"Miss Briscow," said Briggeman. "There is a Sergeant Daniel Callaghan of the New York Police here to see you."

Kathy went white. "What the hell is he doing here?"

"I didn't inquire, miss. Shall I tell him you're not in?"

"Are you kidding? He's only here because he

knows I am."

"Would miss like me to summon her lawyer?"

"That won't help." Kathy laughed. "Sergeant
Callaghan is my uncle. I seriously doubt this is an
official call. I'll be right down."

"He's in the drawing room."

Callaghan sat on the edge of the couch, looking nervous and out of place. The moment he saw
Kathy, all his confident manner returned. He rose
as Kathy went over and gave him a kiss.

"Hello, Uncle Dan," said Kathy, hoping she
sounded as if turning up in a fabulously wealthy
mansion was nothing out of the ordinary. "What
brings you here?"

"Those bruises on your neck."

Kathy's hand flew to her throat. "I'm perfectly all right."

"Katie-girl, you're in a lot of trouble, and I
know it." Callaghan paced. "There was a call in at
the precinct house yesterday evening, some man
was strangling a girl on your block. By the time the
officer arrived, everyone was gone, and only the taxi
man was left to say what had happened. Then there
was a report filed by your Mrs. Lynne. Your room
had been ransacked. Sergeant Reagan told me you'd
left with Mr. Little and a Mrs. Wentworth, and that
you couldn't tell him anything, because you'd been
in an accident and couldn't speak."

"Did the sergeant say why he was there?"

"I know why he was there. I should've

let him have you last Saturday, and maybe you wouldn't be sportin' those bruises."

"I'm fine, Uncle Dan."

"Oh, you are." Callaghan glared. "Then why were you trying to get your Uncle Thomas to tell you about people supplying liquor? And don't tell me Mr. Little's book."

"He is a writer. I happen to be editing his book. It's how I know him."

"That may be true, Katie-girl. But it isn't why you went to Thomas, not when Frank Selby was known for making hooch. And not when Petey Wilson is telling me you're asking him about Selby's customers."

"Who?" Kathy whirled, her interest betraying her.

"He owns a speakeasy on Lexington and 40th. He had quite a lot to say about you and Mr. Swell."

"Oh, him." Kathy sighed. "He certainly didn't have much to say to us."

"Kathleen! What in all the saints names do you think you're doing? They caught the fellow who attacked you last night. The taxi driver identified him and he confessed. He's a paid assassin. Now, why would he be aiming at you, if you weren't up to your ears in business that's none of yours?"

"I have to do something." Kathy sniffed and looked away. "Damn it, I don't care what your connections are. As far as Sergeant Reagan is concerned I killed Mr. Selby, and the only reason I'm free is that he can't prove it."

Callaghan snorted. "I'll grant you, he's a problem. But leave him to me."

"He tried to arrest me yesterday. If Mr. Little hadn't threatened him with dismissal from the force, I would have spent last night in jail."

"Which would be a damn sight safer than where you are! Katie-girl, do you have any idea what you're dealing with? A cold blooded killer, who's already killed once, maybe more, and who just tried to kill you."

Kathy faced him down. "What makes you so certain it's connected to Mr. Selby? There are thousands of criminals in New York."

"Because you been putting your nose where it don't belong, girl! Don't tell me you haven't."

"And you expect me to stand quietly by like a good little girl, while Sergeant Reagan digs up enough evidence to send me to the electric chair!" Furious, Kathy folded her arms across her chest, trying desperately to regain control. "I'm not going to do it, Uncle Dan. I know what I'm doing, and I'm being careful."

"I'm sure you are, Katie-girl."

"I'm not a girl!" Kathy yelled. "I don't need you to take care of me. I don't need anybody."

"Then why are you hiding here?"

Kathy pulled herself up straight. "I am the guest of Mrs. Honoria Wentworth and Mrs. Frederick G. Little, Jr."

"And do they know what happened to you yesterday?"

"Mrs. Wentworth does. I'm here largely at her suggestion." Feeling ashamed, Kathy sighed and walked over to the fireplace.

"And Mr. Little?"

"Which one?" Kathy turned on him. "Mr. Little, Jr., who is the elder of the two here, I might add, is somewhere around the place. I didn't inquire. It is his home. As for the other, I believe he is still asleep. During the course of our conversations, he has mentioned that he prefers to retire quite late at night and rise equally late in the morning."

"And which one has been taking you out every night this week?" Callaghan smiled confidently.

Kathy looked shocked. "Who told you that?"

"Mrs. Lynne."

"That broad has a big mouth, which is no doubt why Uncle Mike likes her so much." Kathy sulked. "Mr. Little, the third, by the way. He's not married, if that's what you were thinking. We're just friends, Uncle Dan. He's excited about his book."

"And Mr. Selby?" Callaghan peered at her knowingly.

"All right. He's interested in Selby, too. And before you get angry at him, he's the one who stopped Reagan yesterday. Speaking of, how did you track me down here?"

"I had a bit of help from your Uncle Mike."

"Wonderful," Kathy groaned sarcastically.

279

"The next thing you know, he'll be demanding Mr. Little's intentions. Well, you tell Uncle Mike he'd better just stay away, because it doesn't matter what Mr. Little's intentions are. I'm not interested!"

Callaghan sighed. "If you insist. Get your bag and come along, then."

Kathy glared. "I'm not going anywhere."

"You're coming with me, girl." Callaghan's look said he would not be argued with. "I'm taking you home, and your Aunt Beth will be keeping an eye on you when I can't."

"You caught the man who attacked me," said Kathy stubbornly.

"Not the one who paid him, and that much we can't get out of the fellow, because he don't know, nor does the grocer that set it all up."

"Grocer?"

"Eye-talian fellow in the Village, and we got him, too, but he doesn't know anything either. It's all been handled by post and phone calls. Now, come along."

"I've got to write a note first. I'll be right down."

Kathy felt angry and betrayed, but there was no help for it. Uncle Dan was not above using force if he had to, and Kathy did not want to embarrass Freddie and Honoria. She finished her note to Mrs. Little first, apologizing for her abrupt departure. She then wrote a second note to Honoria, explaining about her uncle. She hoped Honoria would show it to Freddie.

They walked to the subway. Kathy tried to appear as compliant as possible without seeming as if she were giving in too easily. Callaghan remained vigilant. They took a downtown train to 42nd. In the press of the crowd as they changed to the cross-town train, Kathy fell behind, then slipped away. A minute later, she pounded up the steps to the street. Callaghan was in pursuit, but still a good many yards from the bottom of the stairs by the time she reached the top.

Out of breath, she took a quick look around. Grand Central Station was just a block away. Buses clogged the street. But there was something else that Uncle Dan would never think of.

"Taxi!" Kathy put up her hand, wondering if she would have thought of it a week before.

"Times Square," she told the driver, and looked behind her.

Callaghan had just emerged from the subway and was looking up and down the street. He never glanced at the taxis. He stopped a man entering the subway.

"Excuse me, sir," he asked. "Did you happen to see a young woman with a valise come this way?"

The man looked at Callaghan strangely. "Sure, Mac. Maybe five of them, that way."

Callaghan looked the way the man had jerked his thumb. Grand Central. Silently cussing, Callaghan shook his head.

Freddie checked the knot of his tie with a

satisfied smile, then lit a cigarette. Whoever had said that things always look better in the morning had a point. In the light of the mid-morning sun, the beast of lust that roared within him seemed positively tame. True, even the most casual thought of the ever-delightful Miss Briscow set the beast growling again. But the new perspective Honoria had given the problem sent the beast whimpering back to the corner of Freddie's soul that was reserved for such things.

How he and Kathy would end up, Freddie was not sure. He was not nearly as certain of his intentions as Honoria was, and there were always Kathy's wishes to be considered. Freddie shuddered. He'd had no idea what a woman gave up to marry. How ironic that Honoria's freedom had only come about because she'd given it all up.

Still, taking Kathy as a lover remained unthinkable. There were too many pitfalls, not so much between them, but in terms of the rest of the world. Even though he appreciated Kathy's love of her independence, he refused to leave her completely vulnerable.

Friendship remained perfectly acceptable, and as Freddie thought it through, probably the wisest course. After all, they'd barely known each other a week. He paused. It had been just over a week since they'd met. So much had happened. He couldn't believe it had all taken place in such a short time.

Laying his cigarette in an ashtray, he buttoned up his vest and slid the watch chain through the holes, leaving the fob dangling neatly over the pocket. He wondered if Briggeman had shown Kathy the library, or if she'd remained hidden in the next bedroom. The door had been locked on her side of the bathroom. Freddie hadn't knocked.

"Freddie!" Honoria called hysterically. She burst into his room. "Freddie, she's gone!"

"Who?"

"Kathy." Honoria stumbled to the bureau and took a drag from Freddie's cigarette. "I needed that. Don't fuss. Mummy's out calling." She took another drag.

"Where the hell did she go?" Freddie tried not to panic.

"Who knows?" Honoria shoved the note at him. "Her Uncle Dan came for her this morning. She says her Uncle Mike helped track her down."

Freddie read the note. "Damn that bastard!"

"Watch your language, darling. I didn't know Kathy had relatives in the city."

"They're all Irish." Freddie tapped the bureau thoughtfully, then swept a handful of change into his pants pocket.

Honoria giggled. "This girl's getting more undesirable by the minute. She's perfect."

"I thought I asked you last night to get another project." Freddie glared at her as he slid into his suit coat.

Honoria blew out a mouthful of smoke. "I'm done. Do you want the rest of this?"

Freddie looked at the stub. "Of what?"

He checked his pockets for everything he

needed. Honoria snubbed out the cigarette.

"So what are we going to do?" she asked, worried.

"I am going to pay a call." Freddie read over the note. "Maybe more than one. You are going to wait at my apartment. If she calls, you are to find out where she is, then wait for me. I'll keep calling back."

Honoria put her hand on Freddie's arm. "Freddie, someone is trying to kill her. Are you sure no one is trying to kill you?"

"I'm perfectly safe, Honoria."

Freddie left before she could ask any more questions. He had no reason to believe Honoria would do as he'd asked, but at least Roberts would get the call. If it came. Those uncles of Kathy's were worse than the guards at Sing Sing. Michael Callaghan's interference nettled and wore at him. As they neared 23rd, Freddie told the driver to go on to Callaghan's downtown office.

Rotundity was a definite tendency in the Callaghan family. Living well brought it out. Michael Callaghan was fond of joking that he could tell how well his family was doing by looking at their waistlines. Michael Callaghan was doing quite well, indeed.

He was as proud of his prodigious girth as he was of the happy, rambunctious brood he'd sired, and of his patriarchal status among his siblings, entrusted to him by his father, who'd died some years before. Michael Callaghan was a family man first, and for the first time in a life of scrambling, hard work, and long hours, he had the time and income to indulge it. He took special care of the daughter of his wayward sister. She was just like her mother, Kathleen was, as his brother Daniel reminded him. Daniel had called to let Michael know about Kathy's escape.

"Have you checked with Bridget?" Michael asked into the telephone. "Kathy's fond of Morris, you know."

"Yes, Michael. I've checked with everyone: Mary, Thomas, Colleen, James, Kevin, and Patrick," said Daniel. "Not one has heard from her. I even checked with John."

"He's back in the city?"

"Found him in a flop house near 11th and 46th. I told you, I checked everywhere. She wasn't there, either, thank God."

Michael thought. "She must have gone back to the Littles."

"I don't think so. She was already packed when I got there."

"I'll deal with them. I've been in communication with the younger Mr. Little. He seems a reasonable man."

"Watch your step, Michael. The girl is gone on him, plain and simple."

"Are you certain?"

"She's swearing she's not interested, for starters, never once called him a name, and actually defended him more or less."

285

"That's serious."

"And now she's flat disappeared."

"Don't blame yourself for that, Daniel. When I lost her mother, there wasn't even a subway."

The secretary entered and handed Michael a calling cared. Michael looked at it and lifted an eyebrow.

"Speak of the devil, and he shall come. Daniel, I'll be calling you later. It seems Mr. Little himself is here."

"You think he knows she's gone?"

"I'll be finding out. On with you, now."

Michael hung up and told the secretary to admit Mr. Little.

Freddie was too irritated to be impressed by the fine appointments of the office. He merely noted that Mr. Callaghan was doing well for himself.

"Mr. Little, it's a pleasure to finally make your acquaintance," said the heavy man standing behind the desk. "Is this a social call?"

"I hope so, Mr. Callaghan," Freddie said, shaking Michael's hand.

Michael busied himself with sitting to hide the approving smile on his face. The young man had balls. He'd need them if he wanted Kathy.

"Please, sit down," said Michael. "Would you like some tea?"

"Not at the moment, thank you." Freddie

sat down in the chair, and relaxed just enough to remain serious. "Mr. Callaghan, we have been in communication, and I believe I have made it clear how the situation stands between myself and your niece, Miss Briscow. To reiterate, we are friends. In addition, Miss Briscow has formed a friendship with my sister, Mrs. Wentworth. The entire situation is completely circumspect and without the slightest scandal. Nonetheless, this morning your brother insisted on removing Miss Briscow from my parents' home, where she was staying as an invited guest. From certain remarks she left in a note to my sister, who extended the invitation, and not me, I have reason to believe you were behind the removal. I want to know why you insist on assuming that my intentions are less than honorable, when I have made it plain that this is not the case."

"There is your reputation to consider, Mr. Little," said Michael, struggling to keep his face serious.

"I will confess to some dissipation, Mr. Callaghan," said Freddie after a moment's thought. "But the fact is, my reputation is based more on the people I associate with rather than myself, nor am I prone to pressing my vices on other people. Furthermore, my reputation with respect to women is unassailable."

"But Kathleen isn't, unfortunately, and she was assaulted yesterday."

Freddie nodded. "I assume you also know that I was present at the time. I agree there's cause for some concern. But wouldn't it have sufficed to ascertain that the situation was under control? After all, Mr. Callaghan, your niece is well over the age of twenty-one, and has proven herself quite capable of managing her own affairs."

"True. Better than you know, Mr. Little. But you don't have to answer to her parents. I do. Unless, of course, you'd like to assume that right."

"Of answering to her parents?" Freddie smiled, and chose his words carefully. "Mr. Callaghan, the difficulty lies in that your niece feels no need to answer to anyone."

Michael watched him carefully. "You seem to be good friends with Kathleen."

"It depends on how you define that. Obviously, when a man and a woman find that they are developing, shall we say, a liking for each other, a variety of possibilities come to mind. That your niece and I found ourselves forced to discuss those possibilities somewhat earlier than what one might consider normal in such friendships, I think was only fortunate. In any case, Mr. Callaghan, if you are looking for a husband for your niece, I would recommend a great deal of caution, as she has made it very plain to me that she does not want one."

Michael chuckled. "That's what she says."

Freddie shook his head. "I have good reason to believe she is quite sincere in her desire to remain unwed. Nor can I blame her. She does stand a great deal to lose by it."

"And if she marries you, a great deal to gain."

Freddie was not moved. "So it appears. But, if anything, your niece pities me more than envies me. I assure you, my social position and wealth hold no attraction for Miss Kathy Briscow. The only thing of mine that she covets is my library and the hours I have to spend in it. But even that is not enough for her to be willing to give up her job and her life."

Michael sighed. "Mr. Little, I'm sure my niece sincerely believes she is not interested in marriage. But I know her, much better than you possibly could. Now, you might not believe this, but I have no trouble with seeing her an old maid. However, and I trust you will not take this in the wrong way, Kathleen has been known to, quite innocently, get herself into situations that are, well, less than discreet. I've no doubt, Mr. Little, that you know how vulnerable that can make a woman, even in these modern times. For all the talk there is of free thinking, I see precious few acting on it."

"I am fully aware of all the dangers, Mr. Callaghan." Freddie shifted. "And, as I said in my letter, I think quite highly of your niece, and would not for the world expose her to them."

"You're obviously a gentleman, Mr. Little." Michael got up. Freddie rose also. "As we both understand, to give you permission to call on my niece would be ludicrous at best. But I am considerably eased in my mind. It doesn't matter how independent she is, I do still worry about her. You might try asking her to give me a call when you get back to her."

Freddie froze, trying to conceal his panic. "Pray forgive me, but I was given to understand that she is with your brother."

"In other words, you don't know where she is."

Freddie watched him. "Nor do you."

Michael shrugged. "She gave Daniel the slip

on the subway. We're hoping she'll return to you."

"I doubt it." Freddie sighed. "You found her with me once. She won't give you the chance to do it again. My sister is at my apartment, waiting for her call. Honoria has a remarkable talent for extracting information from people. All we can do is hope Kathy calls."

Michael nodded. "It is disturbing. But I'm not too worried. As long as we can't find Kathy, the madman behind all this can't either. Knowing her, she'll be dragging him to the police first thing in the morning."

"No doubt." Freddie shook Michael's hand. "Thank you for the chat."

"Thank you for dropping by."

Freddie nodded and left. Chuckling, Michael sat back down and pushed aside a brief. He pulled out some personal stationery and began a letter.

"Dear Katie Marie;" he wrote. "Do I have news for you. If I didn't feel so good right now, I'd be hiding under my desk waiting for the world to end. It's finally happened. Your Kathleen has met her match. She won't be saying anything, of course. I don't think she realizes how smitten she is. The same goes for her young man. I've just had the pleasure of meeting him. He's not saying anything, either, but you can tell he's gone on her. He's quite the gentleman, possibly her match for brains (if not, he's close), and he definitely has the backbone to take her on. He'll be able to keep her comfortable, too, a nice little bonus to put yours and Jacob's minds at ease..."

Kathy looked at the little church nestled among the apartment buildings. It was the address she'd managed to coerce out of the butler at the Selby mansion. A Baptist church seemed a little out of place among the staid former glory of Murray Hill, but given their tendency towards hellfire and damnation, it made sense in terms of what Kathy knew regarding Percy Selby.

Taking a deep breath, she went in. The church itself was empty. A little exploring turned up an office in the back, and the minister's residence. Reverend Jameson was quite happy to produce Percy. Kathy asked for privacy, and they were left alone in the office.

Far from being the overwrought, despairing creature Freddie had described, Percy was quite calm, and even pleasant.

"I don't know how I can help you, Miss Briscow," he said. "My story isn't all that unusual."

"The magazine thinks it might be," said Kathy. "And I am interviewing other people, of course. The subject of religious conversion and moral outrage is becoming quite the rage these days."

"Is it?" Percy mused, then leaned back in his chair. "Well, what do you want me to tell you?"

"Why don't you just start with how you came to be converted, and maybe the particulars of how it actually happened." Kathy smiled warmly.

"I suppose you know that I come from a wealthy family. I had everything, cars, women, houses. Anything you could imagine, except one thing. A reason to live. Can you imagine, Miss Briscow, what it is like to get up in the morning, and have no place to go, nothing to do but what my heart fancied? I suppose to a working girl like you, that must sound like heaven. But it isn't. It gets dreadfully boring after a while. The things I did to fill those empty hours." Percy shook his head. "Mostly I drank, even after they passed the Volstead Act. You might wonder where I got my liquor. I had a poor cousin who made it."

"A bootlegger?" asked Kathy. "My goodness. Was he one of the ones supplying the speakeasies?"

Percy's brow creased in thought. "No. He mostly gave it to me and my friends. There was one little place. It was owned by a friend of his. Poor Frank. He passed on recently."

"I'm terribly sorry."

"Anyway, to get back to my empty former life, I drank a lot. And one night, after yet another debauch, I stumbled into this church and slept it off in one of the back corners. When I came to, I heard Reverend Jameson preaching on the evils of relying on earthly wealth to find happiness."

"And that's when you were converted."

"No. That happened a month later. You see, I was like the rich young man in the gospel who had come to see Jesus and was told to sell what he had and give to the poor. I went away saddened because I did not want to be poor. You have to understand that from my former point of view, that was a terrible disgrace. I didn't yet know of the far greater riches God has to offer." Percy sighed.

"And when you actually did convert, what happened then?"

"That most blessed of nights." Percy chuckled. "It didn't start out that way. I was on my way to getting drunk yet again, and I had a terrible fight with my cousin, Frank."

"What were you fighting about?"

Percy's brow creased again. "I assume drinks. He had a nasty habit of aging his whiskey, well, nasty to my way of thinking then. I accused him of doing it on purpose, to torture me because I had money and he didn't. He got rather nasty back, and we fell to blows. Fortunately, a good friend of mine pulled me off of Frank, and took me elsewhere. I do think I could have killed Frank that night. That's when it came to me. My utter depravity, that I was willing to take the life of my own blood kin for a drink. I made my escape and came here, confessing my sins to the good reverend, who showed me God's forgiveness, and here I am, a new man in God's creation."

"You seem very peaceful."

Percy smiled. "I am, at last. I was rather hysterical at first. Satan, no doubt, trying to win me back. Drove my best friend from me as I tried to save his soul." He frowned. "That was the day of Frank's funeral. Freddie thought I was upset because Frank and I had been fighting. Frank's death did scare me. They said a woman killed him. Frank was not kind to women and, I'm afraid, neither was I. It could just as easily have been me that was killed." Percy perked up. "But thanks be to the Lord, I am saved. And no more need I fear the consequences of my former evil ways. I'm living an entirely new life, now. Selling off all my old possessions, and giving them to the poor."

Kathy's eyebrow lifted. "What does your

family think of this?"

"Oh, they've cut me off," said Percy matter-of-factly. "As have all my old friends. Which is just as well. There is no temptation for me to return to my old ways."

"I think your story will do quite nicely," said Kathy, getting up. "May I contact you here at this address if I have any further questions?"

Percy rose also. "Certainly. The good reverend has been kind enough to take me in until I can find some honorable employment."

"I wish you the best of luck, then." Kathy shook his hand.

"Not luck. The Lord will provide. God bless you."

Kathy left, wondering what to do next. She walked back to 42nd and Fifth, to the library where she had checked her bag while looking up Percy in the Who's Who. He seemed so lucid. But he had admitted to being hysterical, and Freddie had spoken to him the previous Saturday, which meant Percy probably had been hysterical the night his cousin had died. But he seemed so certain a woman had killed Frank, as had the speak owner.

Kathy decided she would have to ask Percy why at a later time. With someone interested in killing her, too much interest in Frank Selby's death was dangerous.

CHAPTER FIFTEEN

The melody. It wouldn't stop. The tortured soul paced listlessly, waiting. There would be dinner to go to, but then... Yes, then he would be able to satisfy the music. He paced, humming, waiting for the darkness to fall and the hours to pass.

Freddie paced the foyer of his apartment, sucking furiously on a cigarette.

"Why didn't you keep her on?" he demanded, the smoke streaming from his mouth and nostrils.

"She hung up!" snapped Honoria, who was also smoking.

Freddie ground out his cigarette and immediately lit another.

"All right," he said, regaining control. "She hung up. You couldn't help that. Did you ring the operator and ask where the call had come from?"

"Of course. What kind of an imbecile do you think I am?" Honoria pouted. "The operator just said she hadn't noticed, and disconnected. How was she supposed to know there was anything unusual about the call?"

"Damn." Freddie paced, trying to think. "Once more, Honoria, what exactly did Kathy say?"

"She said to tell you that she was safe, and that she would appreciate it if you would talk to Evans, whoever he is, because she can't, and that she will call you tomorrow. I asked her where she was because you wanted to call her, and she said she couldn't say, but that you were not to worry, and hung up."

"I wonder if her blasted uncles caught up with her after all. That would explain her caginess. Damn."

"I'm afraid, Freddie, you're just going to have to take her word for it." Honoria thoughtfully put out her cigarette. "Who is this Evans fellow, anyway?"

"Nobody," grumbled Freddie.

Even cigarettes weren't calming his jangled nerves. Kathy seemed reasonably sure of her safety, and certainly wasn't taking any chances.

There was a note next to the phone that the repairs on his airplane had been completed and that the engineers had left a couple parts behind so that he could make his own adjustments to the engine. He'd been wanting to go out to the airfield since the accident. But first his book, then Kathy, had driven it from his mind. He needed an excuse to get away, and tinkering with an engine was always soothing. Kathy could easily phone him at the hangar or the nearby inn.

"Roberts?" Freddie glanced towards the servants quarters for the valet. "Have my car brought around."

"The Rolls, sir?"

"No. The Packard, thank you."

Rough men lined the buildings along 12th Avenue, the few not hired in that morning's shape-up on the docks. They were idle, angry, looking for work or a fight, and willing to settle for either. The stench of rotting produce, human waste and simple despair overpowered the fresh breeze from the ocean. The mournful calls of the great ships and tugs underscored the sadness, and the tension.

Still, Kathy felt safer among the waiting men than she had since the attack the day before. Deep in the back of her mind, something whispered that Chelsea had an answer for her, a connection of some sort. And Chelsea also had a place to hide, a place where no one in their right mind would think to look for her. Except, of course, her uncles. But if she was lucky, they'd already tried and wouldn't think to try again. She felt confident her Aunt Mary wouldn't betray her.

The men looked at her curiously as she rang the bell to the convent. A young woman with a suitcase? Kathy knew what they were thinking, and almost laughed. Kathy? Joining a convent? Freddie's form flitted briefly through her mind with a surge of sweet tension. The idea was utterly ridiculous.

"I'd like to visit with Sister Francis, please," Kathy told the nun who had opened the door. "I'm her niece."

Sister Porter showed Kathy to the sitting room, then fetched Kathy's aunt with remarkable speed for the silence of her movement. The former Mary Callaghan had her family's roundness. She swooped Kathy into a hug that was all black robes and rosary beads.

"I'm so glad to see you, darling," the nun sighed. She held Kathy's shoulders. "Your Uncle Dan is very worried."

"I'm fine, Aunt Mary. Really, I am."

Mary nodded. "You don't look that much worse for the wear, although those bruises aren't pretty. What brings you here? Sanctuary for the fugitive?"

"Yes," Kathy sighed. "Please, may I stay?"

"I'll have to ask Reverend Mother, but I don't see why not. We take in guests all the time. It's part of our mission here." Mary chuckled ruefully. "With bruises like that, you'll fit right in with the others."

"You won't tell Uncle Dan, will you?"

"I won't call him. But if he comes asking, you know I'm not any good at telling fibs. Wait here, I'll be right back."

Kathy soon found herself settled in a second floor room overlooking the avenue. It was small and spare, with a straight-backed wooden chair, a simple steel-framed bed, a small bureau and a medium-sized crucifix on the wall. A window overlooked the street. Kathy barely had time to get herself settled when she was called to dinner. The sisters were all kind, but Kathy still felt out of place and restless. After dinner, she retired quickly to her room and spent the evening pacing aimlessly in front of the window.

The clock on the bureau said ten minutes after one when Kathy first heard the song. Wisps of the melody floated up from the finally quiet street. Still unable to sleep, Kathy was resting in the chair. She got up and went to the window.

A lone figure walked the street below. Kathy made out a top hat, and a walking stick with a knobbed head that gleamed in the dull lamplight. The figure paused under a street lamp. Kathy couldn't make out his face, only the white bow tie under his chin.

What in heaven's name was the fool doing walking the streets of Chelsea in evening dress? Doing acrobatics on an airplane was safer. As he approached, Kathy could just make out the melody he was singing. That song from *Lady Be Good*.

Her heart pounding, she grabbed her hat and coat and ran outside. He'd gone half a block past the convent. Kathy shivered with the cold.

"...The neighbors want to know, why I'm always shaking just like a flivver," sang the man.

He ambled along placidly, looking for something. Kathy crept along behind, hiding in the shadows of the building.

"Hi!" The man stopped abruptly, and poked at something with his stick. "Are you awake? Come on, wake up my good fellow."

He dragged the sleeping form to its feet. The bum wobbled a little unsteadily.

"There you are." The man put his hands on the bums shoulders to steady him. "Guess what?"

The man put his hands to the bum's neck and twisted.

"Snap!" he announced in a pleased voice.

Kathy gasped, too shocked to scream. The bum's head rolled at a sickening angle, his body sagged. Kathy looked away, trying to keep her stomach from heaving.

"Fascinating Rhythm, you got me on the go. Fascinating Rhythm, I'm all a quiver..."

By the time she looked up, the well-dressed man had disappeared, his voice silent. The bum's body lay in a heap in the middle of the sidewalk. Kathy's breath came out in small bursts of cloud. She stumbled back to the convent. She debated calling the cops, but there was Sergeant Reagan and Kathy couldn't help being afraid that he'd blame the killing on her. She knew she wasn't thinking straight, but couldn't decide what was the best thing to do, so she went to bed.

Sleep came, but in restless snatches. Visions of the bum's head tore at Kathy, then turned into Freddie's face. She woke up, her breath coming in starts, only to see the vision again when her head returned to the pillow.

She was uneasy through breakfast. Upstairs again, she tried to think rationally through her shock. She opened her valise for the seventh time, not knowing why. Two pages of typescript stuck out between the step-ins and camisoles. Trembling, Kathy drew them out.

"But it would certainly be interesting to feel someone go limp in my hands, the lifespark gone. It's very easy to snap someone's neck, you know, once you get the knack of it. It's in the rhythm. Pop. Absolutely fascinating."

The answer. It made everything clear, except who had actually done the killing. But that wouldn't be hard to find out now that Kathy knew where to look.

A knock on the door brought her back to reality. Aunt Mary stuck her head into the room.

"I just wanted to say good morning," she said, although Kathy could see that she had more to say.

"Aunt Mary, is there a telephone that I might use?"

"Yes. Downstairs. Kathy, are you all right? You seemed so distant at breakfast, and tired. Sister Porter said someone had run out of the house last night, then came back in."

"I'm sorry." Kathy fought to get the trembling under control. "It was an urgent matter."

Mary laid one hand on Kathy's shoulder. "Darling, I'm beginning to think I should call your Uncle Dan."

"Not yet." Kathy turned. Her brain spun with ideas, and clear thought triumphed. "No, Aunt Mary. It wouldn't do any good. I saw something last night. I may know who's been killing those bums that keep turning up. But I need proof. Suspicion won't help Uncle Dan."

"Then tell him where to get it."

"He won't be able to." Kathy folded the pages and stuffed them in her purse. "I've got to make a telephone call, Aunt Mary. Please, trust me, it's urgent."

Mary was not happy, but she showed Kathy the phone. Kathy rang Freddie's apartment. Roberts answered.

"He's not here," the valet said. "But he instructed me to get the number where you are at, and he will call you."

"That—" Kathy swallowed back the oath. "Where is he? I need to know."

"I'm sorry. I was instructed to get your location."

"Roberts, someone is trying to kill Mr. Little. I need to know where he is now!"

Roberts stammered for a second. "He's at the airfield. He has a plane there that he is working on. Good lord. He had an accident in the plane two weeks ago."

Kathy suddenly went white. "Where is this airfield, Roberts?"

The valet gave her directions.

"Call the airfield and make sure he doesn't try to fly that plane," Kathy ordered. She slammed down the phone and picked up her coat.

"Where are you going?" asked Aunt Mary, worried.

"Out." Kathy jammed her hat on her head.

"Now, Kathy, darling." Mary chased after her as she ran down the hall. "Wait. What about your bag?"

"I'll get it later!"

Kathy slammed the door shut behind her and ran for the 11th Avenue El. The trip was time consuming, what with taking two trains and a bus. Kathy fidgeted. All she knew of airplanes was that there was plenty that could go wrong with them. She hoped like hell Freddie wouldn't try flying that death trap of his.

At Junction Boulevard, there was a long wait for another bus. Kathy debated walking. When the bus dropped her at the end of Junction, she was glad she hadn't. There was still another half mile to go before she reached the hangars.

The man at the airfield office was glad to point out Mr. Little's hangar among the wooden barns scattered around the field. Kathy ran for it. Near the door, she paused to get her breath. She didn't want to look inside and find the plane gone. She took a deep breath, and turned the corner.

The huge double doors were wide open. Inside was a custom Curtiss biplane, with Freddie up to his elbows in the engine. He was wearing jodhpurs and boots, and a white shirt with the sleeves rolled up and the collar open.

"That should do it," he muttered.

"Oh, Freddie, thank God!" cried Kathy.

Freddie whirled. "How'd you get here?"

303

"The BMT. I was afraid I'd get here too late, that you'd take off in that..." She glared at the plane. "Thing."

Freddie laughed and gazed fondly at the machine. "It's perfectly safe now. The landing gear and the wings are brand new. There's a new prop, and I just overhauled the engine."

"Oh." Kathy found a stool and sank down onto it.

"Where have you been?"

"Finding things out." Kathy pulled the pages from Freddie's book out of her purse. "Freddie, I know why there's someone trying to kill us, and it's got to be the same person who killed Frank Selby. Only he's not afraid we're too close to him. It's this!"

"What's that?" Freddie picked up a rag and wiped the grease from his hands.

"Part of your book. It's that scene between Thripps and Meabury that I edited out. Freddie, who is Thripps based on?"

Freddie shrugged. "A couple of people."

"The one who wanted to snap necks."

"What?"

Kathy groaned. "Just tell me, damn it!"

"Kathy, it can't have anything to do with Selby's death. He was English, for one thing, and he's dead."

"That's right." Kathy looked at the pages. "Then it must be someone else doing the same thing."

Freddie took the pages. "What are you talking about?"

"The man killing those bums in Chelsea. You must have seen it in the papers. Uncle Dan told me last week. Then last night, I was staying down there in Chelsea. Don't worry, it was a perfectly safe place. And I saw him. A man in evening clothes. I couldn't see his face. But he woke up a bum and snapped his neck. By the time I got my stomach to where I wasn't going to heave, he was gone. Freddie, it was so eerie. He was singing that song from *Lady Be Good*, 'Fascinatin' Rhythm.' Then this morning, I read those pages."

Freddie looked at the pages in his hand. "It can't be."

"It has to be, Freddie. It's too close to what you wrote. Whoever this person is probably knew that Frank Selby was your editor, and killed him, thinking Selby knew about the scene, and that he would call the cops in on it. And this person is trying to kill you. Roberts just told me you'd had an accident in your plane. And remember that night in Greenwich Village? You were going to meet someone."

"Lowell. But he's not killing bums." Tense, Freddie picked up some heavy wire and fidgeted with it.

"No. This man had a flat stomach. But whoever it is, he must have found out that I'm your editor and now he's after me, too."

Freddie shook his head. "Why kill you?"

305

"I'm your editor. I saw the scene. You've introduced me to several people that way, and who knows, maybe someone talked. But you're in just as much danger, Freddie. Maybe even worse. You wrote it."

"Evans," said Freddie firmly. He put the wire onto a shelf nearby. "We know he stole the manuscript. We know he was all but desperate to have it. And the first attack on you occurred the day after you stole it from the office."

"That's right. And he was dumping all that work on me. He had no way of knowing how much I'd read. He was probably trying to keep me from reading it. And, my god, Freddie, he's been whistling that song ever since the show opened!"

Filled with nervous energy, Freddie grabbed a rag and wiped down the side of the plane. "I tried to talk to him yesterday, but he didn't go in to the office."

"We'll have to find him. I think I can get his home address."

"I got it. He wasn't there, either." He looked longingly at the plane. "I'll have to finish this later."

Kathy bit her lip. "Maybe we ought to talk to my uncle first. Evans doesn't have the connections that could get Uncle Dan into trouble without more proof, and he's already tried to kill us more than once. Wait. Where's he getting the money to hire the assassin?"

"We'll just have to find out, won't we?" Freddie grabbed a tweed jacket and took Kathy's elbow.

"Aren't you cold?"

"I've been working." Freddie slid into the jacket. "I've got an overcoat in the car."

With one last sigh, he shut the hangar doors, then, as an afterthought, found a padlock and locked it. He took Kathy's arm and steered her towards the car parked next to the hangar. Kathy held back.

"Who else knows you're out here," she demanded.

"No one but Roberts and Honoria. Why?"

"Someone is trying to kill you. What if they sabotaged your car?" Kathy finally noticed the Packard. "That's not your car."

Freddie looked at her strangely. "Yes, it is."

"But what happened to the Rolls Royce you had the other night?"

Freddie laughed. "I own more than one car."

Kathy gaped. "More than one car? Oh dear. What if someone sabotaged all of them?"

"That seems highly unlikely," said Freddie, helping her in. "Furthermore, I drove this one here without any hint of a problem and I would know if there was one."

"But someone sabotaged your plane."

Freddie just snorted. "The landing gear fell off as I touched down and the right wings folded. It wasn't anything serious."

"It could have been." Kathy's mouth fell open. "Freddie, you could have died!"

"I suppose it's possible, but remember, I've been flying as long as anybody. There are very few situations I can't handle, even if someone had tampered with the landing gear."

"Don't you check things before taking off?"

"I give the plane a complete visual inspection every time."

"It must have been sabotaged. If it were me, I'd figure that would be a darned good way to set a trap."

Freddie sighed. "We can't find a killer in everything. Right now, all our evidence points to Evans. This happened before he would have been involved."

"But it is possible."

"Yes, but not likely."

When they finally arrived at the precinct house, they found that Callaghan was not in. The desk officer said they could wait, which they debated until they found out that Sergeant Reagan was taking his day off. So they seated themselves on a bench outside the detectives' room.

Freddie handed her a newspaper. She opened it, and looked through the contents as she waited.

"Look at this." Kathy folded the paper so Freddie could see the column. "Here's a story on that bum killer. No one has seen him."

"Except you."

"And the killings started right after Thanksgiving, occurring close to once a week, until the end of last week, when they started to hit almost every night." Kathy thought. "I don't remember Evans acting strangely, though."

"I've read that people like that don't always appear mad."

"True. And if your plane accident happened the first week of this month, then Mr. Selby and presumably Mr. Evans both had access to your book, because I got it on the first, and I know Mr. Selby had it before me. Which means your plane probably was sabotaged."

"I hope not," sighed Freddie, even though he had to concede that Kathy had a point.

Kathy gazed thoughtfully at the precinct doors. "Here comes Uncle Dan now."

Freddie looked at the mildly padded man approaching them.

"If that's him, he was at Selby's funeral," he said softly, as the two of them got to their feet.

"So that's how he knew you were looking into this, too." Kathy's lips took on a firm set, as if she were preparing to do battle.

Callaghan saw Kathy, and rushed over to her. "Where the hell have you been, girl?"

"In a safe place," replied Kathy stubbornly. She turned to Freddie. "Uncle Dan, this is my friend, Mr. Little. Freddie, my uncle, Daniel Callaghan."

"It's a pleasure to make your acquaintance," said Freddie offering his hand.

309

Callaghan shook it, still reserving judgment. "Well, Katie-girl, have you finally come to your right senses?"

"I never lost them, Uncle Dan. But Mr. Little and I have found some things out, and have come to a rather startling conclusion."

After a moment's thought, Callaghan led them into the detective's room and found a quiet corner in which to talk. Kathy did the explaining, with occasional comments from Freddie. They showed Callaghan the damaging pages and the newspaper. Callaghan nodded.

"It's not bad," he conceded. "But for one thing. It was not Miles Evans you saw last night, Katie-girl. He's been in the Village precinct jail since yesterday morning for breaking into your room."

"What?" Kathy asked. "How did you catch him so fast?"

"I didn't. Reagan did and that old fellow that lives there, what's his name."

"Mr. Eggleston," prompted Kathy.

Callaghan nodded. "He saw Evans go in that day. Thought he was visiting until he heard about the burglary. Reagan took Eggleston around to the office and he pointed Evans out."

"Which means he isn't the man killing the bums," said Freddie, feeling frustrated.

"It's an interesting point you make about your book and all," said Callaghan. "But I'm not sure it's all connected."

"I am," said Kathy. "It's the only thing that makes sense."

"What did this fellow look like?" asked Callaghan.

Kathy shrugged. "I didn't see much of him. He wasn't particularly tall, but definitely not short. He was kind of stocky in the shoulders, and had a flat stomach. But I never saw his face, and as for coloring, he had on a hat, and the light was bad anyway."

Callaghan sighed. "That's not much, but it's more than we have. Evening clothes, you say. He's a madman, all right."

Freddie was deep in thought. "Stocky in the shoulders... Something tells me I know this person. But I can't think who."

"It could be any number of people, Freddie," sighed Kathy. "It's not an unusual profile."

"I'd best be feeding this to my men," said Callaghan. He eyed Kathy. "I don't suppose I can be trusting you to stay here until I can get back."

"I'm making no promises," said Kathy.

"We'll stay put," said Freddie. "Since it seems that I am also a target, it would appear to be the safest course until we know where the fire is coming from."

"Thank you, Mr. Little." Callaghan sent a quick glare at Kathy. "As far as your manuscript is concerned, we'll have to keep it for evidence."

"I see no problem with that," said Freddie. "I have a friend who has the second copy."

"My notes are on that one," groaned Kathy.

"I might be able to work something out," said Callaghan. "I'll be right back."

He left. Kathy sighed and flopped into a chair. Freddie, equally morose, leaned on the edge of a desk.

"The strange thing is," said Freddie. "Evans had no good reason to steal that manuscript."

Kathy laughed. "He had every reason to. He probably never told Mr. Healcroft that I had taken it. With me gone, he'd be editing it. And even if Mr. Healcroft knew it was gone, Evans still needed that book for his career. It's a very important book, Freddie."

"It is?" Freddie looked at her, not quite sure he believed what she was saying.

"If Mr. Healcroft weren't a wealthy man already, *The Old Money Story* could make him one. And there's a great deal of prestige to be had for the book's editor. It would easily make Evans's career. It would give him the power to take the books he liked, do as he liked."

"But why?"

Kathy smiled. "Because your book is going to sell fabulously, whether it's good or not. People will see your name on it, and buy it."

"Perhaps here in New York."

"All they have to do is advertise that you're a real socialite, and people all over the country will line up with dollars in their hands."

Freddie sank into himself. "Then why are you working so hard on it?"

Kathy got up and leaned on the desk next to him. "Because it is good. It's very good, Freddie. The plebeian rabble may buy it because of your name and background, but it will last because it is an excellent novel. I want it to be the best it can be. That's why I bully you so much. Freddie, you're a good writer, and you have other stories in you, and the gift to put the words together to make beautiful pictures that tell a story. I can't do that. But I do know how to fix a novel. And yours is such a joy to work on because there's so little to fix."

Freddie sighed. "I still don't see myself as a writer, Kathy."

"Don't worry." She patted his arm. "I saw several notes for another novel on your desk. I suspect all you'll need is a stack of foolscap and some pencils, and you'll be at it again. It doesn't matter whether you think of yourself that way or not. You are a writer, Freddie. Trust me."

Freddie nodded. "I do, Kathy." He fell silent for a minute. "This Selby thing. What you said about that bum killer truly bothers me. It has to be the book that's the key."

Kathy shrugged. "Who else could have read it? Come to think of it, Evans probably didn't, or even Mr. Selby, for that matter."

"Lowell did."

"He's definitely not the bum killer." Kathy paused. "Unless he's protecting the one who is."

"That's it!" Freddie bounced straight up.

"Edmund Markham has also been singing that tune, and he has been acting strangely of late. Mother said so at dinner, remember?"

"And Victoria's his sister," gasped Kathy. "The woman at the apartment. Everyone keeps saying it was a woman. Victoria must have read the book last summer."

"Then when Edmund went over the edge..." Freddie scrambled after the newspaper. "When did it say? Yes, here. Right after Thanksgiving. And he does fit the profile you saw. Victoria must have found out it was him, assumed that anyone who read the book would think of him as the killer, and decided she had to protect him."

"By killing you and whoever had read the book." Kathy stopped pacing and turned to him. "Freddie, it was the day after she met me that I was pushed in front of that bus."

"And two days after Edmund insisted on meeting my new editor. He was the one that decorated the stoop, by the way. Victoria could have found out from Lowell that he was meeting me in the Village that night, and I'm sure now that I saw her at that speak we were in that got raided."

"The hired thug must have run around back when the police arrived, and got lucky when we came that way."

"Not that lucky." Freddie's lips pressed shut.

"So what do we do now?" Kathy started pacing. "We have a lot of coincidences, but nothing concrete."

Freddie grabbed Kathy's shoulders. "I know

314

what needs to be done, but I'll have to do it myself. The cops won't be able to do anything. Kathy, please, for once, stay here. She's got a tremendous amount of money, and can afford an army of assassins."

"Freddie, you're her enemy just as much as I am!"

"But she isn't expecting what I've got in mind." He quickly kissed her cheek. "Now, stay put."

And he dashed off.

"Freddie!" Kathy started after him, but realized she'd never catch up. It took less than a minute to think it over. She ran for the subway and changed trains at Times Square.

CHAPTER SIXTEEN

The sun had reached the tops of the trees when Kathy ran up to the mansion on Fifth. It wasn't quite as grand as the twin palaces owned by the Vanderbilts some twenty blocks below. But it was grand enough. Freddie's Packard was parked on the street outside the front.

Kathy doubted that going to the door would do any good. She'd been delayed long enough that Victoria Winters surely knew what Freddie was up to and had prevailed. Kathy stole around to the back.

The servants' entrance was unlocked. Kathy slipped in silently. She was in a plain hallway with a set of stairs across from her. To her left was a brightly lit kitchen. Voices floated out.

"That was Mrs. Markham," grumbled an older voice. "She, Mr. Markham and Miss Elizabeth are staying out for the evening. She wants their evening things sent round to Mrs. Fields."

"What a nuisance," groaned a younger woman. "And Mrs. Winters and Mr. Edmund?"

"Who knows? They've been locked up on the

fourth floor all afternoon. Childs says they are absolutely not to be disturbed."

Kathy's heart stopped. She prayed she was not too late. She tiptoed quickly across the open doorway and hurried up the stairs as fast as she dared, not wanting to make even the slightest sound.

There was a door at the end of the fourth floor landing. Kathy listened first. No sound. Slowly, she turned the knob and cracked the door open. Her head slid out.

It was easy to see she was in the family's living quarters. The hallway featured gold-flecked blue wallpaper, antique chairs and a crystal chandelier. It was also deserted.

Kathy slipped out. She moved slowly through the hall, skittering past the open stairway. The doors to the rooms were all shut. Kathy listened at one. Silence. She went to the next.

"Edmund, you've got to learn to be patient," said Victoria's voice sternly. "It will be a lot easier to get him to the river if he's alive and we can't go until after Mother and Father are at dinner."

"It's almost dark," Edmund whined as Kathy breathed a sigh of relief. "Are you sure Freddie knows about me?"

Victoria snarled. "Very sure. He wrote about it in his book. Isn't that where you got the idea?"

"No," Edmund grumbled.

"The book still connects you to your little mess. Be thankful I'm around to clean it up for you."

"Can we go now?"

Kathy peeked in at the keyhole. It was black, the key obviously still there.

"Do you want Mother and Father asking questions?" Victoria asked. "They will if they see us." A phone handset rattled. "Yes, Childs? This is Mrs. Winters."

Kathy went on to the adjoining room. The keyhole was open. Kathy could just barely see Freddie's legs sticking out. They jerked as if he was trying to move himself.

There had to be a way to get him out. Kathy looked at the lock thoughtfully. They were supposed to be easy to pick. She opened her purse and dug through it, hoping to find something long enough, thin enough and strong enough to release the lock. Her hand closed around it and she smiled at the irony.

Holding her hand steady, she put the buttonhook into the keyhole. She wasn't sure what she was doing, but she felt something give, then something else, and the bolt slid back with a nice, loud click. Her heart pounding, Kathy looked up and down the hall for signs of movement.

Slowly, she opened the door, this time for the sake of silence. She shut it, then turned. Freddie was smiling at her through a swollen and cracked lip and shaking his head. He had been put in a chair too small for his stature and had his hands tied behind him. His right cheekbone was swelling also, and getting ready to produce one rainbow of a shiner. Kathy hurried over and went to work on the ropes.

"I thought I told you to stay put," he hissed softly under the murmur of the voices in the next room.

"Aren't you glad I didn't? Damn it, Freddie, why did you run off like that?"

"I thought I might be able to fool her into thinking I wanted to have it out over Lowell, only Edmund walked in and she pulled a gun on me."

"You're free now. Let's get out of here."

"Wait." Freddie held his position and nodded at the door.

A key rattled in the lock. Kathy scrambled beneath the bed. The door opened. Victoria, holding a revolver fixed on Freddie, came in with Edmund.

"Well, Freddie, it seems as though Mother and Father will not be in this evening," she announced. "That means we can dispatch you now. Unfortunately, we'll have to take you on a little drive first. Edmund, get him up."

Kathy inched her way to the other side of the bed.

"Can't I just snap his neck, as usual?" Edmund complained as he went over to Freddie.

Kathy stifled a sneeze, then inched across some more.

"No, Edmund. It will connect you to the others too easily." Victoria's voice was steady and self-assured. "You'll just have to trust me and do as I say."

The other side of the bed was getting closer,

319

but not close enough. Kathy pushed herself.

The moment Edmund's arms touched Freddie, Freddie leapt to life. He and Edmund rolled together while Victoria tried desperately to get a fix on Freddie with her pistol. Kathy rolled out from under the bed. Victoria's attention was fixed on Freddie.

Kathy leaped on the woman with a football tackle. The gun went flying. Freddie rolled on top of Edmund and rabbit punched his jaw. Kathy's fingers twisted themselves through Victoria's hair. Victoria's teeth scraped Kathy's wrists. With Edmund groggy, Freddie scrambled away. Victoria pulled Kathy's hands free, then rolled on top of Kathy. Freddie grabbed Victoria. Kathy scrambled to her feet and punched Victoria in the jaw. Edmund staggered forward. Freddie backhanded him across the room.

Kathy was already out the door. Freddie scrambled after her, catching her as she headed to the servant door. He tugged her toward the open stairway.

"Not that way!" she hissed, jerking her arm away.

The loud crack of the pistol sent them ducking. Down the hall, Victoria was aiming again.

"Watch it, Kathy!" Freddie yelled.

Kathy screamed at the second shot, then pulled Freddie through the servant door.

"All right?" she hissed as she started down the stairs.

Freddie locked the door. "Yes. You?"

"Fine." Kathy's voice floated up the stair-well.

Freddie nearly fell running after her. Above them, wood splintered as the door was knocked in. Victoria's pistol cracked and little bits of wood flew at Freddie and Kathy from the banister.

On the second floor landing, Freddie spotted a cart and shoved it at the stairs just as Edmund came rushing down. He tumbled with a loud crash, and Victoria stopped short of falling herself. She shot at Freddie and Kathy again.

Kathy burst into the first floor hallway and stopped.

"Catch my breath," she gasped.

"Damn it, you're bleeding!" Freddie said, his breath coming just as hard as hers.

Kathy suddenly became aware of a throbbing in her forehead and something in her left eye. She dabbed at it.

"Blood," she murmured.

Freddie nodded. But a moment later, Victoria and Edmund appeared from the front foyer, and Edmund had a small rifle in his hands. Freddie gently shoved Kathy behind him to shield her.

"How chivalrous, Freddie," said Victoria, smirking. "But it's not going to do your little friend any good. Since it appears I shall have to take care of both of you myself, I may as well do it at the same time."

"You could have saved yourself a lot of trouble and contacted the right assassin," Kathy replied, pressing her hand to her forehead. "But I suppose lowering yourself to go below 40th Street would have been a bit much to ask."

"We'll go through the kitchen," Victoria snarled.

Edmund led the way. As they passed a work table covered with salad greens and silver platters, Kathy wavered and collapsed. The two servants screamed.

"Damn it!" Victoria hissed. "She can't die here. It's got to look like an accident!"

Freddie dove to Kathy's side. She glanced up at him and winked.

"Kathy!" he moaned.

"Freddie, get her up," Victoria ordered. "Carry her, if you must, but I don't want to take all night."

"Give me a hand, will you, Edmund?" Freddie asked.

Edmund reached for Kathy. At that moment, she and Freddie dove for the greens, scattered them and ducked. Victoria and Edmund fired. Servants screamed again. But Freddie and Kathy were already on the other side of the table, grabbing pots, pans, utensils, and trays and throwing them as fast as they could. Keeping low, they ran for the door back into the house. Freddie grabbed the key off its hook as they went through, and he paused just long enough to lock the door.

Kathy was on her way down a long hall that she thought led to the front.

"Kathy, no!" Freddie groaned and chased after her.

"Where's the front?" she hissed as he caught her.

"That way," he growled, pointing back toward the kitchen.

Gunfire and wood splintering echoed down the hall.

"Now what?" Kathy yelped, trying not to panic as her dizziness grew.

Freddie glanced along the closed doors and suddenly grinned.

"This way." He pulled her into a room two doors back and locked the door. "Good. I was right."

"A game room," whispered Kathy, looking in awe at the stuffed trophies that decorated the walls.

"Filled with Mr. Markham's favorite hobby." Freddie went around the billiards table to the glass gun case. "It seems rather rude to use these against his daughter."

Kathy saw a double barreled shotgun leaning against a huge, stuffed, snarling brown bear upright on its rear legs.

"Tying you up wasn't polite," she said. She snarled back at the bear and picked up the gun. "Any shells for this in there?"

Freddie looked and tossed her the box. "Do

323

you know how to use that thing?"

Kathy cocked the gun open and loaded it. "Do you remember the night I threatened to fill your hide with buckshot?"

"Yes."

"It was no idle threat." Kathy snapped the gun shut.

A second later, bullets hammered at the lock. Kathy ducked behind the door and propped herself up against the wall, as Freddie dove for the cover of the billiards table. The door popped open and Victoria and Edmund entered, their pistol and rifle warily sweeping the room.

Freddie propped his rifle to his shoulder and slowly stood.

"It appears we have a stand off, Victoria," he said calmly.

"Freddie, how *outré*," Victoria said. "Using Father's guns."

"Given that you are using them on me, and that I have no other, I think I may be excused."

Victoria glanced around the space behind him. "I see you have your frumpy little friend protected."

"More or less." Freddie didn't dare take his eyes off Victoria, although he wondered what she'd seen that made her think Kathy was behind him.

Victoria sighed. "We might as well fire, Edmund. He can't hit us both."

"But I can." Kathy pushed the door shut with her foot, her shotgun aimed and ready. "That's the nice thing about buckshot. And I can't tell you how much it would please me to pump you full of it. So why don't you set your guns down, nice and easy."

Victoria balked.

"Do it, lady," Kathy growled. "Freddie may be too polite to shoot his friends without extreme provocation, but I don't have that problem."

Edmund set his rifle on the floor. Growing ever more nervous, Victoria shook her head.

"No," she whispered, then louder. "No. I won't let you take him."

"He's sick, Victoria," said Freddie. "He needs help. We want him to get it."

"No. You don't understand." Victoria trembled. "You never did, Freddie. I'm all the help Edmund needs. I can take care of him. You're not going to take him away from me. You poisoned my husband against me. You're not getting my brother!"

Victoria whipped around and fired. Edmund jerked backwards and fell. Freddie fired; the gun leaped from Victoria's hand. She screamed and grabbed the wound. Looking up at Freddie, she glared furiously.

"You bastard," she hissed. "You fucking bastard!"

Freddie swallowed as Victoria sank to the floor sobbing. Keeping one eye on the hysterical woman, Kathy stepped around to Edmund.

"Kathy, I think now would be a good time to summon your uncle and his colleagues and perhaps an ambulance," Freddie said, gathering himself together and coming around the billiards table.

"It's too late for the ambulance," said Kathy quietly as she shut Edmund's eyes. She steadied herself then looked around, trying to focus on anything but the rapidly cooling corpse and the wreck that was his sister.

Freddie picked up the telephone sitting on the end table next to an overstuffed chair.

"Criminy!" Kathy yipped.

"What?" Freddie started.

"They put a telephone in here." Her laugh was small and shaky. "Back home, we'd call that pretty big for their britches."

Freddie paused. Victoria's sobs had softened, but were audible. Kathy's face was still white where the blood hadn't splattered, but she somehow remained standing. Freddie realized his hand was shaking as he rattled the switch.

"Yes, I suppose it is a bit much," he said softly, then answered as the operator came on the line.

It turned out that Kathy had only been grazed, and although the wound had already stopped bleeding by the time the police arrived, Freddie insisted that his personal physician see to patching her up. From there, after they each promised to phone each other, Freddie had to give Kathy up to her Uncle Dan, at whose apartment she spent the evening, letting Aunt Beth make a fuss over her. The next morning she was fed breakfast in bed while her cousins read the newspaper stories to her.

It was front page news, of course. Even the Times had it. Victoria had confessed to killing Frank Selby, ostensibly to protect her brother, as well as hiring various thugs to try and kill Freddie, whose book had supposedly given Edmund the idea to snap the necks of vagrants. Kathy became her second target when Victoria found out that Kathy was editing Freddie's book. Victoria had even bragged that she'd killed her brother rather than let the law have him.

Freddie got top billing as the hero behind her capture, while Kathy noted with disgust that she was only mentioned as a bystander, and in the more spectacular papers, as the damsel in distress. Only one paper credited her with being any help and that was only because they were quoting Freddie.

She was welcomed back to the boarding house that afternoon with open arms. Mrs. Lynne even treated her as something of a minor celebrity. Sunday afternoon, she received two callers.

The first was Sergeant Reagan, who came with hat in hand, mumbling an apology that Kathy was sure her uncle had put him up to. She accepted graciously and sent him on his way.

Then Mr. Healcroft paid a call. Kathy dickered with him, pressed her luck a couple times and won. Monday morning, she went to Healcroft House to a new desk in the junior editors' room. She smiled at Elsie Quinn, who was taking her seat at the secretary's desk.

The holidays arrived. Freddie went away

327

to Long Island with his parents out of duty to them and ended up staying until the twenty-ninth. He called Kathy almost every day to chat and to complain how bored he was. Kathy, herself busy with her new job and her own relatives, still managed to listen indulgently.

But the morning of New Year's Eve found Freddie with a problem.

"I know it's terribly short notice, and if you have plans, don't break them for me," he told her on the phone around noontime.

"Are you sure she has influenza?" Kathy asked with that wicked little smile he could hear over the lines.

"Perfectly sure. I just visited her this morning. She was terribly upset because we've had this date since Thanksgiving. Anyway, Honoria suggested I talk to you before I send my regrets. She says she has a nice evening gown you might like to borrow."

"To be honest, the only plans I had were a good book, a fireplace and Mrs. Lynne's new radiophone. It may be noisy, but your offer sounds a little more appealing."

"Shall I pick you up at eight o'clock?"

"Yes, thank you."

The party itself was noisy, gay and dull as dishwater. Freddie raised a few sympathetic eyebrows when he introduced Kathy as a friend of Honoria's. Honoria's friends were notoriously unsuitable, and Kathy got the feeling that she had dumped one or more of them on Freddie before.

But unlike Honoria's friends, Kathy was quiet and well-mannered, even if she refused to dance.

They left an hour or so before midnight and found a speakeasy. Just before twelve, Kathy dragged Freddie to Times Square.

"Have you ever done this?" she shouted over the braying, shouting and singing of the crowd.

"No!" He held onto her tightly in the press of celebrating bodies. "Have you?"

"Would you believe no?"

The countdown began. Kathy called it out with the rest of the crowd as Freddie chuckled. Then Kathy turned to him and threw her arms around his neck.

"How about a New Year's kiss for your friend?" she shouted.

"We're in a public place," yelled Freddie, who could barely fathom being hugged in public.

"It's New Year's on Times Square!"

And Kathy reached and put her lips to his. Suddenly alone in the swarm of people, Freddie enjoyed her warmth and returned it.

Two more speakeasies and several hours later, a taxi pulled up outside the boarding house. The street was deserted. Bright light whitened the eastern sky, and most of the stars had already faded. There had been snow for Christmas, and just that night another blanket had swathed the street in more white splendor.

"Would you mind stepping in for a minute?"

329

Kathy asked as Freddie walked her up the stoop.

"I suppose." He walked in and took off his hat, spotting a gaily wrapped box on the hall table. "Good. It arrived."

"What's this?" Kathy looked at it in delight.

"A little Christmas present. I'm sorry it's late. But with all the confusion..."

"Let's not talk about that." Kathy swallowed and shook her head. "I can't say things turned out that badly, what with my new job and your book and all. But I would love to be able to forget that awful day."

"Yes. I think I would like to also. And yet..." his voice drifted off as he caught her bright eyes.

"I wasn't sure if I should get you anything," Kathy said, suddenly turning back into the hall.

Freddie laughed. "What are you going to buy me? I have buckets of cigarette lighters, cuff links, handkerchiefs, pens, you name it. I'd barely cleared out last year's trash when this year's arrived."

Kathy straightened with the load she had pulled from under the table.

"You don't have this." She dumped two large boxes of foolscap and a bundle of pencils into his hands. "That's for your next book. I expect you to start on it right away."

Touched, Freddie looked at the load. "Thank you, Kathy. I can't tell how much I appreciate being taken seriously."

"I'm just returning the favor," she said softly.

Freddie bent and kissed her cheek.

"I'd better kick you out of here." Kathy yawned. "Oh, excuse me. Good lord, the street lamps are already off."

As he left, Freddie stopped on the stoop and turned back to Kathy.

"This was quite a pleasant night," he said, brushing snow from the railing and leaning on it. "Do you think you might be interested in coming out with me time and again to see plays and explore clubs and museums?"

"And go to concerts?" Kathy asked eagerly.

Freddie nodded. "I suppose."

"I'd love a concert. They're so dreadfully top drawer that I've always been afraid to go."

"I think I could manage one or two. So you'll come?"

Kathy shrugged. "If I don't have plans. I usually don't, but I'd like a little more notice."

Freddie laughed. "I promise. Fortunately, I don't have any more dates scheduled, so they won't stand me up." He paused. "Well, good night."

Kathy's wicked grin spread across her face. "Good morning."

Freddie leaned over to kiss her cheek. Kathy wriggled around and caught his lips. A minute or so later, Freddie pulled away.

"I seem to have missed," he said smiling.

Kathy's grin grew even more wicked. "You missed in the hallway."

Laughing, Kathy shut the door. Freddie swaggered down the stoop, his spirits rising with the light. He got back into the taxi and rode off into the city. A city alive and sleepy, getting ready to greet the new day, the new year.

Other Titles from Anne Louise Bannon

TYGER, TYGER

When Brenda Finnegan and her animal trainer boy-
friend Bob Zebrinski witness a kidnapping, they end
up caring for the little girl the victim left behind.
Chased by a cult and just angry enough, Brenda and
Bob try to find the kidnappers, helped by Bob's tiger
Sweetness.

WHITE HOUSE RHAPSODY
(www.whitehouserhapsody.com)
A light romantic fiction serial

President Mark Jerguessen is single and there's
a dark secret why. His aide Sharon Wheatly loves
high-achieving, driven guys, but does not want anything to do with their fame. You know there's got to
be a way to get them together.

HOWDUNIT: BOOK OF POISONS
(co-authored with Serita Stevens)

The perfect reference work for writers looking for
realistic mayhem in their stories. The book not only
provides all the facts on toxins, it indexes them by
symptoms, reaction times, etc., to make it easy to
find the deadly dose your story needs.

FIND IT ALL ON
WWW.ANNELOUISEBANNON.COM